The Riddle Box

G. Derek Adams

ISBN: 0692224270
ISBN-13: 978-0692224274 (Lodestar)

DEDICATION

For Mom again. Because once was never enough.

CONTENTS

Sing in me, O Muse

of the dark that hides

quiet and calm

in the center of the riddle box.

Sing with me and hold my hand tight.

                       I am afraid.

1

"Come forth, you rogue," the prince called into the cave. "I have sought you long. Through misty moor and shattered heath, through songbird madness and blood-red dreams. I am Prince Towerlock of the Shining Kingdom, and I will not be denied."

No answer came from the cave. The dark opening hummed with malicious thought and dim portent.

The prince stomped his foot in frustration and unslung his golden bow. From the quiver of white birch he pulled a single arrow. A sprig of blonde hair fell across the prince's forehead and he sighed, then used the point of the arrow to smooth it back into place.

"Come forth, Wizard of Black!" the prince called again, taking aim in a fluid motion. "I cannot miss, even though you hide in shadows deep. Come forth or I will loose!"

A howl of frustration came from the cave. At once two plumes of grey smoke erupted on either side of the opening, and the wizard appeared.

The wizard wore black, as was appropriate. Red skulls adorned the sleeves; skeletal eyes shimmered with wicked glee. His beard was split into two long braids, each end tucked into a wide leather belt. Long, elegant hands clutched the air in wrath.

"I know you, Prince Towerlock -- I know you and your bow that never misses. And I know why you have come, what you have come to ask of my Magic Most Foul," the wizard boomed, grey smoke coiling around him.

"Yes, Sorcerer of Sorrows. I have traveled a thousand-thousand leagues in search of you. All alone I have sought you. Alone except for my will, my golden bow, my broken heart, my determination, my valor, and my manservant Humphrey," Towerlock gestured toward a small cart behind him.

The cart was a low, two-wheeled rig. A coffin lay on the cart, artfully wrapped in blue satin ribbon. Humphrey was a white-haired man wearing a gravy-stained tunic. He quailed at the wizard's fierce attention but managed to wave his hand politely.

"A cart pulled by an ass, ho ho!" The wizard raised his arms with a flourish. "Be careful, good Humphrey, lest your master whip you out of sorts on his fool errand."

Prince Towerlock opened his mouth to retort but was halted by the black-robed mage's next flourish which terminated in a bony finger pointed at the coffin. The prince also inhaled a bit of the gray smoke that lingered and had to take a moment to cough and wipe his watering eyes. The wizard waited, stroking one long beard-braid.

"It's not an errand for fools!" the prince managed at last.

"It is an errand of the purest sort. A quest of justice, a quest to beggar the imagination of a thousand bards -- to drive them mad seeking the proper tune, the true melody, the holy quatrain that can contain its beauty. My quest is made for love. It is made *of* love. And no matter what dark arts you bring to bear, what evil you hide in your cave of shadows, what Magic Most Foul you hold in your hands -- the power of love is greater."

"Love, pfeh," the wizard spat. "That is a strange magic, an old magic. I do not waste my time upon it. Enough idle words, Great Prince. Break open the long wooden box your old ass has hauled across the globe, unbind the ribbons damp with your foolish tears. Show me your Bride! For I know it is she that you carry all forlorn."

Prince Towerlock marched grandly over to the cart, his handsome face wracked with sorrow. Humphrey had to skip out of the way to avoid being injured by the prince's quiver.

The prince composed himself for a moment, his hands on the clean wood of the coffin. Then, with a grunt, he flipped the coffin to stand on one end. The cart had a cunning lever and fulcrum designed specifically for this purpose. Slowly Towerlock began to cut away the blue ribbons with his belt knife as he spoke.

"My beloved Key, brought low by a foul curse. Even as we climbed the stairs to our nuptial bower, her eyes bright with life and joy, her hand grew cold in mine and she slipped into a dreamless sleep. Her beauty and her breath stopped as still as a broken clock, as chill as winter's heart. I laid her on a bier and pleaded. With her, with the gods, with the Thirteen Devils, with the inexorable turning of Fate itself. Nothing brought her back to me. The doctors and sages and wise men of the Shining Kingdom all wagged their heads in despair and told me to let her go, allow her to fall into the earth, into death's embrace. But she did not decay! She stayed as beautiful and unspoiled as the moment she fell under the curse's sway. As beautiful and pure as she appears before you now."

The prince cut free the final ribbon and let it fall to the ground. He unfastened the brass clasps of the coffin and flung the lid open. The lid swung on silent hinges revealing the cursed bride within. Towerlock held the lid open with pride and looked at the wizard in defiance.

The wizard's face was as white as a sheet. His hands moved uncertainly, shaking as they pointed at the bride. The manservant, Humphrey, leaned over and looked into the coffin -- his eyes shot wide with panic.

The Sorcerer of Sorrow managed only a vague grunt of alarm.

Towerlock shook his head in irritation and took a step forward. "Err, yes! Yes, her beauty doth rob even such an evil one as you of the faculty for speech."

"Dammit, Toby!" the prince's manservant hissed. "Look at her!"

Prince Towerlock of the Shining Kingdom turned in confusion and looked full upon his cursed bride.

Blood. She was covered with blood. The blonde wig that she wore had come askew, and it appeared that she had vomited blood all down the front of her white gown. He could see her natural curly brown hair and the pronounced point of her ears that the wig normally hid. Her eyes were glassy and still; she breathed not at all.

"What? Darla?" He moved towards the coffin.

As if on cue, the body toppled forward and landed on the stage with a sickening smack. Blood splattered across Towerlock's doublet, his manservant's tunic, and the skull-ringed robe of the wizard. The Wizard of Black stumbled back in shock, accidentally knocking over his cave mouth -- a simple construction of fabric, wire and slotted wood.

There was a moment of no breath followed by the startled scrape of chairs on the polished marble floor of the manor's feasting hall. The silence was filled with angry and confused voices of many colors. The audience was small, an intimate dinner party. The players had been hired to entertain each evening in the lord's house. They had performed two comedies the night before, a historical the night before that, and on their first night a crude farce and a pair of romances. Tonight was to be a simple adventure story. A simple fable of Good and Evil, the strength of True Love, and how shadows fall before the light.

The manservant Humphrey -- who was neither -- stepped close to the fallen bride, ignoring the slow seep of thickening blood that stuck to his boots. He felt vainly for a pulse in his actress's neck but found none. The wizard was sitting on his toppled cave, eyes wide with confusion. The prince was vomiting loudly behind the cart. The man who was neither servant nor Humphrey sighed and looked out across the shadowed forms of the audience, the guests of the manor. Tonight was to be an adventure story -- but now he did not know what kind of play he was in.

The House of the Heart-Broken Lion was the manor's name in the common speech, and its lord was renowned both far and wide for his wealth and his knowledge. His guests clustered around speaking words of anger, concern and fear, demanding to know what had occurred. How murder could find its way within the stone walls of his house? The lord of the Heart-Broken Lion did his best to calm his guests and promise them answers, but his eyes were focused beyond them. Focused on the two strangers that sat at his table. Everyone within the hall was here at his employ or his invitation. Except for these two strangers, who arrived at his table tonight under the thinnest of pretenses.

Two strangers at his table. And now a murder.

One of the strangers, a young man with a square face, leaned over to the other. He whispered to his companion, face tight with concern.

The second stranger, a small young woman with a swath of bone-white hair belying her age, backhanded her companion's shoulder without taking her eyes off the guests and the players. Her eyes moved from person to person, taking every detail in as if she meant to draw the scene from memory on her deathbed.

"Who are you?" Lord Bellwether asked, his voice quiet.

The two strangers were sitting across from his grand desk. It was all gleaming white, edged with gold. Behind them Funnicello crossed his thick arms in displeasure. The dwarf served as butler, chef, tailor, and sergeant at arms for his household.

The two young strangers exchanged glances. Lord Bellwether ran his eyes over their garb. Travel-stained tunic:, a ragged brown cloak with a hood on the boy, a wide-brimmed planter's hat made of straw in the girl's thin hands. They were both soaking wet, unsurprising as it had been raining for days. His dwarven butler held the only two things they had carried with them: a battered leather satchel, and a longsword with a wooden handle. In the middle of the performance the butler had heard the rude clamor at the great doors of the manor and had moved swiftly to silence it before the performance or his lord's guests were disturbed. Funnicello had glowered up at the two water-logged travelers and dragged them in with a polite ferocity. Over the girl's protestations he'd removed their gear and escorted them bodily to the banquet hall where he could keep an eye on them until his lord was free to deal with them. Two scenes later the bleeding bride hit the stage.

"I am sorry to have intruded at such a late hour, Lord Bellwether. We are newly arrived in Carroway and I have important business with one of your guests. My name is Rime Korvanus and this is my associate, Jonas," the girl said with precision.

Korvanus? The name tickled his memory, but Bellwether could not place it. The girl's demeanor put her as high-blooded.

"I know it must seem unlikely and strange our arriving moments before the body was discovered," she continued, pushing damp white and brown hair out of her face. "But I'm certain you realize that very fact proves that we could have nothing to do with this incident."

Bellwether sighed. "It proves nothing of the sort, young lady. We know very little about the circumstances surrounding this poor woman's death. She died in my household - that is all that is certain. And I take the duties of a host most seriously."

"We had nothing to--" Rime began.

"Please allow me to finish." Bellwether stood and watched the rain batter against the wide bay window.

The window was sectioned with thick channels of iron, splitting the glass into a vast grid. Lightning flashed and he saw his reflection. A long face, auburn hair eroded by gray time, a thick mustache, split into four by the iron lines of the window. He waited five slow heartbeats before speaking again.

"Thank you for your courtesy, Lady Korvanus. Or would you prefer *Doma*?" Bellwether turned to see his butler doing his best to loom over the girl's shoulder and prevent her from interrupting his master's reverie. Her eyes were brittle with impatience. "*Doma* in the old speech, as is common in the Great Houses of Valeria. I apologize that it took me so long to place your family; your current attire and tonight's events have clouded my perception."

"Either is acceptable. I would prefer the customs of your house, as we are your guests, Lord Bellwether," Rime replied.

Intelligent. Quick on her feet. How neatly she has evoked the guest-right, and tied my hands with the manacles of propriety. Bellwether nodded in approval.

"My House of the Heart-Broken Lion is far-removed from the streets of Carroway and the shields of the garrison. The dark forest that surrounds us offers a measure of peace and solitude, but it also teems with the dangers and perils of the wild. My household is small. Only I, my daughter, and Funnicello reside here. We take great care with our safety and even more care with that of our guests. My manor is built like a fortress, iron at every window and

8

stone for every wall. The only point of entrance is the Lobby, two broad doors of darkwood and steel kept barred and locked at all times. The only keys reside safely on my person and on Funnicello's chain."

Bellwether pulled a golden key from his sleeve, securely tied to his wrist by a length of blue leather cord. It was of simple design, with the head of a lion etched in clear relief. The dwarf followed his master's lead and pulled a chain of keys from his pocket. It took him a moment to rustle through the dozens of others that he carried, but in short order he displayed the lion key's twin.

"I'm sorry, sir. Thank you, kindly," the young man in the brown cloak said with uncomfortable deference. "But why are you telling us this?"

Rime sighed in embarrassment. "Because Lord Bellwether is trying to make it clear the predicament that we are in. The door to this manor is always locked. This means that no one can enter or exit without his knowledge. If the actress was murdered, then one of his guests is the killer."

"And they are still here." Lord Bellwether sat down at his desk again with weary calm. "I must find justice for that poor young woman, protect my guests, and discover the bloody hand in our midst. At dawn I will dispatch Funnicello to summon the Third Regiment from Carroway to conduct a thorough investigation. Until he returns, no one will leave this house. And I am afraid that includes you both, Lady Korvanus and Master...Jonas."

"Oh, I'm no 'Master', sir," Jonas apologized. "Just a simple squire."

"A squire? Then where is your knight?"

"Ah..." Jonas' mouth flopped open.

"He is on loan to my family," Rime interjected calmly.

Bellwether peered at the young woman. He couldn't discern whether or not she was deceiving him, but something didn't ring true. "You said you had business with one of my guests?"

"A simple matter of some funds he holds in trust for me. I encountered some difficulties on my journey and have need to resupply and equip myself. Master Waters has been one of my family's financial agents for many years," Rime rose from her seat and Jonas awkwardly followed suit.

"Funnicello will show each of you to one of our guest rooms. I am afraid that my daughter is somewhat older than you, but I'm certain we can find some of her old clothes that would be appropriate. And I believe I have a spare tunic that might suit your associate." Bellwether nodded to the dwarf, concluding the interview.

The dwarf ran a finger through his brush of a goatee and did little to hide his displeasure. He opened the door for the two travelers and shoved his vast chain of keys back into his pocket.

Rime stopped in front of the door and turned back towards the lord's desk. "Thirteen. I counted thirteen, my lord. Is that correct?"

Lord Bellwether looked up from where his hand had come to rest on a book bound in blue leather. "Thirteen what, my lady?"

"Thirteen guests at the dinner. Four members of the

players. You, your butler, and I assume your daughter sitting at your side. Six other guests beyond that. Master Waters, the trader. A priest of the Nameless God. A bard from Gate City. A Nai-Elf shaman. A wealthy woman in red. A Yad-Elf scholar. Is there anyone else in the house? Any other servants or visitors?" Rime asked, the list and questions filling the air with hungry order.

"Only you two," Bellwether replied, bemused.

"I know that we didn't do it," Rime said.

This is the nicest shirt I've ever worn. Maybe touched. Maybe ever seen.

Jonas stared at himself in the mirror.

The shirt was a brilliant white, with black cord to lace up the front. Tiny lion heads were embroidered at the cuffs in black, the stitching so fine that each small tooth could be seen. The squire gingerly tried to push his curly hair into some sort of order, but gave up in defeat. Soft gray leggings had also been provided, along with an immaculate black vest dotted tastefully with round silver buttons.

Only his travel-worn leather boots remained and he had taken a few minutes to rub the grime off of them with a corner of the coverlet on the guest room's wide feather bed.

He slid his hands down the fine fabric of the vest and turned sideways to admire the profile. Jonas attempted a florid bow, bringing his hand to rest over his heart.

"My Lord? My Lord. My Lady? My Lady. My Lady! My Lady? My Lord?" He punctuated each greeting in the mirror with another grandiose gesture.

"Having fun?" Rime asked from the door.

The squire froze. His eyes flicked up to the edge of the mirror where he could see her reflection.

Rime was wearing a simple blue dress with a high hem. It looked slightly juvenile as if intended for a ten year old. She had mitigated the effect with a white half-cloak. Rime turned to shut the door, and he could see a hood with a long black tassel nearly brushing the floor. Jonas turned to face her, hastily assembling the fragments of his dignity.

"I like the cloak. It goes with your hair," he said. "Well, at least the new part."

Rime scowled and tugged on the lock of bone-white hair. When they had met, her hair had been a light forgettable brown, but now a thick swath had been drained of all color.

"I'm glad you approve," she deadpanned, scanning the room. "Where's your sword?"

"Uhhh," the squire began to cast around the room with chagrin.

She crossed her arms in disgust as he began tossing damp articles of clothing around the room in his search. He was pawing through the dripping mass of his travel cloak when she spoke again.

"The dwarf didn't bring it. And you didn't notice. We are locked in a house with a murderer, and you are too busy polishing your buttons in the mirror to notice that the only weapon we have wasn't returned to you. You are proving to be an excellent guardian, Jonas of Gilead," she plopped down on the wooden chair next to the dresser.

"Look, Rime, I'm sorry! But maybe it wasn't a murder. Maybe the actress-lady just got sick, or something. And yeah, I feel really stupid about the sword, but you are a much better weapon if things get murderous." Jonas tucked the beautiful shirt tail into his leggings to cover his absolute mortification.

I was trained better than this. Master must be rolling in his grave.

"If things get murderous. I'm a better weapon." Rime didn't snarl, but the squire still took a step back.

Rime was a wild mage. Jonas was still a little loose on exactly what that meant if he looked it up in a library or queried a scholar. He knew that most people who used magic were called wizards and went to school in a place called Valeria, where Rime's family was from. He knew that they had different ways of making things happen, hundreds of years of study, whole libraries crammed with the rules and laws that governed the correct way to cast spells. And he knew that somehow Rime was different. Somehow Rime ignored all that. He had watched her do amazing things - impossible things - things that were beyond any wizard that he had ever heard of. He also knew that her magic hurt her. That it could kill her if she wasn't careful. That her hair was white because she had gone too far. She had gone too far and saved both their lives.

The mage sighed and pushed the heels of her hands against her forehead. "It's not that simple. We were in the wilds before: no witnesses. Now that we are in the city, no one can know what I am. I had to use my family's name or Bellwether would have locked us in the pantry. As far as the world knows my father and brother are great wizards, and I'm the sad little bookworm deprived of any magical skill or aptitude. If these people discover the truth, we will have a host of problems. Master Waters will not release my gold, for starters. I don't want to have the Third Regiment engaged to execute me, or my name hung on signposts from here to Gorah."

"I didn't know you had a brother," Jonas offered.

"So I will use my magic only if there is no other option available or if I can do so without discovery. It would be best if we were on our way tomorrow before the Third arrives, the better to avoid inconvenient questions. We have tonight and however long it takes that dwarf to bring the garrison tomorrow. We must solve the murder and be on our way before then." Rime punched her palm emphatically.

"Rime," Jonas began, suspicion forming. "Are you...excited about this?"

"What?" Rime replied blandly.

"You just seem pretty excited. Like you're enjoying this."

"That is ridiculous," she sniffed.

"Because that actress-lady is dead. I'm sure she was very nice and her friends are very sad."

"Don't patronize me, Jonas. I am not excited. This is just an obstacle in our way that I am working to remove in the most expeditious manner possible." Rime stood up and straightened her cloak. "You worry about getting your sword back, and I'll worry about solving this mystery."

"Okay. I can handle that, I guess," Jonas said.

"You talk to no one if you can help it. One of them is a murderer and all of them are not to be trusted. You are my manservant. You received your training in Valeria from my father's house guard. You are not very bright, and talking to such grand lords and ladies makes you uncomfortable. Simple enough?" the mage instructed.

"My Lady. My Lady! My Lady?" The squire sketched out three increasingly absurd bows.

"And whatever you do--" Rime put two fingers on his chest just under his right collarbone. "Don't mention that you're from Gilead."

"Why not?"

"Weren't you listening in Bellwether's office?" Rime turned and opened the door. "One of the guests is a priest of the Nameless. It's your religion, so that makes it very likely that he is from Gilead. I won't pry again into your past there. I just don't want it complicating our situation. Now come here."

Jonas swallowed hard, the fine shirt at once feeling like sandpaper on his skin. *Only one life is given...* The prayer came to his mind unbidden. He walked over to the much shorter mage, where she bent his left arm into a crook. Rime placed her arm through his and squared her shoulders.

"Escort me to the parlor. Let's go find a murderer," the mage instructed.

The two travelers walked arm and arm out the door and down the grand hallway of gray stone and white marble.

2

The House of the Heart-Broken Lion was an egg - a granite-gray shell with a golden interior. When Rime and Jonas had finally topped the long winding hill that led to the front gates, it had seemed a rude beast -- yellow eyes burning through the pouring rain. Sharp, triangular edges at the top of its main tower were echoed by flat lines along the shoulders of the great house. The dark forest surrounded it like a vast pelt, thorny-wicked and dense. The mage had not quailed at the monstrous edifice, only taking a long, calculating look back across the dark valley toward the distant lights of Carroway to the east. The squire had simply pulled his hood close around his head and stamped his feet with impatience.

A double dozen steps and a triple dozen knocks on the wide door and the rude dwarf had hauled them inside. Into the center of the egg, golden and white and gleaming. White columns with inlaid brass; a quiet edge of green verdigris left on the metal to subtly remind of the age and time that slept in the house. An ornate staircase descended on either side of the vast marble lobby.

And now they descended the same grand staircase of white marble wrapped carefully with a blue silk cord. Jonas' gait was almost a march, but provided a suitable accessory for the effect Rime hoped to achieve. In the clamor and uproar of the play's sudden finale she was certain that her attire and presence had gone mostly unnoticed. It was very important that she enter into this investigation on an equal social plane with the other guests.

She was very excited. The library of her mind whirred with activity and preparation.

Outside, her body glided down the stairs. One hand lightly clasping her escort's arm, her face composed and wearing a reasonable approximation of demure. Inside her mind, she ran down row after row of books and scrolls, hands going eagerly to choice titles as she passed. Rime pulled the ones she needed and tossed them to the swarm of glowing green numbers that buzzed in her wake. The lambent numerals snagged them from the air but began to sag as the stacks grew taller. A grumpy looking seven dropped his burden with a clamor and floated away to sulk between the pages of a friendly story about cats and their affairs.

Rime directed the remaining numbers to place the books on a long table near the windows. She glanced out of them to see Jonas pulling at his collar, his thumb lingering on the black lion's head embroidered at the lapel. "Someone likes being pretty," she smirked.

The mage touched the spine of each gathered book. *The Unusual Murder*, *Daggers in the Dark*, *The Horror of Marwell Abbey*, *Blood in the Crossroads*. Rime had always thought that it should be 'Blood *at* the Crossroads'. *Sanguine Sundown, Inspector Kyng and the Hazaari Queen, Mother Goodbread and the Case of the Purloined Pups, Murder Most Dwarf, The Collected*

Evidence and Postulated Theories Regarding the Suspicious Events Surrounding the Death of Caliban Dragoon, Gate City Garrote, Thieftaker, Murder on the Lodestone. There were two dozen more, and she smiled a rare smile as she arranged them in reverse alphabetical order. The really interesting stuff was always near the end of the alphabet, and 'A' always seemed entirely too smug in her opinion.

Mystery books. They always began with a murder, then a clever investigator would appear on the scene to unravel the evidence, interrogate the suspects, and bring justice by the next-to-last chapter. The last chapter was usually a bore, just tying up loose ends or the investigator breaking things off with their paramour of the moment in a storm of tears and regretful glances at airship terminals. Rime usually didn't bother reading the last chapter, once the mystery was solved she considered the book complete and avoided the ponderous fluff at the end, leaving it for its intended audience: dowagers, dullards, and dreamers. This errata was not what attracted her.

The puzzle. The questions. The surprise, the chase, the truth shining in the dark. The investigator clasping hands behind his back as the suspects gathered in the parlor; his voice quick and clean as he laid out the evidence and revealed the killer's identity. The books in her head were exact replicas of the books in her father's library and the few she had gleaned from passing scholars, family friends, and her venomous tutor. The mystery books had been few and far between, deemed 'pulp trash' by the sage and 'ridiculous nonsense' by the learned. Rime had resorted to rifling through the servant's quarters in her quest for more, ghosting through her father's house in the middle of the night then dashing back to her room to feverishly cram the new mystery text into her mind. She always tried to return the book before dawn, its content safe forever in her mental library.

The mage turned to a large chalkboard that waited in the clear space near the eye-windows, the white reading stool adjacent. She took one more quick glance outside. They were approaching an ornate archway, the sound of several voices arguing from within. "Not much time," she said and picked up a long piece of chalk.

With deliberate haste she made thirteen columns on the chalkboard. The board was originally only wide enough for nine, but extended itself obligingly when needed. At the top of each column she wrote the name of each guest she knew or the quick descriptor she had assigned in her earlier survey.

Lord Bellwether

His Daughter

Funnicello, the Rude Dwarf

Rime frowned for a split second, then wrote across the first three columns *HOUSEHOLD*.

The next six columns she used for the official guests.

Master Waters, the Trader.

Priest of the Nameless.

Bard.

Sea-Elf Shaman.

Wood-Elf Scholar.

Wealthy Woman, Red Dress.

The last four columns remained for the performers. Rime wrote *PLAYERS* in block letters at the top.

Humphrey [?].

Black Wizard [?].

Toby, the Hero.

Darla, the Damsel.

The mage stepped back to admire her handiwork. The structure comforted her with its thin lines separating each suspect. It was a possibility that Bellwether had lied or been unaware, but for now she would assume that his words were sound. These were the only people in the house; no one else had come or gone. One of these people was the murderer.

One last addition, a chalk slash through the Damsel. Twelve suspects remaining. She would fill these columns with evidence, with facts, with the truth. She would solve this mystery long before the Third Regiment arrived, conclude her business with Master Waters, and be on her way. The puzzle would lay defeated behind her.

Rime turned from the chalkboard and left her library, back to the physical world. She and Jonas stepped through the archway and the hum of voices went quiet.

She was *very* excited.

The grumpy seven floated out of the children's book with a shudder. There are only so many cat antics that a prime number can stomach. The other numerals cavorted near the windows, buzzing over the mystery novels and considering the list of suspects with airs of studious curiosity. The seven floated the opposite direction with sour disdain, toward the edge of the library.

It settled on the end of a bookshelf and looked out into the dark. Things moved beyond the light of the library. Large shapes made of teeth and scales and cicada-chitter. Madness walked beyond the library and waited.

The seven yawned with scratchy boredom and flopped over for an impromptu nap.

Jonas tried not to stare - at the room, at the seven people gathered around some finely appointed couches and divans, at the table piled high with cheese, meat, and other oddments that made his stomach moan - but most of all he tried not to stare at the princess.

She floated towards him. Well, she was floating towards him and Rime, but he was positive that her eyes were fixed on his fancy new shirt. The other people in the room faded into obscurity and the squire wished desperately that he had his sword. Partly from a knee-jerk terror, but mainly because he was certain he'd cut a more dashing figure that way.

The princess approached.

She was blonde-strawberry, not the common reverse. Her gown was distinctly a gown, and the fabric was a color. She smiled, and Jonas realized his brain had deserted him.

She had a tiny scar on the bridge of her nose, and her eyes were also a color.

"Welcome!" the princess said. "My father has asked me to entertain our guests while he and Funnicello see to the security of the manor. I am afraid I have shared your names and a tiny part of your tale with the other guests. All of us were understandably alarmed after what happened during the play, and I wanted to reassure them that you were not strangers and could not have caused this awful event. Please forgive my lapse in courtesy."

She inclined her head in apology, a stray curl falling across her forehead. *Her eyes are...green? Blue? Is light a color?* Jonas thought in desperation. *Oh no, she's looking back up--!*

"It is no lapse to comfort your guests, Lady Bellwether," Rime said. "I completely understand."

I don't understand. What is happening to me? Jonas shifted nervously but found his movement halted by the mage's fingers pressing firmly into his forearm.

"Oh, please don't stand on formality, Lady Korvanus," the princess winced. "I'm so bad at this! Here I am asking you not be formal with me, but then I call you by your proper title. Just call me Neriah. Even Neri would be better."

Neriah...Neri.

"That is just fine, Neri. And you can call me Rime if you would be so kind."

"And your guard only goes by Jonas, so no way I can mess that up," Neri laughed with relief. "I'm afraid I must seem like a country girl to you. Compared to your city of Valeria this must be like a trip to the dark side of the globe."

She...she said my name. Jonas felt his stomach fold over and he moved to flee the parlor. Rime's fingers dug in like a rake's teeth.

"Not at all," Rime said airily. "My guard was just leaving to take his customary place near the window. It's part of their training to keep an eye on the surrounding terrain, having all exits and entrances from the room in clear view. I'm afraid his training doesn't cover much in the way of etiquette."

The mage removed her hand from his arm and gave the squire a subtle push.

Are they brown? Light brown? No, her eyes are darker than that.

Rime sighed and gave him a much less subtle shove.

"Now, if you would be so kind. Could you please introduce me to the other guests? It seems we must spend some time together and it would be best to spend it in the company of new friends." The mage took Neriah's arm and nearly dragged her away from the entrance.

"Of course, Lady Rime! It would be my pleasure, and--" she looked back over her shoulder in a flash of blonde-strawberry curls. "--your guard can help himself to any of the refreshments. We don't have any servants but Funnicello, so we don't stand on a lot of ceremony. I hope you won't find us rude, Rime."

"Not at all, Neri. Not at all." The mage's voice fluttered with false bird-sound then faded as the two women moved away towards the other guests.

Jonas stood where he had been left like a mushroom flicked from a cutting board for having a bad spot.

"My name is Jonas. It's nice to meet you, Neriah," he said to his princess' back.

After a few minutes of blank time his brain reported back for duty and his stomach moaned. He took Rime's advice and moved to a window where he could see the whole room, snagging a tray of cheese and bread on the way. He munched disconsolately. Out the window the rain and dark revealed nothing but the watery outline of the distant trees.

Rime added information to the column freshly labeled '*Neriah*' on her mind's blackboard with quick strokes. *Lord's daughter. Mother dead or absent. Pretty.*

Why had she written that? The mage considered Neriah again. She was attractive; Jonas transforming into a songstruck cow was evidence enough of that. Her face was wide with frank lips and a few stray freckles, and her hair seemed to curl without artifice or rancor. Rime estimated that Neriah was only a few years older than her. The mage found herself gazing at the older girl's pleasantly curved chest with a vague sense of unease.

"I'm so glad to have someone here closer to my age," Neriah's bosom confided. Rime corrected her vision upwards. "Father's guests are very nice, but they're a little difficult to talk to about girl stuff."

"I completely understand," the mage made herself smile

and pour more sparkling glitter and lamp oil into her speech. "I am pleased too. Do you know the other guests very well - are they common visitors here?"

Rime despised conversation without purpose, but she had to admit that slipping into the elevated vernacular her despised tutor had drilled into her contained a surprising appeal. She felt like Mother Goodbread, affecting the speech and manner of a simple country woman to allay suspicion while she teased information from her unsuspecting quarry. At the end of the book, the murderer's rage upon realizing the old woman's steely intellect and how easily she had manipulated the situation always gave Rime a small, fierce smile. Now she could do the same, pretend to be a vapid young noble far from home, cordial and curious and eager to hear the guest's tales. Every conversation could contain evidence - clues - to help her unravel the mystery.

"Only dear old Trowel and Master Waters. Trowel is a scholar and comes here often to use my father's library, and Master Waters conducts some of my father's financial affairs. But let me introduce you officially!" The two young women had arrived at the far end of the parlor.

Three people sat on a low divan. The scholar, the trader, and the sea-elf looked up at her with curiosity. Rime made note of the others in the room. The woman in red sat alone sipping her wine with the quick motions of anxiety. The bard stood with his back to the room, a floor-length coat of cobalt blue shining with reflected lamplight. He seemed to be leaning over something, his shoulders arched oddly. From a nearby open case she surmised that he was fiddling with his instrument. The priest was nowhere to be seen.

Trowel was a plump Yad-Elf with gray hair twisted into a

tidy bun. Her ears came to slim points that curved slightly around her head. She wore a brown coat that seemed large even on her generous frame. "Ah, our new guest! I'm so sorry that you have arrived under the auspices of such a horrendous event. Are you familiar with the word 'auspice' child?"

"She is," Neriah said with a practiced haste. "She is from Valeria after all, some of the finest schools in Aufero."

The older girl gave Rime a sideways grin. Trowel's face seemed to manifest a pair of brass spectacles as her plump hands erupted from her sides, placed the lenses on her broad nose, and went to dancing in the air.

"Ah, Valeria! Home of the Archivus Eldracon. Many of my colleagues argue that it is the finest library in the world, though I personally lean towards the Primex Loghain in Pice because of their expansive collection of primitive texts. Actual scrolls, tablets, even part of a Precursor ring excavated from near--" As Trowel's hands soared with mounting enthusiasm, the blue-skinned sea elf adjacent rolled her eyes and reached for the cheese tray.

"This is Lady Rime Korvanus," Neriah blurted. "I believe she is already known to you, Master Waters, but I wanted to introduce her to Scholar Trowel and to Coracle. Coracle is a shaman for the Nai-Elf Dragonfish Tribe."

Coracle popped the last morsel of cheese from the tray in her mouth and stood. She bowed and the bones and shells knotted in her hair rattled as she moved. White silk wound around her body in intricate knots. Rime could see in the elegant blue of her skin markings and whorls of darker flesh. *Tattoos perhaps, or are they naturally occurring?* Nai-Elves were a reclusive race, rarely bothering to emerge from their ocean home. *What is she doing in Bellwether's manor?*

"Winds and waves and the spirits of the lost. Banu bless your journey, your memory, your spear, and your fertility." The shaman pulled a small vial of white sand from her belt and sprinkled it liberally in the air around both Rime and Neriah. The sea-elf reached out with both hands and seemed to grip the air that the sand fell through, and her head reeled back, transfixed. Rime started to say something but was immediately forestalled by Neriah's quick gesture and Trowel's imperious shush. They both seemed enthralled by the shaman's trance; the mage bit her tongue and tried to brush the sand off her cloak surreptitiously.

Coracle sat back down next to the scholar, clattering. Rime blinked and looked to Neriah for a cue. The young noble shrugged and reached over to assist the mage in getting the sand out of her long hood. Rime decided that the shaman must have done this to each guest and no one had yet mustered the temerity to question the practice.

"Thank you for that…" *dusting? T*he mage searched for a proper euphemism. "…greeting, Shaman Coracle. I'm afraid I know so little of the Sea-Elves, perhaps you could teach me of your religious traditions, tribal practices, and--"

Coracle's eyes narrowed slightly. The shaman shrugged with mystical patience and went back to her cheese tray.

Am I going too far? My voice is getting so high pitched, I sound like a flash terrier. Rime berated herself. She turned to the trader to cover her misstep.

"It has been some time, Master Waters. How are you?"

The trader was an ink-quill. Thin, black, and bristly at the top. He had attempted to fold himself up properly on a nearby ottoman, but his long legs still bent in half like an awkward arachnid. He frowned in response, sourly collecting some words in his mouth before begrudgingly pushing them out the slot.

"*Doma* Korvanus. I am well. Your trip, successful?"

"Quite," Rime replied. *If you consider a prolonged period of being death-adjacent punctuated by discomfort and pain successful. All to discover the thing you've sought for years - the thing that you were so certain would save you - was a foolish fantasy.*

"Your gold. It is safe in my counting house."

"Good."

"We will speak more of this later." Waters closed the iron vault of his mouth.

"Absolutely." Rime did enjoy conversation with the taciturn trader.

The mage turned back to the two elves on the divan and smiled. "I'm sorry to discuss business. I did encounter some difficulty on the final leg of my journey, and Master Waters is holding the balance of my travel expenses."

Coracle waved a hand in disinterest, but Trowel perked up at the word 'journey'.

"Where were you traveling, child?" The wood elf had wide eyes; an errant strand of gray hair flopped between them as she leaned forward. "Please be as specific as possible. The history of this land is filled with secrets both shallow and deep. Did you pass any Precursor sites? Perhaps some Dwarven constructions?"

I am terrible at talking. I'm supposed to be finding out about them, not prompting questions about myself.

"Some family friends a few days journey to the north. It was lovely to meet you, Lady Trowel and Lady Coracle. I'm sure we'll have more time to talk later. Neriah, let's go." Rime scooped up the blonde girl's elbow and set a course for the anxious woman in the red dress. *The less people know about me the better. I don't want questions hunting me when it is time to leave. I'll come back to these three when the attention is off me.*

"Thanks for saving us," Neriah snickered. "When Trowel gets wound up, it's best to get out of the way as quickly as possible. She's in rare form ever since her presentation last night."

"Presentation?"

"Oh, I didn't go. I stayed in my room and read. She found some relic on her last expedition."

"I see. I'll have to ask her about it later. I find matters of history interesting." The *Trowel* column on Rime's mental chalkboard began to gather notes. "Though I will make sure I have a chair ready and some free time."

Neriah laughed as they approached the next guest.

The woman in the red dress was staring into her nearly empty wine glass, eyes unfocused. It afforded the mage a moment to inspect the woman's fingernails. They were painted a ceremony-shade of violet. Rime's sharp eyes picked out some flecks on the left ring finger and pinky that appeared to be tooth marks. *What do you have to be so nervous about?* The woman was fine boned and thin, her face drawn in acute angles.

"Lady Karis? I'm sorry to bother you, but I wanted to introduce our newest guest." The blonde girl gave the mage's name and Rime inclined her head.

Karis' eyes came into focus and stared at the mage intently. Her gaze spoke of a natural sense of humor that had been brutally murdered behind a shed in her formative years. "Another buyer? A representative from the Orvales?"

"I'm sorry, I am afraid you are mistaken. A buyer for what?" Rime's curiosity growled, but she kept her tone level.

Karis smiled and put her wine glass down on a table, delicate and precise. Her hair was dark brown, and her eyes were purple. The irises matched her fingernails if not her dress. Her age was unclear to Rime, somewhere in the wilderness between youth and middle age. "I see. I am interrogating a child. That is where I am at. That is the fact that I am presented with."

"Please, Karis. I'm sure that what we all just saw has upset you, but there's no need..." Neriah began.

"My apologies. I need more wine. This wine is less than satisfactory. Excuse me, ladies."

Karis rose and stalked away with a slight wobble in her gait. Neriah grimaced and watched her go. "She arrived before the rest of the others last week, so I had a day or so to get to know her. She's really not that bad, just crazy wound-tight. Everyone is here to bid on the relic that Trowel found and I've gathered that she's under some intense pressure to win the auction. She is an agent for Seafoam Trading Company."

Rime's chalk danced. *Relic. Auction. Bidding. Motive?* She was already familiar with the Seafoam Trading Company, a merchant conglomerate mainly concerned with airship travel and ocean freight. They were at the forefront of Precursor research, using rediscovered technology to power their ships, to make them faster and more efficient than any other in the world. Their corporate headquarters was in Gate City, outposts in most major trade hubs, and an expansive research site in Kythera, the ruined capitol city of the Arkanic civilization. Rime had devoured a travelogue describing some of the ruins and there had been expansive footnotes about the STC as they had underwritten the publication.

"This is a strange group to all be here to purchase the same object." The mage looked around the room. "You have no idea what it is?"

Trowel is interested in Precursor artifacts and sites. The Seafoam Trading Company is very interested in Precursor artifacts and sites. She switched to red chalk in her mind and drew a bold connecting line.

"Oh, Trowel explained it to me once over dinner a few nights ago. She lost me about two paragraphs in, partly because of, well *Trowel.* But also because I was seated next to Geranium that night." Neriah gave an appreciative sigh.

"Geranium?" Rime said distantly, completing her internal notes. *Don't jump to conclusions. Meet all the suspects. Objectivity is key.* Her instructions were sound, but her hand had a lot of red chalk dust on it as she returned from her mental library.

"Oh, no. You haven't met him yet. I saved him for last. The best for last." Neriah carefully pushed her long blonde curls over her shoulder and tugged at the front of her dress. "Do I look okay?"

"I guess?" Rime hazarded. "What's so special about this Geranium?"

"You'll understand as soon as you meet him. I am *so* glad that there's another girl here now who can fully appreciate him." The older girl straightened and gently took Rime by the shoulders. "Let's go meet a god."

This is the best cheese. I can't remember ever having better cheese than this.

Jonas had attempted to remain vigilant at his post, but after his first bite the storm of flavor had completely distracted him. It had even temporarily pushed the princess out of his thoughts. He was engaged in scraping the tips of his fingers across the plate to gather the tiny morsels of cheese that remained when he felt a tap on his shoulder.

He spun around in alarm and stared at the Past.

The Past wore a black cassock and an amused smile. His gray hair had abandoned the top of his head and was establishing its last line of defense just above his ears. On his chest a blue circle was stitched,three blue swords crossed within.

Rage. Fear. Despair. The three weapons of the human soul. Bound in a thin circle of Valor. This is Faith, my son. The words came unbidden to the squire's mind.

"Hello," the priest said, then pointed at the empty tray

Jonas clutched. "Good cheese here, right?"

The squire did his best to swallow and nod emphatically. "Yes. Yes, Father."

"Ah, are you a follower of the Nameless? Most of the other guests here go to great lengths to avoid calling me 'Father'. 'Master Gallowglass' or 'Andrew'. That's the best I can expect from this pack of heathens." The priest grinned and slanted his eyebrows towards the rest of the room.

"Oh. Heathens, right." *Stupid, stupid, stupid. The one thing I'm supposed to do is not let people know that I'm from Gilead.* Jonas waved his empty tray around, vainly looking for a place to stash it. He finally settled for tucking it under his arm.

"I'm sorry, son. I didn't mean to catch you off-guard." Father Andrew folded his hands together. "I was just excited to meet a new guest here. It's been a long few days of being patted on the head by the more worldly members of our company."

The priest reached over and pulled the tray gently free from Jonas' armpit.

"Scholars and wizards and businessmen. A bunch of sharp knives that like to think a man of the cloth is a dull spoon. As if faith was a feature of a weakened brain," Father Andrew snorted.

"My father is from Gilead -- he taught me the Faith." Jonas blurted. The squire had heard somewhere that lies were best if they were close to the truth. *What did Rime tell me to say? What was the name of her home town?* "I grew up in Valeria. I'm Lady Korvanus' manservant."

He almost sighed in relief but caught himself. He had managed to repeat what Rime had told him to say and cover the mistake about his religion. *See, I can do this spy-stuff.*

"Manservant?" the priest cocked an eyebrow. Jonas realized that Father Andrew used his eyebrows like battle flags signaling the march of his thoughts. "You seem more like a house guard that's been stuffed into a dandy costume. The buttons on your vest are all crooked, and most gentlemen don't tuck their shirt only in the front."

Jonas looked down in horror. The bottom of his vest gaped, a spare button shining in the lamplight. He had been so proud of his reflection in the mirror; how could he have missed this?

Father Andrew chortled and tucked the cheese tray under his arm. With a grandfatherly air he nimbly undid the buttons as the squire's face burned with embarrassment. Jonas risked a quick glance back towards the other guests. Everyone's attention seemed to be focused on Rime. She and the princess were moving towards the tall man in the blue coat.

"Just a little moment of humility, son. The Nameless sends me plenty, I assure you. They are reminders of our simple natures, deflate our pride. They are healthy and harmless and help us remember to show kindness when we witness others in their own tiny moments of shame." The priest smiled as he fastened the last silver button. He handed the cheese tray back to Jonas with calm deference.

"Thank you, Father." Jonas turned his back to the wall and shoved the errant shirt tail down the back of his leggings as stealthily as he could manage.

"Nothing to it. Now that you are properly chastised and attired, shall we exchange formal introductions? As you may have gathered, I am Father Andrew Gallowglass, a simple Shepherd of the Nameless from Corinth."

Corinth. The capitol city! I must be careful. He may have heard about the trial and Master. He considered offering a fake name but didn't trust his fledgling skills at deception. And after all, his name was as common as dirt in Gilean families. "Jonas is my name, sir. It's nice to meet you."

Plus, I'd probably forget whatever made-up name I said.

"Walk on, Jonas, that the Nameless may see your path." Father Andrew bowed his head after saying the old blessing.

The squire wondered how long it had been since he'd heard the old words. Weeks? Months?

"Only Once." The words came as if from a stranger's lips.

"*Only Once,*" the priest echoed with a trace of surprise. "Your father taught you well."

Jonas nodded, not trusting himself to speak.

"We must find a time to pray together." Father Andrew's eyebrows waggled with elation. "A shepherd doesn't feel right without a flock to tend."

The tall man in the blue coat was standing with his back to the room, in front of a window filled with night and rain. Rime meticulously noted the fine material, the deftly stitched buckles and piping, the high collar studded with machine-forged snaps. The bard was still hunched over his instrument, his shoulders and arms tight with concentration. All at once he relaxed. His head straightened first, revealing a brush of cotton-candy hair floating over dark skin the color of coffee. The neck of his guitar appeared, cradled by his left hand. He wore a pink, fingerless glove that matched the shade of his hair with mathematical precision. The bard's fingers tightened on the strings of his guitar and an expectant vibration filled the air.

"Oh," Neriah sighed. "This is my favorite part."

The strings yowled and dipped into a steady beat. A melody skipped into view and began to unfold itself like a tiger stretching, low and hungry. Then the tall man turned to face the room.

Rime watched her thoughts turn into letters made of glass. *He is beautiful. So beautiful.* The bard's eyes were closed as he turned, lips pursed as his hands flew across the guitar strings. His face was thin and sharp. Nose, cheekbones, chin all drawn with a razor -- the face of a cat, fine and precise. *Cinnamon coffee, the expensive kind*, Rime amended. The parlor grew still as the bard opened his eyes and sang.

His eyes were the same color as his hair and his gloves, though they seemed to shine brighter than the lamplight.

Watch all this wither
Watch as we gather
the leaves and grass
and broken things
threadbare heroes
and three-cross kings,
we sleep in the heart

we wait in the dark
until the cobblestones give way...

Watch all that glitters
Watch all that stains
the sun shines on the city
but tomorrow will rain
but tomorrow will rain
we dream in the earth
we dream of the sky.
Green bone and promise
even blue dreams can die.
When the cobblestones give way
When the cobblestones give way...

The music grew in concentric circles, rippling through the parlor. Rime's temples itched as she sensed the bard's magic at work. She had read several books concerning the strange manner in which the bards of Gate City had learned to harness magical energy in the form of music, but this was her first opportunity to witness it.

The melody and lyrics were mournful and odd, but the tall man's voice rang with easy sincerity and joy. His voice was higher than she expected but clean and true.

"Isn't he amazing?" Neriah whispered. Rime could only nod in agreement.

The bard sang a final verse, then let his fingers fly across the guitar strings as he brought the song to a close. The guitar itself was a gleaming ebony with white inlay that appeared to be some sort of bone. The pressure in the mage's head increased as the musical spell began to resolve. *What is he doing? All spells have a purpose, a function. What is he trying to do?*

The guitar sang out, and the bard added his voice again in final harmony. The notes faded away into silence, and the pressure in Rime's head vanished. A smattering of applause came from Trowel and Coracle; the others in the room simply nodded with appreciation.

"Lady Rime, I am most pleased to present our honored guest--" the older girl gushed.

"Geranium." Fluorescent pink eyes flashed and a fluorescent pink glove took Rime's hand. "Geranium the Eruption."

Rime blinked once. The bard was extremely impressive, but she would not allow herself to be overwhelmed as the blonde girl was. Not by his music, not by his unknown magic, not by his perfectly symmetrical cheekbones.

"I enjoyed your song very much, Geranium the Eruption. Lady Neriah tells me that you are a bard of great renown. Are you putting us all under an enchantment?" The mage did her best imitation of a winsome smile.

Geranium laughed and flew through a sudden chord on his guitar. "Nothing so grand, kitten. Nothing so grandiose. Just a simple song."

Rime's eyes narrowed. *I know you did something.*

The bard let his ebony guitar fall and it hung in the air, as certain as a hummingbird. She saw that there was no strap holding it in place.

"The shadows hang, kitten. They hang on us all after seeing such a sight, a sight of horror. My song, my simple song. It lets you feel the shadows' weight and nudges you to step out from under them," Geranium said.

The blonde girl leaned in eagerly, hanging on each word. Rime realized Neriah's fingers were digging into her arm. *I don't know which is more irritating: her fingernails or that ridiculous explanation.*

The mage pried herself free from the older girl's grip and took a step closer to the bard. Geranium smiled wide -- a cat looking down on a canary. *He is very pretty*, Rime admitted to herself.

"What brings you here? The auction, I presume?" She kept her face still.

"Of course, kitten. The technology at work in the Sound Crystal would be immensely valuable to the Symphony. Are you planning on buying it out from under us?"

Sound Crystal. That's what they're all here to buy. More chalk danced in her head.

"Perhaps," she replied nonchalantly. "I know I missed Scholar Trowel's presentation, but I'm hoping to convince her to give me an abbreviated glimpse."

"It was remarkable. Even if I am not successful in the auction, it was worth the trip alone to hear such an amazing thing." Geranium turned to put his guitar away, ebony instrument floating obediently towards its case at a simple gesture. "Sounds from a forgotten age, kitten. Worth much travel, and even the horrible sights we have seen this night."

Doesn't seem too shaken up by the murder, for all his words of horror and terror. 'Sounds from a forgotten age'? I need to find out what that means, but I can't show too much interest. Also, it should probably bother me that he keeps calling me 'kitten', but it really doesn't. What does that mean?

"Ah, you have reminded me. I had hoped to visit the Players and offer my condolences. They, of course, are struck the hardest by this foul happening. Neriah, would you be so kind as to take me to them?" Rime turned to the blonde girl.

"Huh, what?" Neriah said, her eyes glassy and wide, reflecting Geranium's tall form.

"The Players. I want to visit them. To tell them I'm sorry for their loss." Rime grabbed the older girl's arm and spun her away from the bard.

"Oh, okay." The blonde's eyes still trailed back towards the shining blue coat, but her faculties seemed to return as Rime increased the distance between them and Geranium.

The mage shot a glance toward her guardian. He was refilling his plate, while carrying on a lively conversation with the priest of the Nameless. Rime let her nails scratch down the chalkboard of her mind to unleash her frustration. She snapped her fingers until Jonas finally looked up with a guilty expression. He said his farewell to the priest and lumbered over. His eyes came a little unfocused as he approached Neriah. The blonde girl nodded politely, but she still beamed across the parlor towards Geranium.

Rime sighed.

She took Neriah's arm gently and indicated to Jonas with a stern expression that he should follow them.

The main doors lead back into the lobby of the manor and the grand double staircase. The mage lead her small entourage towards a single door on the north wall that, according to her quickly expanding mental map of the House of the Heart-Broken Lion, would lead to the banquet hall where the performance of *Towerlock's Travels* had ended so abruptly.

Rime made note of all of the information she had gathered on the chalkboard of her mind but refrained from drawing any conclusions as yet. It was time to meet the Players.

3

The Banquet Hall was dim, lit only by small lamps on the long table and a cock-eyed stage light still illuminating the Prince's cart. Funnicello scowled as they entered but continued to clear the discarded plates and goblets. The dwarf scraped the food into a large bowl, stacked the plates one by one and made no effort to conceal the rude gulps he took from the half-finished wine goblets.

The stage was only raised knee-height off the floor. Neriah led them to the cunning wooden steps on the left-hand edge of the stage. Rime noticed an identical set on the opposite side. The floor was dark burnished wood that seemed to drink in the spotlight, an amber circle of golden light.

The mage's eyes moved immediately to center stage where the damsel had collapsed. Not a speck of blood remained. Jonas stared up at the stage lights, squinting into the one that was still lit. The silver buttons on his vest shone.

At the back of the stage was a freestanding wall. From behind it spilled the quiet sound of sobbing and a little

43

more light. The lord's daughter led Rime around one side of the wall. Jonas trotted quickly to catch up.

Behind the wall, four hammocks were strung and three battered chests spilled over with tattered finery: robes for kings, gowns for penniless match girls, cloaks for villains, and armor for heroes. Wooden swords sprouted from a pea-green barrel, gilt flecking and thin. Crammed into the far end of this space was the wooden coffin that had revealed the murdered woman. It was from this that both the tears and the wobbling light originated.

The three players stood around the coffin like a tableau. The Sorcerer had removed his beard revealing a sallow face dotted with moles His skull-ringed robe hung off one shoulder, showing a doublet that was equally as spotted. The erstwhile wizard had one long hand on the shoulder of the weeping Towerlock. *Toby is his real name, and he called out hers. Darla.*

The man who was not Humphrey was fussing with a lantern shaped like a globe. He looked up in surprise at their approach. He smoothly hung it from a nearby hammock and stooped into a florid bow.

"Ah, ladies. Please excuse our disrepair. You have come upon us in our grief and our masks are all askew." His voice was deep and rang with quiet skill, a voice familiar with a thousand speeches in a thousand strange tales.

"No, it is we who must ask your forgiveness," Neriah said. "Lady Rime suggested that we come and offer our condolences."

"Most kind, most proper." The player bowed again. His hair was almost completely white and close cropped.

Rime adjusted her impressions of the performers. She had assumed that the Sorcerer would be their leader, but the older man spoke with calm authority. The long-jawed villain had made no move to speak, keeping his attention on the weeping hero.

"I know this must be horrible for you," the mage said in her best imitation of concern.

"Horrible. Yes, my lady. Horrible and most strange. I only thank Providence that supplied us with a coffin for poor Darla. If we had performed *The Rickett Tragedy*, we would only have had a pair of sawhorses and a prison facade."

Toby's constant sobbing paused for a moment in shock. The handsome man looked up, his face a classical ravage. He then flung his arms across the coffin and wept with redoubled ferocity.

"Sand," the Sorcerer sighed with quiet reproach.

"I apologize, Vincent. My glib tongue works overmuch, I fear," the white-haired man grimaced.

"Tell me, Master Sand, was Darla ill? I know that Lord Bellwether plans to investigate and ensure our safety, but is it possible that this was some unfortunate sickness that took her?" Rime asked.

"Not likely, my lady. Darla was hearty, smiling and fine when we took our places for the performance. I closed her in the coffin myself and there was nothing amiss." Sand gestured toward the swinging hammocks. "And as you see, we've been in close quarters. If it was a sickness, than the rest of us would surely show some sign of it. No, our Darla was taken from us."

The crying hero seemed to absorb the older man's words and his voice rose in pitch until he was nearly keening. Rime had to speak loudly to be heard over the din.

"Your friend seems very upset. Were they lovers?" the mage asked.

"No, no." Vincent laid a fond hand on Toby's golden hair. "He shares my bed, but he cared for Darla greatly. He's a sensitive sort, feels things deeply. It's what makes him such a fine actor."

"And a bit of a mess in situations like this," Sand said with careful projection to be heard over the sobbing.

"Perhaps we should leave him for the moment, then," Rime nearly shouted in frustration.

Sand nodded his agreement and walked with them back onto the darkened stage. Vincent and Toby remained in their tableau. The leading player paused briefly to undo a bit of twine that hung ragged on the broken cave-front from earlier, clucking with concern. He bowed again, focusing on Neriah.

"My lady, could you do me a kindness? Could you speak to your uncle about perhaps a small cask of wine for our troupe? We would drink to Darla's memory, but I also pray it will calm poor Toby's nerves."

"Of course," the blonde girl replied. "Let me go fetch you one myself -- I am so sorry that nothing else has been offered to you. I'm afraid we were all very caught up after the show."

"No need to apologize. Your uncle did offer us some kind words, and the Father spoke a few more for Darla's soul.

But the wine would be the kindest of all. We are actors you see, and wine is our sacrament." Sand spread his hands.

"Will you be okay, Lady Rime? You have your escort, Job." As Neriah spoke, Rime could almost hear the squire deflating behind her. "I will rejoin you in the Parlor shortly."

The lord's daughter took the mage's smile for assent and turned to leave, threading her way past the sour dwarf who was carrying out folded piles of table cloths. Jonas watched her go with an absurd level of attention. The mage rolled her eyes.

Rime tapped the chalk on her board. *Details. Specifics. I need more information.*

"Such a tragic affair," the mage turned back to the white-haired player. "Surely there must be some reason why this --"

Sand was staring at her directly, his arms crossed. "You are a terrible actor."

"Excuse me,sir. I--"

"I mean, you're fine for those fine lords and ladies in the other room. But please have a little respect for my craft. Your eyes dip slightly when you deliver your lines; I've seen more convincing smiles painted on dolls." The actor laid a hand on his bosom and let the other float out with consummate grace. "You should have chosen another role. The Damsel is not for you."

Jonas snickered, then covered it poorly by coughing into his sleeve. The chalk snapped in her mind's hand.

"Very well. Did you kill her?" Rime retorted.

"No. Nor did Toby or Vincent." Sand let his hands drop. "I don't know why you are concerned with our Darla's murder, but you are our best chance. That miserable dwarf made it quite clear that we were not to leave this room under any circumstance. I want to know who killed my girl."

The white-haired actor's eyes blazed and for the first time Rime thought she was seeing a true light from him.

"So do I," Rime nodded.

"I will help you however I can. Though your acting is going to perhaps take more time than we currently have at hand to improve," Sand gestured with sarcastic aplomb.

Jonas started to chuckle again, but she ignored it.

"Then answer my questions. How long was she in the coffin? Did she have any encounters or conversations with the other guests? Did you notice anyone backstage before the performance? Why was she wearing a wig? How come there is only one woman in your troupe? What is Darla's background? Where does she come from? And can you get that lump away from the coffin long enough for me to inspect the corpse?"

Sand's eyes widened as the questions hammered. He looked over her shoulder and asked Jonas, "Is she always like this?"

"Only when she's in a very good mood," the squire replied.

Rime pulled on her half-cloak in frustration. She opened

48

her mouth to speak, but the actor held up a hand to forestall her.

"Please, let me tote the first pile before you stack more on my barrow. Let me get some wine in Vincent and Toby before you peek in the coffin. They're good lads, but the less explaining we need to do the better. Any show that needs more than one woman, Vincent or I can easily don a dress and heels to fill the cast. She was wearing a wig because of Towerlock's speech in Scene Three, 'By secrets and songs and riddles untold, I care for naught but Key's bright hair of gold'." Sand counted on his fingers as he answered.

"I saw when it slipped off that she is a Wood Elf. Pointed ears, delicate skeletal structure. What grove is she from?" Rime demanded.

"No grove. Her family is from Quorum, that greasy stack of metal and smoke. All the Yad-Elves there swore off the land in exchange for a steady paycheck and fancy top hats. We winter there, get factory work, repair costumes, brush up our speeches and wait for the first wind of spring to get back out on the road." Sand smiled at the memory.

"Yes, very nice."

"I'm almost through, don't rush me." The actor paused to review her questions again. "The only people that came backstage were Geranium and the dwarf. The bard hit it off with Vincent and Toby and wanted to wish them well before the performance. The dwarf just dropped off our evening meal, just as he has before each of our shows. The show tonight is a short one, she only would have been in there half an hour. I closed her in myself, as I said. She was fine, smiling and laughing."

The chalk danced in her mind. *So if she was fine when she went into the coffin, somehow she was poisoned inside of it. Unless it was a slow-acting poison.*

"Did any of you eat the food that Funnicello brought?"

"We all did, nothing amiss."

Another note. Darla's column was filling quickly. She tapped the chalk on a missing spot.

"You left something out. Did she talk with the other guests, any strange conversations?"

Sand laid a finger aside his nose and sighed. He walked a few steps away towards the edge of the stage and peered out across the dim chairs and table in the banquet hall. The dwarf was nowhere to be seen. Rime pursued with her arms crossed in impatience.

"I don't like to speak ill of my troupe. But Darla always took the hammock on the end," he said with quiet reluctance.

The hammock on the end? The mage looked at the backstage wall. She thought of the cramped space she had just seen, and it appeared in green chalk on the wall. The two hammocks at the back, the third spaced a bit further, then the three trunks of costumes, then the final one swinging near the entrance. A chalk-Darla slept in the final one, then swung down her face careful and sly. She slipped out of the backstage while the others slept, chalk snores scratching.

"She was seeing someone in the manor," Rime said, not bothering to conceal the triumph in her voice.

50

Sand nodded.

"Did she say who? Give any indication?"

The white-haired actor shook his head. "Not a whisper. I only knew because I spied her slipping out last night. I know she didn't tell Vincent or Toby either -- no secrets kept in a troupe."

A tryst. The mystery books in her head gaped open in excitement. Almost all of them had a sexual transgression of some sort, secret assignations, daggers in the lovers' bower. *If I find Darla's lover, then I've found her killer.*

The door banged open as Funnicello re-entered. He glowered at the actor, but saved a helping of eye-stone for Jonas and Rime. The mage didn't leap back into her full simple young lady act, but she did straighten her posture.

"I shall return later, when your players have drowned their sorrows. You've given me something to go on, but I still want to inspect the body." Rime bowed and swept away down the simple wooden stairs. She looked back to see Jonas pat Sand on the shoulder in rough comfort.

"Do remind Lady Neriah about the wine," the actor called after her. "It is darker than usual in our Twilight Kingdom. Wine and light, if you would be so kind."

The squire's beat-leather boots squawked on the burnished floor in his haste to follow Rime out of the Banquet Hall. The door to the Parlor closed behind her; she had neglected her Escort Accessory. *Maybe she won't bother as much with the act, now that Sand shut her down so hard.*

Jonas found himself across a table from the ice-river eyes of Funnicello.

The dwarf was pushing a white cloth across the long table, mechanically dunking it in a silver pail after each section of the wood was cleaned to his liking. Jonas felt his gaze like two gaping cannon mouths and tried to side-march out of the firing lane in as dignified a manner as possible. The wet slap of the dwarf's rag on the table startled him, and it turned into more of a crab-scuttle.

Funnicello's eyes hung on Jonas. The squire felt himself getting heavier with each step. The dwarf's disdain was a bricklayer slathering hate-mortar and disgust-stones all over him. Lord Bellwether's manservant wasn't particularly imposing in appearance: thinning red hair and a well-kept moustache and goatee. But his eyes made the room groan with slow time.

Crossing laterally around the table took a decade. Each chair Jonas passed was five months of hatred, a signpost. *Slap*, the wet rag on the dark wood.

The door to the Parlor was only a few weeks away, when a thought wiggled its way into the squire's brain. *'You worry about getting your sword back...'*

Jonas sighed. He was going to have to talk to the glacier.

"Ah Master Funnicello, sir?" The squire tugged on the bottom hem of his vest.

The dwarf glowered in response and tore the wet rag in half. A quick, squelching rip and half of the rag was sailing through the air in his direction. Jonas caught it, soapy water scattering across his face. He lowered the dripping cloth and peeked over it.

Funnicello continued to swab the dark wood of the table, his eyes trained on Jonas. But now an air of expectation seemed to have entered the fray.

Uncertainly, Jonas dabbed at a the corner of the table closest to him. The dwarf's moustache twitched. The squire leaned into the task of scouring the table with the damp white cloth.

The two white cloths moved across the table, the only sound in the room their husky slide. Jonas risked a quick glance at the dwarf, and saw that his gaze was finally averted. Funnicello's thick fingers prodded a dried up spot of food, excavating it from the wooden landscape.

"So, I was wondering. If I could get my sword back?" Jonas made sure to keep his rag moving while he spoke.

Funnicello exhaled sharply, flaring the pointed ends of his moustache.

"I am Rime's, Lady Rime's, Lady Korvanus' guardian." The squire's rag nearly flew across the table. "And there's most likely some sort of killer in the manor. I won't do much good with my bare hands."

The dwarf slapped his half-rag down into the silver pail. He held the bucket before him and approached Jonas. Without a word he looked down into the soapy water.

"I can promise you that I will use it only to defend my Rime, I mean my lady."

Funnicello raised the bucket slightly.

Jonas sighed and dropped his cloth to join its other half.

The lord's manservant turned and stumped away, but he stopped at the door that led out into the grand lobby. His back stiffened for a moment, then he turned and locked eyes with Jonas. Then he turned right back around in a crisp about-face. The dwarf rapped his knuckles on the pail, four staccato beats, a pause, then two slow beats.

Funnicello walked out the door.

Jonas stared at the blank door. "Okay. What?"

WHO WAS DARLA TARGHOS?

In a city of smoke and steel, she was a glow-worm.
Not particularly bright or piercing but a stubborn
illumination. Not enough to guide one through the smog-
filled brick horror-streets of Quorum, but if one happened
to stumble. If one happened to stumble upon one of the
few sickly shrubs that dotted the iron-wrought medians of
the Thoroughfare, and one's eye focused for a moment in
the brown branches of the dying plant. One could see her.
Green-glow shine and shout, inching along. The arrogance
of joy. Common and casual, bioluminescent defiance.

Quorum is a new town, though it has labored fiercely to
coat itself in smoke-stack centuries of grime. Fifty years
gone the Yad-Elves of Riddlewood turned their back on
the forest, on their forest, on their sacred bond to the
wood. They joined forces with metal-minded humans and
built a city on the coast, a hub of trade, a garden of
squares, a warehouse world.

Darla was born here. Her mother was a dockyard
mechanic; her father repaired roofs. Plain elves, simple and
sturdy, they were unprepared for her arrival. Her father

knocked together a ramshackle crib while her mother cried out across the room. Their shifts were long and their home-strength was short, but the dark-morning joy she brought them with her first wails did not offer itself for easy calculation. Her mother and father held her in exhausted reverence as the sun did its best to shine through the morning smog. Then they wrapped her in a clean blanket and went to work with no breakfast.

They were even more unprepared for her first words. Her first dance shocked them all the more. The small plays she would perform with her crude toys and sheets, the rambling stories she would tell born from her dreams, the pictures of monsters she would paint on the walls: all these wearied and shocked her workaday parents but also filled them with a solemn light. Their girl was something. Their girl was worth a story.

Their girl glowed.

Darla grew older and learned that she was reckless with hearts. She cut out of work to listen to a travelling bard. She slipped through the greasy window of her room to watch a troupe perform *Fast Jack and the Incorruptible Widow* in the courtyard of a local merchant. She ran away from home for a week when a tall goblin bought her a blue dress with white pearls at the neck. Her parents despaired and railed. But their glow-worm came back, and they were not so secretly pleased at the clamor and light that followed her unrepentant inching.

When she was nineteen, Darla met the players.

She was running through the midnight streets of Quorum, hand in hand with a black-haired human girl. They had heard of a secret session in the heart of the city, a trumpet player of rare skill and verve. Her friend had talked about it all day across the steel track at the factory, and Darla had nearly flown home to pick out the perfect outfit for their excursion. Dark enough for shadows, light enough to move, but with a little flash for dancing in a crowded basement. Jazz requires the proper attire.

Darla and her friend turned the corner, and there they were. Vincent was dressed as a devil, red fabric stretched across his long frame. In his clutches was Toby, wearing a simple white tunic and his gorgeous face. Sand wore a fake beard and a strip of bloody fabric wound around his right eye. The older man's hands were clenched, white-knuckled with anguish. He was mid-way through a long speech as Darla dragged her disinterested friend closer.

She had seen players before, but this was the first time she had ever seen them perform for empty air. Their cart was parked in a narrow alley, a brace of round lanterns cast clean light on the space. The shadow and smoke of the city retreated in alarm but hovered close waiting for the play to end. Darla guessed that she had stumbled upon a rehearsal of some sort, but it captured her. The light and the pain that sang in the old man's voice captured her.

"Name your price, Demon of Old!" Sand cried out. "Treasures or tortures or my own shining soul. Ask it of me and it is yours. What would I deny for my beloved?"

She leaned against a wall fascinated. Her friend grew bored quickly and left. Darla didn't offer an apology or an explanation. The one-eyed man wept, the devil laughed, and the handsome young man died. Her applause seemed to echo in the alley when the players were finished.

Toby laughed, Vincent gasped in surprise, but Sand swept into a florid bow without missing a beat.

"It was so good," Darla glowed. "Why was it so good if you're only rehearsing?"

"Only rehearsing?" The old man arched an eyebrow and pulled free his false beard. "Lovely lady, you do not understand our ways; you have not walked in the Twilight. Each time we visit the kingdom we must journey as honest guests. Eager and thankful for the light we may reflect. Also, a sloppy run makes a sloppy play."

"And he loves that speech. That doesn't hurt either." Vincent wrapped a long, red arm around Toby and bared pointed teeth. From that close Darla could see that they were false and made of wax.

"I see you have a cart. I suppose that means that you travel." She folded her hands.

"We do," Sand replied.

"When do we start?"

And in moments it was done. She joined the troupe; she became their Damsel. As quick and easy as two drops of water meet. Her father shouted while her mother threw a dish, but Darla went anyway.

She went anyway, down the long and twisting roads of Wander. Toby taught her stage makeup, and Vincent taught her the Nine Proper Villainous Stances. They performed for kings and merchants, for paupers and farmers. The rain fell on their backs when the cart broke a wheel near Valeria. Their stomachs groaned with rich food when the king of Flenelle bought their services for an entire season. Sand taught her how to lie with conviction, to love with clarity and brevity, to destroy with three fingers touching her neck. She most often played the

58

Damsel, in all its thousand shades. The Shy Lover. The Prudent Daughter. The Chaste Princess. The Lost Love. The Fairest. The Childhood Dream. For a lark, she tried her hand at a few murderesses and crones, but her easy glow proved a hindrance. No audience could dislike her, her charm either made the witch too unlikely or the villain too sympathetic.

The glow-worm inched on. Her light did not pierce as a star or burn as a sun. It simply shone on, reckless.

Until she toppled out of a coffin onto the stage. Until the House of the Heart-Broken Lion.

4

Lord Bellwether stood in the center of the Parlor with his guests clustered close. His hands were shoulder-level, fingers splayed wide in contrition. Rime caught the last of his words as she entered.

"--manservant will summon the proper authorities, the Third Regiment from Carroway. I am not certain if there was truly any foul play, but no chances will be taken. The front door is sealed and will remain so until the Regiment arrives," Bellwether said.

"The door is sealed?" Karis seethed, purple nails clutching another empty wine glass.

"Yes. If one of our number has done this deed, I will not have them escape justice," the lord replied.

"Then you have sealed us inside with a murderer. Or perhaps with plague, if disease carried off the girl. Wonderful." The woman in red raised the glass to her lips, then blinked in embarrassment at the empty crystal.

"This does seem an extreme passion, my lord of Bellwether," Coracle grimaced, shells rattling in her hair as she spoke. "Shall I consult the Balance? Perhaps they can shed some wisdom on this dark affair."

The sea-elf folded her cobalt hands in an intricate lace and closed her eyes. The whorls in her flesh that Rime had noticed earlier began to gleam, then shine like golden sun through dark blue ocean. Coracle began to hum an atonal melody.

"No, no thank you," Bellwether said hastily, interrupting the shaman. "I know you had planned to leave tomorrow morning, immediately after the final bidding. But I'm afraid that I must insist that everyone remain an extra day or two."

The gleam faded from Coracle's dark skin, and she opened her eyes.

"As you say, my lord of stones and rain. I will abide and wait for the Balance to guide my steps," the shaman murmured and raised one hand to the heavens as the other pressed towards the floor. In this odd contortion she glided away, her eyes at peace. The sea-elf sailed out of the Parlor without looking back. The jangle of shells in her hair followed.

In an uncomfortable silence, the balding priest with who Jonas had earlier conversed, cleared his throat.

"I can pray as well," Father Andrew smiled. "But I think everyone bolting their doors tonight would be more prudent."

Trowel and Master Waters nodded agreement.

"But still pray," the priest said with mock severity.

"Do the tenets of the Nameless God of Gilead allow you to advocate or allow prayers to rival deities?" Trowel asked, her eyes wide with curiosity.

"Well, ah..."

"It is a topic that I have not given sufficient study, but I find it fascinating. With the endless physical evidence of multiple deities, how can a monolithic religion such as yours take root?" The scholar's nostrils flared as she gathered steam. "There are so many other belief systems, spread across the world. The pantheon of the Balance: Seto, Banu, Jocasta, Marrus. The goddess of Fire and Law, Nasirah, worshipped by the Sarmadi. The odd dwarven mysticism of the First Stone, the Cat Spirit, the fallen god of mathematics, Nomus--"

"So many names," Father Andrew interrupted. "So many splinters of--"

"Another philosophical tangle, wonderful," Karis interrupted his interruption. "Can we return to the matter at hand? Our rooms have locks, but could not anyone with a key open them?"

"They lock from the inside," Bellwether assured her.

"So you say," the woman in red sighed as she pinched the bridge of her nose with two fingers.

Neriah stepped out from behind her father's shoulder where she had been standing with a careful mannered smile. The smile frayed, leaving only gentle concern on her face. She took Karis' arms and gave her a squeeze.

"I'm sure that the poor actress died by some strange accident or was sick as you said. No one else here has shown any signs of illness, so I am sure that we are all fine," the lord's daughter said.

Karis laughed with a brittle-black tone. "Fine. All fine. Yes, if you say it, Neriah."

"Perhaps we should all turn in for the evening. Please lock your doors as we've discussed, just as a precaution. Funnicello and I will walk the halls at regular intervals. I am your host, and that is a duty that weighs on me. Now, please excuse me. I will see you all tomorrow morning at breakfast. If you have any needs or further concerns, come to my rooms in the tower." Lord Bellwether inclined his head and left the room.

Neriah and Karis followed, arm in arm. The scholar and the priest picked up their debate while snagging a few more tarts from the ornate display, then departed as well. Master Waters shot a blank stare at Rime before making his way out of the parlor.

This left only the bard, Geranium, who had said nothing. He was leaning over his ebony guitar, working at a bolt with a small silver tool. Rime realized that her hands were unconsciously smoothing her white half-cape and ordered them to return to their posts. They went with no undue shame.

Unacceptable. He is extremely attractive and has a beautiful singing voice. But I do not react in this way. I am not some flighty little girl with a brain full of ponies and nail polish. Now I will calmly approach him and obtain some more information. Everyone is a suspect, and I need to know more about the strange manner in which his magical skill operates.

Her right hand was fussing with her hair. Rime grimaced and marched forth to battle. She would fight with the army she had, limb insubordination notwithstanding.

"Such a strange and frightening situation," she gushed as she approached. Rime concentrated on appearing as a harmless, excitable young lady. The actor's appraisal of her ability to deceive concerned her, but it was too late to change character.

The bard looked up, the silver key held between his perfect teeth.

"I am glad that we have a Bard of Gate City to protect us," Rime fought to not grit her teeth as she simpered. "I have heard tales of their strange musical abilities."

Geranium strummed a dark chord on his guitar.

"I am glad that you have chosen this moment to speak with me. This moment alone," he crooned.

"Oh, well. I am glad too, if you have something you wish to share with me."

"Ever since I first saw you, I have had a question to ask you. A question of great importance," he continued as he summoned another chord.

"Yes?"

"I must know. What do you use to color your hair?"

Rime rocked back on her heels, fingers summoning frustration knots from the hem of her dress.

"I mean, it's really well done," Geranium continued. "It

goes right to the root. I color my hair often, but I've never been able to get that pure white."

The bard ran his spider-fingers through the brush of pink hair, holding it back to demonstrate his point. Rime could see the barest bit of nut-brown color at the base of each strand of hair. His sharp features twisted in a mockery of a pout. He let one hand drift languorously towards her face as he spoke again.

"Is it some magic, an enchanted elixir perhaps? Or some secret family recipe passed down for untold ages in Valeria? It is so pure and --"

For a moment, even through her frustration, Rime was spellbound. Something about the tall man in the blue coat skipped beyond the hold of numbers or the pages of her library. She could see each perfectly cut nail on his hand as he reached up to touch the white in her hair. His pupils seemed to spin.

Then the moment burst like a soap bubble. The mage slapped his hand away with all her might.

Geranium the Eruption laughed with surprise, a flute's scale. He clutched the offending hand with the other and cradled it like a broken bird.

"Keep your secrets then, kitten. A woman's beauty is a fortress best guarded by silence. But have a care, my hands are my life. A few more swats like that and I will be reduced to playing drum for a dancing monkey show. And then who will serve at the feet of my Lady Moon-Death?" the bard asked with reproach, sliding his hands nimbly along the guitar's strings.

It took the mage a moment to respond. Her reaction

confused her. She had no fear of the man with the ridiculous pink hair. Her magic could tear him apart, consume and burn and erase him no matter what his silly music did. The same magic that she had leaned on too much, pulled on too deeply from a short stack of weeks ago. It had marked her, turned her ordinary brown hair to bone-white. A slash of blank hair that the bard had tried to touch.

Am I angry? Afraid? Offended? Her heart beat enough that she was aware of it. *I can smell him like candy in the oven. Burning sugar, but not unpleasant.*

"Please accept my apology," the bard bowed almost in half while his hands summoned a lament from the strings of his black guitar.

Rime echoed the gesture, then turned and walked away. She considered offering some bland pleasantry to cover the strange moment, but her eagerness to be away from the bard howled in her veins like adrenaline-wolves.

She pushed at the door leading out of the Parlor and stopped. The bard was singing again.

Oh--
Strange and mysterious ways
Songs of the Lost
Please brighten our days
Remember the beginning
and obscure the end
the two-button knight
is the loner's best friend.

She felt nothing in her temples, there was no magic in the melody. But it gripped her spine all the same.

Oh--
Fallen and fearful ways
Songs of the Lost
Please remember our days
Hiding and hidden
lost and alone
the King of Forever
topples his throne.

Rime fled into the shining lobby of the manor. She needed to get as far away from the words and bard as quickly as possible, though she did not know why.

Jonas watched his companion flee the parlor and looked at the blue-coated man with a new respect.

I didn't know anyone could spook Rime. I didn't know that she was even spookable.

The song was strange, all sliding guitar notes and odd, wailing rhythm to the vocals. It wasn't to his taste. The squire liked simple songs that could be best remembered when marching or drinking. Or march-drinking.

The squire straightened his vest, thankful again for the kind priest's attention to his buttons. He moved forward through the room to follow Rime, when the pink-haired bard's song came to an end.

"I don't believe we've been introduced," the bard crooned to his back.

The squire squeaked and turned to face the tall man in the bluc coat. *Don't talk to anyone. Don't talk to anyone.*

"Hi," Jonas said.

The bard left his instrument hovering in the air. He smiled as he crossed the room.

"I am Geranium the Eruption. May I have your name?"

"I'm Jonas the - Umm - Jonas?" the squire hazarded.

The coffee-skinned man laughed, flashing perfect white teeth. "Of course you are."

"Do all bards have floating guitars, or is that one special?" Jonas' curiosity overcame Geranium's odd attire and his cat-like features.

"Lady Moon-Death is very special. Most unique and divine, an instrument of rare power. Would you like me to sing a song for you?" Geranium leaned over the squire, nearly a foot taller than Jonas.

"Uh, sure?" the squire replied.

Rime stood alone in the middle of the lobby, eyes trained on the surprisingly diminutive gold lock that held the doors of the manor shut.

As opposed to the shining white marble and muted brass gleam of the rest of the lobby, the doors were thick brutal steel. She hadn't been paying close enough attention when they entered, but her memory told her that the doors were nearly a handspan thick. Rivets and reinforced bands of steel, the hinges inset within four feet of stone on either side. The mage was certain that she could rip through the wall if needed with her magic, but nothing short of a small army with a battering ram was going to get through.

That's what made the lock itself so incongruous. A gossamer-thin golden chain was wound around the handles of the steel doors. From the chain hung an ornate lock that would fit comfortably in one of Rime's small hands. The sides were etched with roaring lions; the mage was already growing tired of the preponderance of the grandiose felines in the manor's decoration. In the center was a simple keyhole.

The lock was small and the chain looked thin enough that even she could break it if needed. Small and thin was bad. Coupled with Lord Bellwether's confidence, it meant problems. It meant that the lock was enchanted. The small size and elegance of the lock further suggested that it had been crafted by a master.

That meant getting the doors open might not be as simple as punching a hole in the wall.

The doors of the Parlor opened and revealed Jonas, looking a little wild around the eyes.

"Where have you been?" Rime crossed her arms.

"Uh, talking to the dwarf about my sword, and then the bard sang me a song." The squire crossed the lobby and pointed at the doors. "That's the lock?"

"Geranium? Did he say anything about me?" The mage almost reached up to stuff the words back in her mouth but kept her arms firmly crossed.

"About you? Geranium?" Jonas furrowed his brow as he

tried to remember. "Nope. I don't think so. Why?"

"The lock is enchanted. I was just about to investigate it when you came stomping in." Rime evaded the question and turned back to the ornate lock. *Let it go, Jonas.*

"Oh, are you going to..." The squire wiggled his fingers, completely forgetting his question. "Do some magic stuff?"

"Yes. Keep an eye on the doors. There shouldn't be any visible emanation, but we want to avoid all suspicion," the mage instructed.

The squire shifted to a guard position. Legs wide, stout as an oak, eyes moving from door to door in regular patterns. It was the most obvious thing Rime had ever seen. She sighed and concentrated on the lock.

The mage dipped a hand down into her magic, gently skimming the surface.

She had drained herself a few weeks ago, almost to the point of death. Even after being told to wait 'a moon's turn' she had plowed on. By the sea, in the sand, with salt air in her lungs she had collapsed and slept for nearly a week. Jonas had kept her safe, justifying her trust. *Trust or exhaustion?* A cynical voice chirped in her head. The voice sounded familiar, like the witch's voice that had told her to wait before using her magic again.

Rime had followed the witch's instructions for weeks. Weeks of boredom, weeks of walking on her feet, weeks of having to do things with her stupid hands. Only the fear of how close to death she had come kept her away from it for that long. With great relief, she had conducted some private tests over the past few days to make sure her magic was ready and available.

It was, as eager and fierce as ever. Ready to be used, *begging* to be used. She needed no incantations or foolish wands, only her imagination and will. An image flashed into her mind of the lock held in the Magic Wild's grip. The golden device pulled apart at her will, each shining piece hung in the air for her inspection. With a step more, the heavy steel doors flew open, bent into the shape of crude gliders. and sailed across the dark forest that surrounded the manor, held aloft by her will alone. Another step more, she pulled the guests of the manor from their beds and they hung in the air before her. She questioned them each, before finally reaching into their ears and pulling out their secrets.

She saw it all, even with her fingers barely dipping into the well of her power. It would be so easy.

Rime shuddered and banished the image. *Easy and deadly.* She could almost hear the dragons in her head coiling in excitement as she contemplated the use of so much power. *I'd pass out halfway through that sort of display and Jonas would be left to deal with the stragglers to make sure none escaped to tell the tale.* The mage smirked at the last. Her guardian was not known for his ruthless nature; he would be like a puppy set to bring down a quarrel of cats.

Enough. Let's see what this lock is all about.

Rime reached out -- her magic was invisible tendrils approaching the lock. She hesitated, picking up a very slight vibration coming from the lock. It rippled through her temples and whispered of danger. *It's geared to sense magical interference. It may have some sort of natural defense or perhaps an alarm that is triggered.*

She pulled her magic back and put knuckles to chin in

thought. Just like every other mystery in the manor, she would need to know more before proceeding.

Rime took Jonas' elbow and shook him out of his absurd stance. The squire started but then remembered his role as her humble escort. The two of them made their way up the shining marble staircase and were met by the glower of Funnicello. He was carrying a simple lantern in his right hand, but the dwarf clenched his fist in such a way as to make clear that his purpose was not for a quiet stroll.

The lantern creaked as the dwarf gestured towards their rooms. Rime acquiesced without comment. The other guests would already be in their rooms for the evening. *Except Geranium*. She shied away from that thought and concentrated on the case. The night would give her time to review the evidence she had collected, prepare her next line of inquiry -- and also time to slip out in a few hours to get a closer look at Darla's body.

Her eyes slid across the open space of the second floor -- a mezzanine where one could look down into the lobby below. The guest rooms were on the east and west walls, with a broad oak door to the north that lead up into the lord's tower. All of the doors on this level were shut, and the powered lights were dimmed. They gave no clue to which guest occupied each room. She made a note on her mental chalkboard to discover that information as soon as possible.

The mage offered a paltry smile to her guardian and the manservant, as a young lady should. She walked into her room and shut the door, overhearing a snatch of conversation as Jonas quizzed the dwarf about some sort of cleaning implement.

She stood with her back to the door for many long

moments, her thoughts whirling around the chalkboard, filling in every scrap of information she had gathered, overheard, or observed.

It was a few minutes before she realized that she was humming. With trepidation, she recognized the song about the Lost that the bard had sung in the Parlor.

5

Jonas stared out the window. He had slipped out of his worn travel boots, enjoying the feel of the cool marble on his bare feet. The rain poured an endless curtain, leaving the three moons a vague smudge above the dark forest that surrounded the manor.

The squire had a simple mind. The strange encounter with the dwarf, the even stranger song of the tall bard, the overpowering impact of the princess: his mind simply could not keep that many rocks in the wheelbarrow. Jonas would try to pile them all up but at the first bump, the first distraction, the thoughts would all fall out. The smaller stones went too -- the grisly murder, the actors, the button mistake. Greater intellect like Rime could keep everything moving, flying through the air, juggling them as if they were weightless. Jonas could only carry one rock at a time.

Jonas held the Stone of the Past in his hands.

It was heavy.

For no particular reason, he prayed aloud. Quiet, as if a

dozen ears pressed against the walls were eager to catch a whisper. Jonas spoke the old words for the first time in many long miles.

"Time and wave, sun and wind, night and fire, moons and stone," the squire said to the rain. "We walk through the world only once. Only one life is given by the Nameless."

Jonas put his hand on the glass, fingers splayed wide. He did his best to catch the blurred moons between his knuckles. Red, white, and dark purple.

"It is a gift, a burden. A challenge, a duty. To not waste it. To serve the Highest. To the end of the path with our honor unbroken."

His hand squeaked on the glass as he clenched it into a fist. The words burned him. He had not done his duty; he had failed the challenge. His gift lay covered in blood at the top of a grayscale tower in Gilead. He had no honor left to carry.

The squire with no knight leaned his forehead against clenched fist and watched his breath smoke on the glass. The rain and the moons showed little concern.

His door popped open, and Rime slipped inside. She shut the door with speed and great care, to keep the latch from sounding.

"I thought I locked that," Jonas said, greatly relieved to see his companion. *Maybe a little bit of honor left.*

"You did." The mage crossed to the bed and plopped down on the edge.

The squire made his new *magic-rime-stuff* hand gesture but

kept it faced towards the window. There was no need to attract her ire at the moment.

Rime folded her legs and steepled her hands in thought. She stared into space, then pointed across the room at nothing.

"The components of murder can be distilled down to three essentials, the Three W's. The Will, the Way, and the Walk. From my extensive research it is clear that no murder can be completed without all three of these parts. The murderer must have the Will - a reason to kill and the fortitude to complete the dread task. The Way: an opening, an opportunity to attack the victim. And finally, the Walk. The actual steps that the killer takes to complete the deed, whether it be a brute-simple ploy like storming across a room and clubbing their victim with a piano leg or as elaborate as a chess game. These are the three fields of our investigation; the evidence we gather will help us eliminate suspects based on their lack of any of the W's."

Her voice was clinical yet with an excitement buried beneath the surface. Jonas shook his head trying to follow her words.

"Okay. Why are you talking to me about it?" the squire asked.

"I'm bored. It's too early to go and inspect the corpse. I need to give the actors time to become sufficiently inebriated, and then I must wait for a lull between Funnicello and Lord Bellwether's rounds. I don't expect you to solve the mystery, but it helps me to focus and--" Rime trailed off, a strange expression coming over her face.

"And what?"

"Nothing. Now, do you understand what I've said? I don't want to have to stop and answer questions later." The mage laced her fingers with impatience.

"Okay," Jonas sighed. "You're saying that whoever killed Darla had to have a reason."

"And an opportunity, and a plan to carry it out," Rime ticked off on her fingers.

"People kill people for no reason all the time," the squire said.

The mage frowned and began to twine the shock of white hair around a few fingers before responding.

"Madness is a motivation. Then the killer still needs an opportunity and a method. While it is possible that the killer's motivation is so esoteric that it cannot be determined through investigation, the bald mechanics of the murder still remain open for our inquiry. Especially when the victim was killed while in a locked box in full view of a dozen witnesses," Rime argued. "This isn't helping. You are a terrible sounding board."

"I'm just saying it's not that simple. People aren't puzzle pieces. Especially when it comes time for killing," the squire said stubbornly.

"What do you know about murder?" Rime demanded.

The Stone of the Past was heavy, and hearing the girl's words it flared with dull heat.

"What do you know about it? 'The Three W's'? You got that out of a book somewhere, didn't you?" Jonas scowled.

"A series of books actually, though I've only found the second, fourth and fifth volumes. *Detective Corrective and the Innate Prelate* is my favorite. They are an excellent primer for investigation techniques and…"

"That's stupid. This is stupid. You can't pretend that we're in a mystery book. It's real, Rime. It's real." The squire's anger slid across her mounting excitement.

"You're stupid," Rime snarled. "I know that it's real. I know that…"

There was a sudden, crisp knock on the door. Jonas whirled and took a half-step towards the sound when the quick rustle of sheets made him look back. The mage had neatly tumbled off the bed and was sliding herself far back into the shadows underneath.

"What are you doing?" Jonas kneeled next to the bed and craned his neck to peer at the mage. Another knock made the squire bellow over his shoulder. "Just a second!"

"It is completely inappropriate for a lady of my status to be alone and unchaperoned in a young man's bedchamber in the middle of the night," Rime hissed, sliding further back. "Now get rid of whoever that is."

The squire shook his head and stood up. He crossed to the door, wrapping his hand around the knob and mentally preparing himself for some serious deception. *Spy-stuff, spy-stuff, spy-stuff.* Jonas opened the door.

The sea-elf stood before him, cobalt blue and marble white. Coracle was wearing a diaphanous sleep-shift that enhanced and revealed far more than it concealed. Her face was pressed into the palms of her hands, and she looked up as the door opened. Her dark eyes were damp, overflowing with tears. She rushed forward, clutched at the squire's vest and buried her face in his shoulder.

Spy-stuff? Jonas cleared his throat and tried to simultaneously retreat and remove the weeping shaman, all while keeping his hands as far from her body as possible. Coracle's grief pushed him further into the room and her left foot kicked out as she sobbed, swinging the door shut. The Nai-Elf collected herself for a moment and looked down into his eyes. It was only at that moment that Jonas registered that she was several inches taller than he was. She had needed to hunch over a good deal to weep on his vest. It was also at that moment that Jonas' brain informed him that he was eye level with entirely too much uncovered blue skin. The dark whorls that had glowed with her prayer in the Parlor spiralled over her collarbones and plunged down into her -- *SPY-STUFF*.

Jonas was in trouble.

"I am sorry for this storm," her breasts said. "The Balance whispered to me in my pain and told me that you were the one that could help me."

The squire realized that her words were probably coming from somewhere to the north and managed to raise his eyes to hers. Coracle beamed down at him with relief, the shells in her hair clinking.

"Help you?" Jonas took a step back and felt his back foot connect with the side of the bed.

"Yes, Bright Lady Seto be praised, Sky-King Marrus be feared, Water Lord Banu be honored, Dark Mistress Jocasta be respected: they told me to seek you out" The sea-elf clutched at his vest, her eyes glazing. "There is a dark thing loose in this manor, a Beast of Breaking. Only a true Hero stands a chance, and they whisper that it is you who can defeat it."

The shaman continued to press forward as the squire leaned further and further back over the bed.

"Please forgive my weakness, I grew frightened alone in my chamber. And I knew I would be comforted, feel safer in your presence." The Nai-Elf pressed against him with relief. "Can you tell me of your adventures, of your travels? What brings you and the lady you protect to this dark place?"

"I, uhh." the squire blinked and tried to think of a polite way to extricate himself, but gravity and the gibbering monkey-beat of his heart were making that more and more difficult.

Three things happened in metronome-succession. First, the squire felt a small hand clutch his ankle and fingernails dig painfully into his skin. Second, Jonas yelped and toppled back onto the bed while the shaman's dark eyes and breasts fell eagerly down with him. Third, there was another knock at the door.

Coracle's eyes widened in shock and she rolled off the squire with lightning grace. Jonas hopped off the bed, neatly ejected as the shaman artfully tousled the sheet and coverlet. The sea-elf wrapped the covers around herself and twisted herself into an innocuous hump. If he hadn't seen her do it, he could easily believe that the bed unoccupied except for fabric and pillows.

"How did you learn to--"

"My people are naturally skilled at camouflage. Now get

the door," Coracle's pillow hillock replied.

The knock sounded again in the room.

Jonas sighed and risked a brief moment to hang his head below the bed. Rime's eyes were inches from his own and brimming with irritation, but she raised a hand as if to say, *Well, what else can you do?*

The squire crossed to the door and opened it just as the dwarf's knuckles were coming down on the polished wood. Funnicello retracted his fist with reproach and raised the globe-shaped lantern that he carried.

"Oh, hi Funnicello," the squire attempted.

The dwarven manservant leaned into the room, his feet never crossing the threshold. The lantern hung between them, and Funnicello peered over it, eyes locked with the squire's.

A tiny eternity transpired.

At last the dwarf sniffed and lowered the lantern. He nodded once and walked away back towards the staircase that led from the darkened mezzanine.

Jonas swung the door shut slowly, doing his best to puzzle out the taciturn dwarf's purpose.

With a rattle of shells, the sea-elf's blue face popped up from beneath the covers. "What did that thing want?"

"I - I have no idea. I feel like he's been trying to get something across to me, but I can't figure out what. What do you mean 'thing'?" the squire replied.

"Ick. I've never liked his people, so stumpy and weird." The shaman pulled down the coverlet in a most distracting manner and smiled. "I thank you, Hero, for keeping him at bay and safeguarding my reputation."

The squire couldn't actually see Rime's eyes rolling underneath the bed, but he was fairly certain he heard the icy clink of her eyes revolving.

"Sure, I guess?" Jonas wasn't sure how he felt about the dwarf being called a 'thing'. The strange manservant did have a sour demeanor, but the squire felt a strange kinship. *Whatever that thing with the rags was all about. Maybe because we're the only servants in the place.*

"I am incredibly grateful," Coracle gushed. "Only you could…"

A knock at the door. The covers flew, and the sea-elf was camouflaged again. Jonas leaned over to peek at the hidden mage. Rime was digging fingernails into her forehead in exasperation.

Jonas opened the door. "Did you forget something Funnicello?"

Two hands jutted forward, wrapped in neon pink fingerless gloves. One held a pair of empty wine glasses, the other a dark green bottle.

"Yes, I did forget something," Geranium the Eruption leered. "Though my name is far grander than that absurd cavalcade of wonky syllables. You left so quickly before. We did not have time to become properly acquainted. I thought perhaps a quiet drink in your chambers would be a lovely way to remedy that."

Jonas was in trouble.

The bard took his stunned silence by the arm and glided into the room, pushing the door shut with his elbow. He deposited Jonas on the edge of the bed and wrapped the squire's fingers around the two glasses. Geranium's blue coat squeaked slightly as the tall man helped himself to a small armchair in the corner of the room and dragged it over near the bed.

The squire risked a quick look at Coracle's lump; she was still well hidden. Jonas wished that he could trade places with Rime under the bed. He had never known such an active social life.

The tall man's boots thumped down next to him, narrowly missing the edge of the hidden shaman's toes. Geranium smiled as he leaned back in the chair and waggled his spider-fingers until Jonas understood to pass him a glass.

"Now that we are getting cozy..." Geranium pulled the bottle's cork out with his teeth and spat it out onto the floor. "Tell me about yourself - Jonas? You spoke so hurriedly in the Parlor, I wasn't sure I heard your name correctly."

"That's right, my name is Jonas," the squire managed over the quick rattle of glass as the wine was poured.

"A fine name, kitten." The bard took a sip from his glass. "Difficult to rhyme, you must admit. But not without a certain music of its own."

"I - I guess?" the squire replied.

"I will sing a song of your name, my friend," Geranium mused. "A bright name, an auspicious name, a name that travels well. Oh, but you are not drinking."

Jonas raised the glass to his lips and slurped. The wine was dark and red with a hint of fall apples. He immediately felt more confident about his current situation.

"There you are." Geranium's smile twanged wide like a longbow. "Have you travelled long with your Lady?"

"Who? Oh, yes. Lady Rime, quite some time. Years." Jonas finished his glass and held it out towards the bard.

Geranium leaned in to pour, his eyes calculating.

Jonas refused to be surprised when there was a knock at the door.

In a bound, the tall man leaped from his armchair and dragged it back into the corner of the room. The bard carefully folded himself up behind the chair until not a hair of his cotton-candy head was visible.

"Um, why are you hiding?" The squire set his glass down on the floor, where Rime's hand could slip out and conceal it.

Jonas heard the clink of glass again and the sound of wine being poured.

"It's traditional!" Geranium insisted.

Jonas sighed and went to the door. He steeled himself. Surely the next visitor would be a small parade band, or a talking cat who granted wishes, or his grandmother.

He opened the door, and Lord Bellwether was standing outside.

I am so glad that I put the wine glass down.

"My lord!" Jonas bowed with respect.

Bellwether nodded curtly. "I am sorry to bother you, but I went to check on my daughter and she was not in her room. I knew she had become friendly with your mistress, and there was no answer at her chamber door. Do you by any chance know where she is at this moment?"

The man's concern and ire were clear; the squire scrambled to produce a reasonable response. He chucked rocks into his wheelbarrow at breakneck pace and then tossed them all right back out again.

"My lord, I…" Jonas' mouth was dry.

A scream echoed through the manor. A high pitched voice cried out in horror and despair. It seemed to go on forever. Across the open mezzanine doors flew open: scholar Trowel in a faded robe of red and brown, Father Andrew still in his black cassock with the three blue swords of the Nameless.

Bellwether turned in alarm. "Neriah? Neriah?!"

6

They found her at the bottom of the stairs.

Rime had seethed with impatience under the bed as she watched the bard trot out the door, followed a few moments later by the half-dressed sea-elf. Jonas had lumbered over and offered her a hand up. She clawed her way out and distilled the abundant comments she had brewed during her captivity down to the most essential for the moment. "I sleep with ear plugs. I didn't hear the lord knocking. We'll open my chamber door as we pass. Sea-elves lack the ability to cry. Whatever she wanted had nothing to do with the spirits."

"What about Geranium?" The squire had seemed somewhat relieved.

"Not now."

The guests clambered down the eastmost staircase in their haste. The squire and mage were last, and Rime grabbed Jonas' elbow to keep him a handful of steps higher than the rest so she had an unimpeded view.

Neriah stood on the last step above the polished marble floor of the lobby. Her hands were twisted in the green fabric of her simple sleep-shift. One green slipper had been dislodged from her foot and propped toe-down between the last step and the floor. The fuzzy fabric was sodden, and a thick stain spread up the slipper like a wick. Blood puddled at the base of the staircase and marooned the weeping girl on a spit of white in a red sea.

"Oh no. It's Funnicello," Jonas said.

The dwarf lay face-down in the red ocean. One hand was folded under his body; his right hand splayed out wide pointed towards the door. A few crimson bubbles still lingered on the right side of the dwarf's face where the blood had trapped his final breaths.

The guests on the stairs stood absolutely still until Lord Bellwether broke the spell by moving towards his daughter. The others started to shift down the stairs, questions already forming on their lips. Rime made her mind go faster. She needed to take in everything, every detail, and commit it all to memory. As soon as the other guests stepped off the stairs information could be compromised by ignorance or malice.

There were no footprints. The pool of blood surrounding the dwarf was unbroken and undisturbed. The killer had fled before the ocean formed. This meant that there was no clue to where the killer had gone. Funnicello was wearing the same innocuous black coat, and no wounds were apparent on his back, legs, arms, or head. The mortal wound must be on his chest. The position of his arms was intriguing. The left arm was crumpled and folded under his body as if covering his wound, but the right arm stretched out painfully towards the door. The angle of his body and the thrust of his feet with toes pointed out suggested that he had actively been reaching towards the door when he died. *Trying to flee?*

Neriah turned her sobbing face into her father's shoulder in slow motion. The other guests moved forward, ponderous as oak-sap. Rime's eyes ignored them and continued her inspection. The lord's manservant had appeared at Jonas' door not fifteen minutes past. The murder, the killer's escape, and Neriah's discovery had all occurred in that time frame. *There must be some detail, some clue that the murderer left in their haste.*

The dwarf's right hand was twisted oddly, too specific to be accidental. The mage willed her vision to increase, praying that her eyes wouldn't suddenly start glowing. The edge of the pool of his blood stopped at Funnicello's right elbow, but she could just make out some tiny daubs of red underneath his hand. A few swirls and lines.

Letters. He wrote something. Rime snapped forward, pushing her way through the other guests. Any concern about her role as a simple young lady shattered in the overriding desire to be the first to inspect the victim's final words.

Trowel clucked with agitation as she elbowed past, stumbling back into the arms of Father Andrew. Rime stopped on the bottom step next to the weeping girl and Lord Bellwether. The pool of blood spread across the entire floor at her feet; her only option to avoid it would be to attempt an ungainly hop to the far side of it or quickly run up and around to the other staircase on the far side of the lobby. The mage grimaced, hiked up her skirt, and put her feet down in the red. She was barefoot and it would wash off easily later.

The other guests gasped; Geranium covered his mouth

with both hands in artful disgust. Rime ignored them and tiptoed through the blood, careful to not spatter any on the other evidence. She stepped out of the blood, and leaned over Funnicello's right hand. With great care she seized the cuff of his coat and lifted his hand straight up, then moved it several inches over revealing what he had written on the white tile floor.

The dwarf's thick fingers had smudged every stroke, but Rime could still make out a symbol and what appeared to be letters beneath it. The symbol was three large dots, connected by lines into an equilateral triangle. A final dot rested in the direct center of the triangle. The symbol tickled part of the mage's memory, but she forced herself to remain focused on observation for now. The letters at the bottom appeared to be where Funnicello had been attempting to write a word, but his pain had proven too great for him to write legibly or complete the word. Amidst the bloody scrawl, Rime felt reasonably confident that she could make out an 'O', a 'T' and an 'I'. She could not be certain if there were supposed to be letters between or after.

These letters mean absolutely nothing to me. The mage stood up to face the panel of horrified stares that greeted her, not least of all Jonas. Neriah had even calmed her tears enough to be watching Rime's inspection with a confused gaze.

Rime rolled her eyes. "Get down here and help me. We need to flip the body and discover the method with which he was dispatched."

The squire pointed at himself quizzically.

"Yes, you." The mage crossed her arms in frustration, and addressed the crowd. "Playtime is over. This is far too serious for any more playacting. Funnicello came by my room fifteen minutes ago. The killer dispatched him and escaped in that window of time. This does not fit the circumstances of the actresses' death at all. We need to know what's going on. We need to know it now, and my patience for clever repartee has evaporated. I am much smarter than the rest of you and I will discover the truth of these events, but only if people start doing what I say *when* I say it, and are you still just standing there?"

Rime pointed at Jonas in accusation. The squire jumped in embarrassment, and began to sidle his way down the staircase.

"Smarter than us, Lady Korvanus?" Lord Bellwether's voice cracked out. "I believe these horrible events have unsettled your nerves."

"Questioning our intelligence seems a bit uncalled for," the wood-elf scholar said with wounded pride.

"And, how smart can you be, kitten?" Geranium spoke through his clasped hands, voice quavering with nausea. "You're the one walking through all that dirty - blech - fluid."

"I didn't want the rest of you to get in my way." *Or hide any evidence.* "And, yes, I do believe I'm the smartest one here, as I'm the one who instantly realized that Funnicello had one of the two keys to the front door." Rime's eyes blazed figuratively, but she kept enough rein on her anger to keep them from becoming green torches.

At once, everyone looked towards the great steel doors leading outside. They did not appear to be disturbed, and the thin golden chain and lock were still wound around the handles. Like iron filings to a magnet, their voices and eyes flew as one to Lord Bellwether.

Bellwether shifted his daughter to one side and reached into his sleeve. His golden key appeared, still secured by the cord to his wrist. "Everyone, please calm down. I have my key, and the lock is still secure. Funnicello's chain of keys is ever in his right pocket. You! Do as you were instructed.Lady Korvanus is young and her tone insulting, but we have no time to judge etiquette while we stand in danger's shadow."

Jonas started again, realizing that he was still being referred to. His time as the only remaining servant in the House of the Heart-Broken Lion did not promise to be pleasant or filled with an abundance of concern for his feelings.

The mage crossed her arms in impatience as the squire quickly cuffed his gray leggings high on his bare shins. Trowel, Coracle, and Geranium huddled close together, seemingly transfixed by the ghoulish tableau. Neriah's eyes were hollow and wide, and the priest was whispering quiet words of comfort to her over Lord Bellwether's shoulder.

Rime crouched down, lowering her gaze to the floor under the dead dwarf. The squire waded through the blood with equanimity, though his gaze was sorrowful. She saw the squire's hands move quickly on his chest in a quick three slashes. *The sign of the Nameless God. A battlefield benediction.* Before she could help it, her mental chalkboard flipped. A new name was written on the blank slate. *Jonas. The Deserter.* She didn't have time for another mystery right now, but the chalk danced regardless. Everything she knew about the squire's past, about Gilead, about the way he walked to turn a dead body with quiet familiarity. *Another mystery - but one for later.* Rime flipped the chalkboard back around to the list of suspects and swiftly crossed out Funnicello's name.

Jonas walked to the opposite side of the body from Rime and took a firm grip on the dwarf's shoulder and right arm. In a swift motion he pulled the dwarf's body towards him revealing a mangled horror.

Rime's eyes recorded everything.

The dwarf had not been stabbed or slashed or shot with a crossbow bolt. He had not been shot with a musket or blasted with arcane fire.

He had been gutted. His entrails slid out of his body in a gout of red, the flesh of his stomach curled in pink tatters. The dwarf's left hand was pressed to one end of the horrible wound as if attempting to halt his life's escape. Funnicello's eyes were cold and blank, his face slack. Rime moved in closer, inspecting every part of the corpse. A hair on the collar, a tear at the cuff, a smell of cinnamon. All of these had solved the sing-song mysteries on the shelves of her mind, the killers in yellowed pages, the detectives of ink. As she watched Jonas square his jaw and reach into the dwarf's right hand pocket, she felt a shadow gather. These murders would not be solved so neatly and the killer would not wait his turn and come to the penultimate chapter of revelation, meek and proper.

"I am going to vomit," a prim, well-modulated voice came from the doors that lead to the banquet hall. "Right now. Vincent, hold my hair."

Rime's eyes flicked up in surprise. At the door, the three actors stood. At least they did, until Toby kept his promise and expelled purple-wine sick all over the white wall adjacent. His lover sighed and tottered over, doing his best to comfort the golden-haired hero. Sand blearily kept his position, wine bottle in the crook of his arm and a large tankard in his left hand.

"What - what has happened? We came when we heard the scream," the actor managed.

"Dead dwarf," Geranium called. "Very messy."

"We heard the scream, and after some brief discussion decided to come investigate." The lead actor shook his head. "To lend whatever aid we may."

"Some aid," the sea-elf shaman sniffed.

"The three of you have been together this whole time?" Rime demanded. "None of you slipped off alone?"

"Why would we wander, when the wine is so good?" Vincent asked, patting the convulsing actor's shoulder.

Fair enough. Rime decided to ignore the actors for the moment, and turned her attention back to the body. A smell was rising, apparently his bowels had been punctured by the force of the attack. *Not cinnamon at all.* No helpful threads or tears on his clothing presented themselves, so she forced herself to closely expect the horrible wound. The edges were jagged - no clean cuts as a blade would make. To her best estimation it appeared that the dwarf's stomach had physically been torn open, tearing and splitting.

"He must have been in immense pain. Why did he not cry out?" the wood-elf scholar asked.

The mage frowned. She had been about to ask the same question.

"Funnicello had no voice. He never speaks," Neriah said, propriety overriding her grief. "That's why everyone thought he was so awful and grim. But he raised me after my mother died, as much or more than my father. He would play Castle with me, and sit through my tea parties, and make my favorite waffles at any hour of the night if I had a bad dream. How could this have happened, Father?"

Lord Bellwether sighed. "I don't know, child. I don't know. Have you discovered anything? The keys?"

Jonas straightened up, his search complete. "I looked through all his pockets and his coat. The keys are gone. I'm sorry, my lord."

"The killer must not have had time to make his escape!" Coracle pointed towards the door. "They could be waiting in the shadows right now! We should guard the front door."

"Let them go," Geranium cooed.

"Let them go?" the priest and the lord asked in unison.

"Of course…" the bard began.

"Why would you let the killer go?" Toby interrupted, his back pressed against the vomit spattered wall and a clean white handkerchief pressed to his lips.

"So he doesn't kill us." The tall man in the blue coat spread his hands wide in finality.

"Look, everyone stop talking," Rime said. "If the killer's plan had been escape, he would be long gone. Any assailant that could dispatch the dwarf so brutally, take his keys, and flee -- all before Neriah discovered the scene -- could easily have left the manor. Clearly, the murderer has a darker plan."

"Why do you keep saying 'the murderer' or 'the killer'?" Geranium smiled like a cat. "We know perfectly well who did this."

"What?" Rime scowled at his knife-edge leer.

"Oh, did I figure something out before you?" The bard placed his neon-pink gloves over his heart in mock surprise. "I thought you were the smart one around here."

"There is absolutely no way from the current evidence that you can correctly identify the murderer," she laid words like stones on the tall man's grave.

"Oh, but there is." The guests of the manor leaned in close to hear Geranium's next words. "Look around the room. Everyone that isn't dead is standing in the lobby. Except one."

Rime's veins dripped lightning, and she flew to the chalkboard in her head to the names and faces of the guests, her finger flew across the columns. Her eyes widened, and she took a quick inhalation. The bard watched her face, then pointed when she reached the conclusion. He clapped and proclaimed to the other guests who were still glancing around the lobby and counting on their fingers.

"That's right. The only one not here is Master Waters. That sour old stick is the killer."

WHO WAS FUNNICELLO DELMARR?

Once upon a time there lived a family of dwarves. A mother, a father and five stubby children, round as pebbles in the stream. Mother and Father loved their pebbles and did their best to polish them and keep them bright.

The oldest son was quartz and the eldest daughter pearl. The middle son was amethyst and the middle daughter was ruby. They sparkled in the sunlight and lay in their parents' hands cool and clean.

The last son was agate. Dim purple stone shot through with a vein of granite. And he was bad. He was the worst. He refused to be polished: the water of the river sharpened every edge. He slipped from every hand, cutting and tearing. The last pebble was heavy and cruel. In anger he was flung against the earth, into the waves, across the sky, but he would not break. The stubborn granite would not break.

His parents looked at the shining gems they had polished, then to the bitter brick they had been burdened with. Mother nodded twice and Father sighed and went back to peppering the pot roast. Mother picked up the last pebble and carried him far away from their home, from the gentle river. She carried him for a brace of days, a pile of weeks. Then she pulled the angry stone from her pocket, her last son from her pocket, and she buried him. Under the bones of the wind and the memory of the river, she buried him. She buried him, and she walked away never to return.

And for the last time in his life, Funnicello wept.

But even a bad stone can have purpose, a cruel stone with a vein of granite can be turned to many purposes. He became a tool. A weapon.

He sat in the hands of evil men and learned the joy of breaking. The elixir of destruction was sweet on his lips, and he shouted in the dark streets, lawless and resolute. He brought his sharp heart down on the world's brow and howled in glory as the blood flowed.

A brace of months, a pile of years. He became strong and horrible and as empty as a gourd. Death grew weary of totting up his score and idly considered hiring some freelancers to mind the vicious dwarf, or at the very least provide sympathetic ears that he could bend with complaints across his metaphysical water cooler.

The bitter stone thought nothing, remembered nothing. Eat and sleep and shatter, bread and wine and bone.

Until the monk in the road.

Funnicello was going from Somewhere to Somewhere when he saw another dwarf coming his way in the road. The traveler wore a simple robe of faded green and was chomping contentedly on a long piece of straw. He had a gray beard and an eye-patch the same color as his robe.

The monk waved to Funnicello with gentle disregard.

That's when the bitter stone knew. He knew he would break this smiling old man.

His hand smashed into the old monk's chest and tore the soft leaf-green fabric in rage. The stone cut and tore and Funnicello howled with fractal glee.

At last he was finished, and he found himself pushing the battered and bleeding old dwarf down into a muddy ditch. The eye-patch had split revealing an empty socket and the scars of fire or acid. Fresh blood oozed from a cut on the old man's head, but somehow he still clutched a stump of straw between his swollen lips and his good eye was clear and alive.

"Is there anything else I can do for you?" the dying monk asked the bitter stone.

"What?" Funnicello pressed the old dwarf harder into the mud. "What are you saying to me?"

"You needed a victim, you needed something to break. I am pleased that I was the one, and not some other. I am old and ready to return to the earth, though this is a bit literal," the one-eyed monk chuckled. The cruel stone heard the monk's words and saw in the ebbing light of the monk's eye that he spoke the truth.

For the first time in his life, Funnicello was afraid.

The dwarf stood up to flee but his feet would not move. He was agate and granite, a weapon still. He had no purpose but breaking, no recourse but ending. He could not escape and he groped for words to cover the precipice.

"What happened to your eye?" he asked the monk.

"I lost it." Quiet words as the old dwarf slipped away. "I lost it on the day that I learned. I learned what you are learning now. At the beginning of all things, in the heart of forever, every spirit was given a choice. Every spirit, great and small, dark and light. A simple choice. Serve or Destroy. Will you serve? Or will you destroy?"

The empty-eyed dwarf died in the mud.

Funnicello stood and was alive and was still a cruel stone.

But he had heard. He heard from where he was buried under the bones of the wind and the memory of the river.

A bad stone can still have purpose. And a cruel stone with a vein of granite can be turned to many purposes.

It took time. He tried to blunt the knife-edge, but that was impossible. He listened to the words in his head; he made the choice again and again. He learned the words were easier to hear if he did not speak.

He became a servant.

He found a kinder master and a lonely house of gray stone. He walked on eggshells, the edges of his granite heart sharp as ever. He made his quiet choice again and again.

Until he bled to death on cool marble. Until his final moment in the House of the Heart-Broken Lion.

7

Rime steepled her fingers and waited for the blood on her feet to dry. Her guardian had likewise trudged free of the red pool and now stood uncertainly like a wet dog too terrified to shake on the carpet.

"I, for one, am shocked." Geranium continued his triumphant proclamation, one fist balled at his hip, the other thrown across his brow. "Shocked!"

The mage took a moment and slipped into the library of her mind. She calmly walked past the dog-eared mystery books and the chalkboard crammed with details. From a shelf she pulled a red clay pot filled with black earth, neatly dislodging a napping seven. Rime took the pot and laid it in the center of the library. The rudely awoken numeral floated close to get a better view. With infinite care she placed a finger into the soil to make a small depression, then placed a small green seed within and covered it with exacting diligence. She produced a small silver can from the ether and sprinkled a few drops of clean water. A stick of chalk floated through the air and Rime wrote the name *Geranium* in smooth strokes on the red clay.

She picked up the flower pot and held it up to eye-level. A green sprout had already appeared. Then, with a vicious grunt she hurled the pot against the wide windows of the library. It shattered.

How could I have missed something so simple? Why didn't I count the guests? Rime snarled inside her head. She glanced at the labyrinth of chalk that was filling up her blackboard. Too many details. The mage chewed on her rage until it was manageable and kept her eyes trained on the maze of information, questing for the way out.

"Why would Master Waters do this terrible thing?" Lord Bellwether kept both hands sentinel on Neriah's shoulders.

"I don't know, Lord of All Lions." The bard kept his stylized stance.

Trowel and Coracle both rolled their eyes with similar disdain but individual style. A Sea and Tree Double Elven Eye-Roll is an uncommon occurrence, but it was not remarked upon. Geranium was clearly enjoying his moment in the spotlight and was in no hurry to abandon it.

Rime shook the shards of mental pottery and hate off her fingers. "I think a more pertinent questions is *how* could Master Waters have done this? He is a frail man in the latter third of his life expectancy. From the vicious damage and short time window for the attack, immense strength would be required to inflict this wound, as well as a great deal of speed to escape before Neriah arrived. Lord Bellwether, was your manservant a skilled combatant?"

"Very." The lord did not elaborate.

"And I understand that you have had financial dealings with Waters for many years -- just as my family has. Do you think it very likely that he could have overpowered Funnicello?" The mage took a test step on the marble floor. The blood was almost dry.

"You point is made, Lady Korvanus," Lord Bellwether stared down at the dead dwarf.

"I don't know if it follows." Father Andrew ran a hand across his balding scalp. "I understand your point that it is unlikely that the tradesman had the physical skill required to perform this awful act of butchery, but as far as we know there is no one else in the house. Every other guest is accounted for. If Master Waters did not do this, then who did?"

Every eye turned to Rime, and she briefly considered returning to her library to smash some more imaginary objects. The priest had a point. *Every other guest...*

She snaked a hand into her hair and gave the white blaze a vicious tug. She had missed it; she had missed it completely. *Again.* The ridiculous bard and his gleaming blue coat and his smile or the murder itself had distracted her. Waters was not the only guest missing.

"Where is Karis?" Rime demanded. "Have any of you seen her since we left the Parlor?"

The others looked around in consternation. She watched their faces carefully but none betrayed anything other than surprise or rueful embarrassment at overlooking the sour woman's absence.

"I think you should have spent a little bit longer counting, instead of preparing your grand announcement, my friend." Father Andrew gave Geranium a crooked smile.

"I...I..." the bard bristled like an irritated alley cat, then collapsed boneless on the nearby bannister. "Maybe they did it together."

Cats and their shame are like midnight and noon - impossible to glimpse at the same moment.

Rime scoffed. She set to work constructing a vicious response coated with slime and fire-ants. The cinnamon-coffee bard *bothered* her on a level that she did not fully understand, but she would make absolutely certain that no one in the manor questioned her intelligence again with such gleeful impunity.

"It is possible," the lord's voice interrupted her spite-construction. "I fear we have entered a time where all dark things are possible and must be guarded against with care."

"We must search for them," Coracle spoke in shimmering tones. "If one of our fellow guests are not the murderer, then they are surely in grave peril. We should search the manor right away."

Father Andrew and the bard both began to speak at the same time in reply but were quickly bowled over by the strident voice of the wood-elf scholar.

"That does not seem wise, or warranted, or worry-free. None of us are armed or equipped to deal with a killer in the shadows." Trowel wrapped her pudgy arms around herself and shivered. Rime noticed that she had a large, ugly purse thrown over her left shoulder.

"I have a sword," Jonas finally spoke up. "Though Funnicello confiscated it."

"It is most likely stored in his quarters, guardian. As well as a few other simple blades and…" Lord Bellwether took a breath to finish his sentence but was forestalled when the bard finally sprung from his pose of studied apathy and bounded up a few stairs before placing his fists on his hips.

"I have a weapon," Geranium sang.

"Err. What?" Father Andrew raised a hand in confusion.

"The greatest weapon, the only blade any true Bard of Gate City could need." The tall man in the cobalt coat let his voice fly up a careful scale, the last words an arpeggio.

Rime bit down on her frustration and slogged back through the blood to throttle the bard. "Can't you all tell? He's been waiting to say this. He's been dying to perform this little scene and I won't…"

Trowel, Coracle and Neriah all shushed her, then turned their attention back to the bard. *All of the female guests.* Rime spluttered.

Geranium the Eruption snapped his pink-neon fingers.

"Lady Moon-Death, come to me!" He held his hands up high with ecstatic abandon.

A metallic twang, a gryphon-roar of music came from the second floor. The black guitar howled through the air and stopped directly above Geranium. It lowered itself slowly, a quick rainstorm of notes spattered from the strings. The bard's face was beatific, and he cradled the instrument close as it came to him.

"Forever, my love," he crooned.

The three female guests applauded and were quickly joined by the priest and the almost forgotten actors across the lobby.

"Thank you, thank you," Geranium smiled with thousand-stage familiarity.

"Everyone, please be silent." Lord Bellwether was rubbing his temples with irritation. "Clearly we must take great care to ensure our safety until dawn. A search is needed but should only be performed by those who can protect themselves. My daughter and I will remain here and do what we can for brave Funnicello."

His daughter looked into her father's face and seemed to draw strength from his resolve. "Yes, I will go to the kitchen and bring clean linens and the mop bucket."

"In a moment, Neriah. Let us make our plans all together. Sand. I assume that your fellows are in no condition to defend themselves." The lord waited half a second for the actor's bemused nod before continuing. "You will remain here in the lobby."

Where I can see you. Rime saw the unspoken words take shape and glare at the performers. She wasn't sure what impulse made her speak to remove some of the sting from them. "It would be wise to have someone focus on the door to keep watch. Just in case I am mistaken about the killer's intentions."

"Yes, fine." Bellwether waved a hand. "The guardian and the bard are armed. Lady Coracle, you too have the protection of your shamanic arts, do you not?"

"The Balance guides and protects me," the Nai-Elf bowed

her head.

"That only leaves the the three of you. Scholar Trowel, you were opposed to the search anyway, so you are welcome to remain here in the lobby with us."

"Oh, I'll be going," the portly wood-elf grinned. "It's surely unsafe and unusual, but I can't stand to be kept in the dark."

"Before you offer, I will also help conduct the search." Father Andrew smiled.

"Father! It isn't safe," the squire blurted out, then hung his head in embarrassment.

"Nor is it safe for any of you. I can at least be an extra pair of eyes. Thank you for your concern, young blade."

"Very well. Now, Lady Korvanus," the lord's tone grew brusque. "You have made great claims to the power of your intellect - and I'm sure you would like to be a part of the search as well - but I must insist that you remain here with me and my daughter."

Rime's brain smoldered at the insults, both implied and overt, but still managed to spit out a suitable solution. She forced her hands to move slowly, as she kinked each finger in a precise pattern and whispered terse words in an ancient tongue. She completed the fake spell, and allowed a tiny, tiny burst of her magic to manifest as a green flame cupped in her right hand. Rime spoke a final word of command, and the green flame formed into a simple shield shape that hovered at her side. The mage took special care to make it look as generic and cliche as possible.

"I'm sorry that I've been keeping a secret from you," she

said. "I am a wizard."

It had been a stressful few hours, filled with heightened emotion and increasing danger since they had arrived at the manor. Rime couldn't help but feel that it all might be worth it, just for the look of absolute terror that appeared on Jonas' face.

It was quickly decided that they would split into two groups. Jonas, Geranium, and Coracle would do a room by room search of the second floor, saving a search of the lord's tower for last when the second group could join them. This group was decided when Jonas asked Lord Bellwether where the dwarf's quarters were, and the shaman and bard both swooped up on either side of him to claim an elbow.

"The second floor, northwest corner," the lord sighed.

Father Andrew, Scholar Trowel and Apparent Wizard Rime would search the bottom floor, doing a quick survey of the lord's study and library as well as the kitchen and other storage rooms.

"And I must take time to inspect the first victim," Rime insisted.

"She's where we left her," the white-haired leading player said, leaning against a column. "And we passed no one in the banquet hall, so it should be safe."

"If you see anything - hear anything - call for the rest of us. My manor is not over-large, but the walls and doors are thick. Do not close doors behind you, and do not go anywhere alone. We will all fly to your aid," Lord Bellwether instructed.

"And *wait* for us to go into the lord's tower." Rime repeated the instruction for the fourth time, hissing it into Jonas' ear. "I doubt that the killer would linger so close to the scene of the crime, especially since we've all been standing here shouting for minutes on end. It also gives us the chance to inspect Bellwether's living quarters for further clues.

"Okay, okay," the squire grumbled. "I get it. Do you think Neriah is going to be okay?"

"Of course, now go." Rime gave the squire a little push.

The blonde girl had departed briefly to the kitchen, but now returned with the promised cloth, a short mop, and bucket of soapy water. Neriah had wrapped her hair in piece of the white linen and her face was composed, though tears still trickled down her cheeks.

"Be careful, Rime," The blonde girl instructed wanly. "And you too, Josh."

"Thanks," The mage forced herself not to whip around and ogle at the preposterous expression that was surely forming on the squire's thick face.

"Thank you, my lady," Jonas bowed, his voice a goopy misery.

Rime cleared her thoughts and considered about the layout of the first floor. The Lobby in the center with the Parlor and Banquet Hall on the east side. Study and Library taking up most of the west. Kitchen and storage to the north.

She walked towards the Library; it was the most sensible location. The actors had come from the Banquet Hall, Neriah from the kitchen. The Library and Study should be checked first, but the mage was almost certain they would not find their quarry.

As the layout of her mental landscape was an easy sign, she believed the first place to look for answers was on shelves lined with books. The dying Funnicello had taken great pains to draw that symbol on the cold marble floor: the least she could do was try to look it up.

The scholar and the priest took several moments to notice her departure, then hurried to follow her through the tall doors of the Library.

8

"I guess if we're looking for Master Waters, then the first place we should check is Master Waters' room?" Jonas managed to disentangle his arms from the bard and shaman with a quick leap as they reached the top of the stairs. "Or should we try to find that other lady first?"

The second floor was laid out in a square-edged horseshoe: matching rows of guest rooms on the east and west walls, and on the north wall, just slightly off-center, a grand archway of gold-flecked stone that lead to the Lord's tower, with a solid door of stained oak. The squire turned to his left and looked across the open space of the grand lobby. He knew which rooms were his and Rime's, but he had no idea about any of the others.

"I think the first place we should check is wherever the weapons are." Coracle crossed her arms with a wry smile. "Just in case we do find Master Waters in Master Waters' room. Or that 'other lady'."

"I don't think it particularly matters who we're actually looking for." Geranium languidly twanged his guitar.

"We'll find who we find when we find them. Weapons first."

Jonas angled towards the room in the north-east corner that Lord Bellwether had indicated. It was the first room on the same side of the mezzanine as his and Rime's. The squire noticed that most of the doors on this side of the hall were ajar except the one he was about to open and the room adjacent. He spun around and saw that the bard and the shaman were already making their way towards the opposite wall where three doors were shut. One was cracked ever so slightly.

"Where are you two going?" Jonas called.

"I'm wearing my night dress. The Balance and my sense of modesty require a quick change. Especially if we're going to be fighting vicious killers at any moment." Coracle didn't stop moving and entered one of the closed doors.

"I forgot what we were doing," Geranium admitted. "I was just watching the elf's backside and got distracted. Girl's got some serious business happening back there. Serious *blue* business."

The squire chuckled despite himself. He felt a vague sense of unease; they really shouldn't be splitting up like this in contested territory. *Units should stay within visual range of each other at all times.* He wrote it again and again on his academy parchment until Scholar Dryden was satisfied that he absorbed it. The instructor had been most displeased when Jonas had responded "shouting distance" initially, and his ire had been further invoked when the squire had tried to explain that he was thinking about fog, or trees, or you know, steep hills.

"Could you…" Jonas began.

"Yeah, yeah. I'll stay here and watch all the doors. Go grab your thing." The bard waved a hand to dismiss him, and began to pick out a somber melody on his black guitar.

I wonder what Scholar Dryden would say about giving away your position with a melancholy guitar solo? Jonas shrugged his shoulders and turned the knob to enter Funnicello's quarters.

He had already been thinking about his days in the Academy, so the dwarf's room was almost familiar. Unlike the understated opulence of the guest rooms, this seemed more like a dormitory: a short bed with a plain blue quilt, cotton sheets folded back. A gray wooden trunk at the foot, a simple steel rail on wooden stanchions that hung with many duplicates of the servant's plain black coat. A small white tub with dragon's feet stood in one corner, surrounded by a surprisingly jaunty shower curtain with blue polka-dots. Through the expected door, Jonas spotted a simple privy. The room was devoid of clutter and as frank as road-brick. This made the eight-foot tall silver statue of a cow all the more preposterous.

Jonas ran his eyes over it as he approached. The bovine monstrosity took up most of one wall. The cow appeared to be caught mid-frolic its head thrown over one shoulder, mouth wide in a distressing, boisterous manner. The silver gleamed in the light thrown from the burn-light torch in the ceiling showing not a speck of tarnish. The udders gleamed the brightest of all. *I don't want to know why he spent extra time polishing those.*

The squire turned in a slow circle. He squatted, peered under the bed, and took a furtive peek inside the trunk. The dwarf was dead, but it still seemed a bit improper to be rifling through his underwear. That and chunk of fragrant cedar was all that the trunk contained. That left only the silver cow. Jonas moved his face inches from the shining skin of the farm animal and squinted at the entire length. He could just barely make out a hair's breadth seam that ran down the cow's stomach. Somehow, the statue was a container; it had to be where his sword was stowed. He was going to have to figure out how to get it open.

Jonas took in a breath to call for Rime but then stopped himself. The embarrassment of marching back downstairs *in front of Neriah* to ask for help was more than he could possibly bear -- not to mention the venomous reaction Rime would surely have. The squire crossed his arms and stared at the leering cow with determination. He wasn't going to be much help solving the mystery of the manor, but he could solve the Mystery of the Silver Cow unaided.

He continued his inspection, looking at the statue from every angle. He poked the eyes and the teeth, pushed down on the tail, hoping to find a secret lever. Jonas ran his hands over the extra-bright udder, giving each a distinct tug.

"Thirsty?" Coracle's voice made him jump. "Or just like the feel of them?"

"Both. I'm hoping for both." The bard leaned in the doorway next to the shaman, completely at ease. The somber tune he had been playing still filled the air.

They could have said something. Jonas tried to appear nonchalant, even though his face was bright red. "It's a safe, a container. I was trying to figure out how to get it open. Wait, how is the music still…"

Geranium waggled his long fingers in delight and jerked his head back in the direction of the stairs. "Lady Moon-

Death can play for some time without my supervision. Simple melodies lacking in my verve and swerve, but still a useful trick."

"One does need their hands free from time to time," the Nai-Elf agreed. She was wearing the same simple tunic that she had worn earlier, and she now carried a large cream-colored conch. "If I could make my Spirit-Shell float at will, it would make certain rituals easier to perform."

Jonas found himself staring at the conch. It wasn't the same type or color of the one he'd seen in the Wheelbrake. *But still...*

The squire shook his head to clear his thoughts. He was still completely puzzled by his encounter with the Gray Witch, and like most things that confused him, it was far simpler to allow them to fall off the edges of his flat mind.

"Do either of you have any ideas?" Jonas indicated the rest of the room. "There's nowhere else in the room to hide anything. My sword has to be inside."

"I know little of locks or safes," Coracle crinkled her nose. "And even less of this land-beast, whatever it is."

The bard approached the statue, his eyes for once sparked with natural curiosity instead of artificial grandeur. Geranium rubbed his chin for a moment, then snapped his fingers.

"The dwarf was a dwarf," the bard exclaimed. "Dwarves are very cunning with machines, always. There must be a secret way to open this."

"That isn't particularly helpful," the shaman said as she shifted her shell to the opposite elbow.

"I've tried everything. That's why I was fussing with the teats. I've poked and prodded every inch of this thing, but there doesn't seem to be a button anywhere," Jonas complained.

"Awww, no button, so sad." Geranium whistled a quick melody that landed in perfect harmony with the tune that still echoed from Lady Moon-Death in the hall.

The squire crushed both fists into his temples and concentrated. *I'm not going to run and ask Rime. I'm not going to run and ask Rime. I am going to open this stupid dwarf safe. There has to be an answer--* His eyes popped open with an unfamiliar sensation. He smelled burnt coffee as two thoughts in his brain groped and searched for each other.

"One time we had to open another lock made by a dwarf," Jonas said, hoping that speaking aloud would help the process. "And to open it we had to dance. And there was a song. But mainly we had to dance. Maybe you open this one by..."

The squire let the last word drag out, the final syllable rising with excitement then slowly dying in defeat. He had been really close.

"A sound-lock!" Geranium said with delight. "I have heard of such devices! If you know the tune, it opens as easily as farmer's daughter's innuendoes!"

Coracle laughed and clapped, caught up in the excitement. "That is neat. Now, how do we figure out the song?"

"I have no idea!" The bard scooped up the shaman, and spun her around the room with elated glee.

Jonas held up a hand and the other two slowly came to a halt. Coracle started to speak, but the squire gestured urgently, his eyes locked on the grinning cow. He needed total quiet to concentrate. He was close, so close. The coffee burned to sulphur and two thoughts clasped hands in the dark wilderness.

With delicate care he extended a fist, and rapped on the statue's side. Four quick beats, then two slow. It was the same beat and rhythm that Funnicello had done in the Banquet Hall.

The statue gave off a series of audible clicks, then the seam in the center split as the two halves of the silver cow swung open. Inside was a fairly large cavity, one side was stacked with smaller boxes; the other was a weapon's rack. There were a pair of cutlasses, some wicked looking daggers, a battle axe, two or three rapiers, a narrow-blade, and three short swords with matching pearl handles. Wedged in between two of the rapiers - a plain longsword in a wooden sheath with a red cotton rope for a strap.

I can't believe it. I solved the Mystery! Jonas pulled his good steel free and slung it over his shoulder with habit-worn pride. The red cotton didn't go with his borrowed black and silver finery, but he felt complete. Not without a little swagger, he turned to face the waiting shaman and bard.

"Really, that one? Take a cutlass at least." Geranium rolled his eyes.

"This is mine," the squire said simply. "You have your guitar. Do you need a weapon, lady?"

"I have the Spirit-Shell. And the trust and guidance of the Balance." Coracle raised her head, the shells and bones in her hair clattering. "I have no need of steel."

"Okay. Because the cutlass *is* really nice." Jonas eyed the open gut of the Silver Cow with speculation. "Maybe I will…"

A woman's scream and the sound of shattering glass cut through his sentence. Geranium flung himself into the hall. "That's close. I think it's coming from next door!"

Jonas and Coracle followed close enough on his heels to see Lady Moon-Death sail through the air to the bard's hands. The three of them converged on the door, Geranium pounding on it first. The scream had been short and guttural, more of anger than fear.

"Hello, hello! Lady Karis, is that you?" Jonas yelled at the door.

The bard stopped knocking and they all leaned in close to listen. There was the sound of feet shuffling, then the click of the door being unlocked. Jonas turned the knob, and at Coracle's urgent hand on his shoulder, opened it with slow care.

Karis sat in the center of the room with her back against the far wall. She was still wearing the ornate red dress from earlier, but a fresh stain marred the entire front of it. Her knees were pulled up nearly to her chin, and her hands clutched a large wine glass. Karis sipped from it as they entered, barely acknowledging their presence. The remains of a wine bottle littered the entryway. Jonas was still barefoot so he walked with great care.

"Lady Karis. Are you well?" Coracle broached the stony silence.

"Well. Well, I am well." The short-haired woman stared

117

directly ahead and took a long slurp from her wine.

"You've been in here since you left the Parlor?" the shaman continued.

"The Parlor. Sure."

Jonas shared a quick look with the bard. Karis was drunk.

"Did you not hear the scream before?" Geranium asked, suspicion clear on his long face.

"I screamed before. I was mad. It's been a long day," Karis stared down into her wine, then added emphatically. "A long day."

Coracle turned and shrugged. "I guess let's drag her down to the lobby. She can fill her cup with the pretty boy actor, and they can keep an eye on her."

"I will not be dragged." Karis' voice was frosted slush. "I will not sit with pretty actors. I will stay here. And I will drink alone."

"Okay, Lady," the bard said with squeak-soap comfort in his voice. "We'll be right back."

Karis flipped her hand in a signal of disinterest.

At the bard's gesture, they withdrew from the drunken noble's room to confer.

"I still say the quickest solution is to just pick her up and drag her downstairs. I can do it, if you two are too shy," the sea-elf whispered.

"Are you sure? She's clearly not going anywhere." Jonas

peeked back into the room in time to see her take another long draw from her glass, wine dribbling out the corners of her mouth.

"She could be faking." Geranium pushed his floating guitar back to hover behind him. "You have to consider it. She could be putting on a show. It's a pretty good explanation - a little too good - if you ask me."

Jonas furrowed his brow. He wasn't sure what to do, but what the bard was saying made sense. "Even if she's not faking, we can't leave her alone with the killer prowling the halls."

"Agreed. Simple." The bard snapped his fingers again. "She's a fancy lady, you're a servant. Go serve her."

The squire peered back into the room. Karis was staring poniards into the empty air.

"Okay, I'll try," he sighed.

He took a moment to adjust his vest into something approaching proper alignment, tugging at the silver buttons. His back straightened in proper Academy-fashion, but immediately kinked as he navigated the broken glass with his bare feet. *Next stop after this: Shoes.*

"Uh, my lady--Karis?" She did not break her staredown with the abyss, but simply held up her empty wine glass. "Lord Bellwether sent me to bring you downstairs. It's not safe right now."

"It's never safe, boy," Karis sighed. "Jobs, slobs, hobbled horses, the grind of the quill and the ink spatter on the parchment."

"Okay. Okay, my lady. Those are some words you said there. Could I perhaps escort you downstairs?" The squire folded himself in half, offering his elbow in what he hoped was a courteous manner.

The bedraggled lady reached up past his proffered limb and grabbed a fistful of his hair. Jonas yelped as she pulled herself off the floor using him as an anchor. She glanced into his face, her eyes whirling and dark. The squire realized that since entering the house he had been brought in intimate proximity with some fairly attractive women in a short span of time. Karis' hair was cut in a severe fashion. Her eyes had the weight of primed cannons, but the clean line of her jaw and lips had a surprising appeal. The pain from his wrenched scalp seemed distant, and the squire found himself gently taking the drunken lady by the shoulder to guide her from the room.

"Want to feel the udders some more? Let's go!" Geranium hooted from the hallway.

Karis did not act as if she had heard; she just took a few deep breaths while staring straight ahead. "I can still get it. I can still get the Box."

"Uh..." Jonas began.

Karis pulled her spine taut and walked forward, the squire had to move quickly to keep pace with her. She walked through the broken glass without stopping. He was forced to hop in ungainly haste and was amazed to see that her feet were left unblooded.

The bard and the shaman rewarded him with polite applause as he lead her out of the room. Karis' eyes flared and she pushed herself away from the squire, nearly toppling in stomach-sick haste. The red-clad woman threw herself at the mezzanine rail overlooking the lobby, and seemed to be fighting the bile back. Karis breathed deeply, and managed to spit out a few curse words but she kept her gorge in check. Jonas shrugged at his two companions, then he smelt the tiniest whiff of burnt coffee.

"She mentioned something about a Box?" The squire gestured towards the recuperating noble. "Do you know what she meant?"

The levity on Geranium and Coracle's faces vanished instantly. Like whips their eyes flew to his face: cold, calculating and alert. They exchanged a glance of neon-pink and dark-sea blue.

"No idea," they said in unison.

9

"Why the Library?" Trowel demanded, shifting her battered red leather purse. "There is very little held within these pages that my own intellect cannot provide. *'Mundum interreliacce'* -- the world in my brain -- as the poet says."

Rime did not answer immediately. She was looking at the books. She was smelling the books. She wished that she was alone so she could run her hands along the spines and press her face against the pages. The mage spent so much time in the library of her mind that sometimes she forgot the impact that these piles of leather-bound paper could have on her.

Lord Bellwether's Library eschewed the polished marble and brass of the Lobby and the Parlor, leaving the gray stone of the manor unembellished. Tall shelves of dark wood held the standard tomes and books arranged neatly with a long slotted rack in the center of the room for a few scrolls and more esoteric forms of literature. Four well-polished tables neatly quartered the room along with a set

of comfortable looking leather couches and chairs. A red blanket was strewn over one arm of a couch as if begging to be wrapped around the knees of some chilly reader. Like
the rest of the manor there was no open fireplace, only the clean illumination from burn-light glass set at regular intervals in the walls. It was different from her father's library, yet the same. It was heaven.

Rime collected herself and turned to face the irritated scholar. The wood-elf's ears were nearly thrumming with her ire. The black-robed priest was standing a few feet behind, listening politely. The mage considered her options.

Do I tell them about the symbol and letters that Funnicello left? Controlling information is paramount at this point in a case, but I can't very well hide the books I want to look at with them in the room. Maybe I can get them to leave? Unlikely. She frowned, then decided. *I will tell them about the symbol but not the letters. Remember every part of their reaction.*

"I'm sure you are very knowledgeable, Scholar Trowel. But what I need to research is very obscure." Rime gestured for Father Andrew to come closer. "Funnicello left us a clue. A mark on the floor."

"A mark?" The balding priest's eyes were intrigued. "The name of his killer?"

"No. Something else -- a symbol. Here, let me show you." Rime cast around the room before finding an ornate lacquer box on a table holding fine parchment, a simple quill and inkstone.

"Why would he write a symbol? If he did it moments before his death, wouldn't it make the most sense to write the name of his killer? Are you sure that it was a proper symbol and not just the pained scratchings of a dying dwarf?" Trowel took a seat at the table, hooking her purse over the chair back.

Rime took a seat across from the Yad-Elf and laid the parchment out flat before her. *The name of the killer. 'O', 'T', and 'T'. Maybe, but those letters don't fit any of the guests' names -- unless one of the letters is incomplete or incorrect.* Father Andrew leaned on the edge of the table between them to get a good view of the blank paper.

She drew the symbol carefully from the pristine record of her memory. She spoke as the ink flowed. "This symbol was immediately familiar to me."

Three tiny circle-dots evenly spaced. "I knew I'd seen it before but decided not to dwell on it while I was gathering evidence."

Three lines connected the dots into an equilateral triangle. "It is geometric in nature. Simple lines and dots. Vectors and angles, points and routes. Which suggests a certain mathematical bent to the culture that this icon originated from."

A final small circle colored in the center with the dark ink. Rime carefully laid down the quill without spilling a drop. "Which has lead me to the conclusion that…" the mage broke off as she saw the priest and the scholar trading shocked glances.

"That this is a Precursor hieroglyph," Trowel said. "Like much of Arkanic script it has several nested meanings, better expressed by the context in which it is found. It makes the language nearly impossible to translate beyond the most basic of concepts; only a fraction has been unlocked by my colleagues. This symbol presented alone signifies the number zero, emptiness, darkness, void -- but also wisdom, understanding, lore. I presented a paper in Pice theorizing that they viewed knowledge as an emptiness. Not a concrete value to be gained, but an absence -- a recognition of all that they did not understand."

"You are an expert on the Precursors," Rime sighed. The obvious conclusion slid out of her and spattered her half-cape with residue.

"She is," the priest nodded. "The days before your arrival, it was rare that she *wasn't* telling us all about the Precursors. It was very interesting at first, but then around the third day…"

"It became even more fascinating," the scholar said without rancor. "The entire civilization vanished thousands of years ago, leaving technological wonders in their wake like discarded toys! Almost all of our own advances are built upon what they left us -- why the very lights in this room are based on glow-globes discovered in the Gryphon Ruins near Quorum. The more efficient airship engineering that powers the vast fleet of the Seafoam Trading Company, the salt processing plants in Jacradam, the Glass Towers of Vo!"

"The white bridge in Jericho," Rime offered, swept up in the wood-elf's excitement.

"A minor site, of course, but not without its charms. Clean and unbroken while empires rise and fall around it." Trowel smiled, and past the braided gray hair and the seams in her face, Rime glimpsed the young student who had fallen in love with the wonders of a forgotten age.

"This is why you both recognized the symbol. You from your studies, and you because she showed you in a demonstration or on the back of a napkin at dinner?" the mage asked Father Andrew.

"Ah, not quite." He ran a hand across his bald pate. "There was a demonstration of sorts, but it didn't have to do with this symbol directly."

Rime blinked as her fingers ran across the chalkboard in her mind. Several facts and chance comments aligned and she saw the pattern emerge.

"The auction. Every guest is here to bid on something. Trowel gave a demonstration; she's the seller. What are you selling, Scholar? And what does it have to do with this symbol?" The mage tapped her finger on the paper, careful lines of ink smearing.

The wood-elf sighed and turned to pull her battered purse into her lap. "I can't imagine how it is related. I don't know what came over me when I heard Neriah's scream. I have a perfectly good lockbox in my quarters. But I just knew that it wouldn't be safe -- that I should keep it on my person."

Trowel reached into her purse and pulled out a small box. It was a quiet green like newly formed leaves, and it fit easily in the scholar's hands. The box had rounded corners and showed no obvious hinge. Etched into the lid of the box was the same symbol that Rime had drawn in ink and Funnicello had drawn in blood.

The mage felt her stomach tighten and her pupils dilate. The pure force of curiosity and expectation ripped through her. She clamped down on her magic so she wouldn't start floating out of her chair. Good mysteries always contained such things. A box, a chest, a locket. Some secret unknown that would be revealed at the flip of a lid.

"What is it?" Rime demanded with as much diplomacy as she could muster. *What is it, what is it, what is it?!?*

"It's a box." Trowel smiled, then held up her hands at the mage's instant agitation. "Forgive me my small jest. The box is of Precursor manufacture, beautiful and perfect as one would expect, but it is its contents that are more impressive."

The wood-elf pressed down on the lid, and it popped open with an audible click. She pulled the lid open, revealing a small sheaf of folded parchment covered with writing. Trowel clucked and pulled the papers aside to reveal the box's true contents. Set into a simple recess was a blue crystal wound about with silver wire and a jet black base. The crystal glowed, drawing the eye. With the pride of a farmer presenting his prize tomato, the wood-elf reached in and removed the object. It fit easily in her hand, and from the way her fingers wrapped around the base Rime could see that it was designed to be held thus.

"What is it?" she repeated in awed reverence.

"It is a sound-crystal. The Precursors used these to record music, voices, anything audible. Very few have been found. It still operates perfectly and holds the words of a being long gone from this world." The wood-elf gestured towards the folded parchment with her free hand. "This is the translation."

"Actually, question. I meant to ask you when we all listened to it the first time. If the language is dead, and only a fraction of their symbols have been figured out, how were you able to translate this entire recording?"

Father Andrew tugged on his nose in embarrassment.

"Magic." The scholar wiggled her fingers and chuckled. "A spell of translation is a complicated and costly affair, but easily within the reach of a well-funded researcher. This is why these recordings are so valuable! A wave of the wand and we can unearth entire conversations while our colleagues can spend a decade parsing out a single sentence on a stone tablet. Which--wait, you are a wizard, dear Rime! You are clearly new to the Art, but perhaps you have learned some advanced spells with your vaunted intellect we heard so much about in the Lobby?"

Rime shook herself free of her fascination. "No, I'm sorry. I don't know anything that advanced yet." *I wouldn't have any idea where to start. That's something I should start working on: more indirect and fine-tuned applications for my magic. I can't solve every problem with fire.*

"Ah, too bad then," Trowel said regretfully. "Then I shall do as I did for the other guests. I will play the recording and read you the translation."

"Who is the speaker? Do you know?"

"I do. But he introduces himself nearly right away, and please allow me the delight of seeing your reaction. Any educated person will recognize the speaker, as you clearly are." The scholar pressed her index finger down on the silver trigger.

The sound was perfect. It was as if whoever recorded it was standing in the same room, not a trace of echo or corruption in the voice reproduction. The modern devices based on this technology -- jukeboxes, song-casters, doorbells in the finest of homes -- none emitted any sort of sound this pure.

Rime folded her hands beneath her chin and listened to the words of the long-dead Precursor. The words were incomprehensible, but still spoken in a clean and easy tenor. She could deduce that the speaker was educated, older, male -- and that the words were spoken while under a great deal of pain and fear.

Trowel allowed a few sentences to pass, so her audience could appreciate the strange timbre and cadence of the Arkanic language. Then she began to read the translation.

My name is Teon.

There was a time, and there was a place where and when that name meant something. A bright name, a fell name. East of the Sun and West of the Moon in the place we once called home. A place that is lost, a time that will never come again.

Now my name is rubble. My name is a relic. Here in the shattered foundations of Kythera it echoes and lingers. The voices of my people scream out my name in pain and despair. I want to tell them that it wasn't me, that it wasn't my fault. I didn't bring the Machine.

It was my left hand.

It lies quiet now, folded on my stomach. Black blood whimpers out of a dozen small wounds,
inflicted by the sharp instrument I hold in my right hand. It is a delicate instrument, best suited for aligning tiny wires or adjusting the fine components on a word-board. It served this purpose ably, plunging again and again into my skin. There was pain -- but distant — not my pain. My

left hand mimics true feeling, but it is always false. The pain is no different.

I will die soon. At least, that is my hope. I fear that if I fall unconscious before my heart ceases to beat, my left hand will rise and repair my wounds. I must stay awake until Death comes. I have fled him all my life, running further and faster than any others of my kin. But now I welcome him as my dearest companion.

To stay awake, I will tell my story. This sound crystal is fully powered. It shall last longer than I will. I will speak the story of my name. How we, who the people of this world call the Lost, came here trying to escape the dark, on our silver ships made of song and steel.

But we brought it with us.

I brought it with us.

Light help me, I brought it with us.

What can I tell you about Home? I have tried many times to describe it to the people of this world, but something is always lost in the telling. Home is a feeling, a knowledge — and no matter how many times I described the towers of glass, the river bank where I learned to swim, the smell of my grandmother's library — I could not catch it.

It was a place not much different than this world. The sun rose, the wind blew. We only had one moon instead of the three that dance in this world's sky. Such a greedy world, this Aufero. How could it have less than three moons?

I wander. It is what I do. In speech as well as deed. Even now, even as I wait for the end. There is something to that. Something mundane and comforting.

Our world shone. That is all I can say. It gleamed more brightly in the heavens than any other star. Every one of the Lost can point to it in their sleep, even though it shines no more. It was our Home, and we knew as we left it that we would never return. And we knew that we would never stop grieving the loss of it.

The Dark swallowed it whole, and we fled. The entirety of my race crammed on half-a-hundred silver ships, flung into the sea of stars. But that is not the true beginning of my story.

My story begins with falling.

The fastest ships were chosen, to seek out a place to land — a place to begin again. My father was the captain and he slept not at all as our ship plunged ever forward into the dark. The far-singers hummed as we approached barren planets and balls of molten fire. Every one was discordant. Ugly noise and static.

We flew on and on, day after day, hoping to find a place that the Dark had not touched. A whole universe of empty rock and death. In desperation we returned to the fleet and found the same answer in the weary faces of the other captains.

I remember how my father took my mother's hands and laid his forehead on hers. They looked into each other's eyes and she nodded. They knew what must be done, and the risks. The other ships would wait, and ours would risk Beyond.

My mother sang the Song of Away.

The universe grew thin and we slipped through the walls

as she sang. I stood next to my father and listened hard for the tune of another place -- any place -- that we could go.

I think I heard it before my father but maybe just a heartbeat before. I still remember the joy in his eyes when he heard the faint melody.

And then the melody was a march — Aufero, the greedy – Aufero, the thief — reached out and *pulled* us in.

We erupted into that universe like a comet being born. The silver ship bucked and spun, the songs of my people becoming screams. Through the windows I caught my first glimpse of the planet.

It was blue. I fell in love.

Then the glass shattered, and I fell towards the greedy planet.

My story had begun.

Did my left hand just move? Did my eyes shut a little too long?

I must stay awake. Awake until the end.

I fell. Through the skies of the blue planet, my body tumbling and burning with heat.

The Lost are stronger than we appear. It was always a wonder to the creatures of Aufero that such frail golden-skinned things as we could hide such might. I fell through the atmosphere, clouds fleeing from my descent.

I was young then and I was afraid. I cried out for my father to save me, for my mother to save me. But the clouds gave way to empty air, and I rushed faster and faster towards the earth below.

I saw an ocean, larger than any from Home. A desert, a range of mountains, then finally a dark forest.

I spun in the air, my eyes toward the skies hoping to catch a glimpse of the silver ship. Nothing.

The forest wrapped itself around me, and there was pain. Pain like I had never known.

I do not know how long I abandoned the seat of my mind to the God of Pain. Hours, days, the lifetime of a stone. But at last I crawled back to sanity and looked out of my own eyes again.

I wished then I had not. To return to the abyss and drift away. Better if I had. Perhaps, some part of me would like to still say. But I look at my left hand, and I know. It would have been better if I had died then.

My body lay at the base of a vast tree. The bark was black and the leaves were gray, edged with blue ash. And through my left side pushed a great root, right through my heart. In horror I pulled away the cloth from the stinking bloody thing. It was gnarled and vicious, ending in a sharp point. In my pain I glimpsed the truth, even then. This root had been waiting for me. The tree had grown just so, in this exact spot – patient and vile.

Feeble, I tried to push myself up off the evil spike. But I could not; it had me by the heart. I would die before I was free. As I have said, the Lost are stronger than we appear. Even a mortal wound can take quite some time to claim us. But without food or aid the end marched closer.

I wept. I was young and alone. My people had fled the Dark, thrown themselves into the unknown to escape, and I had fallen immediately into another trap. How strange I must have appeared -- a small golden child at the foot of a dark tree. A spike of wood through my chest, tears spilling down my face. But there was no one to see. At least not right away.

The sun moved above me. I saw the three strange moons again and again. Days passed, and I was alone. Blood drained out of my heart and I waited for the end. A bud formed on the root piercing my chest. It opened slowly, its petals a deep blue.

And then he came to me. Jalyx was his name. So strange, as my name echoes throughout the pages of history that no one remembers his name, his beautiful name. Much later he told me that his name meant something ridiculous -- an odd waterfowl with bright red plumage. I was appalled and insisted that we give his name a new meaning like moonlight or the smell of autumn leaves. He laughed and said his name could mean anything I wished.

Anything I wished. Such power so casually tossed at my feet.

I wander again.

He moved cautiously into my little glade, morning sunlight behind him. His skin was dark; long green hair threaded through beads of bone and glass. A native, his eyes wide with wonder and horror. Finding me dying, impaled on the root of the black tree. I cried out in surprise and relief, alien words to his ears.

But Jalyx was not afraid. He stepped into the glade and looked me over with severe caution. He gripped my shoulders and pulled me off the root in one quick motion. Relief mixed with fresh pain; I cried out. He picked me up and carried me out of the glade.

My last view of the dark tree was of the blood stained earth around an empty spike. The blue flower was gone, disappeared somewhere inside my chest.

It is important to say the tree had no flowers. Not before, nor after. The malevolent blue flower bloomed from a seed that I brought with me all the way from Home.

My left arm is moving. Every time I blink, it inches forward. I do not have the strength to kill this evil. I must speak faster.

Days passed, and weeks. I slept and ate and healed and learned to speak the strange tongue of Jalyx and his people. He was my savior -- my first friend on Aufero – and I swore that his kindness would be repaid tenfold.

My left hand. It moves.

So much that happened, so many years. Must speak faster. We found the survivors of the crash and the wreckage. Both my parents were dead. I found myself made Captain of a shattered craft.

Must speak faster.

With time and skill we repaired the music hall in our ship and called the fleet to the planet. We faced many dangers and complications, but I was determined to make Jalyx's home a paradise — a place where we could share our knowledge with any who desired it. I should have guarded our knowledge more carefully; there were many who sought to abuse it. But the years were golden, and the songs we sang knew nothing of doubt.

Inside me the flower of evil slowly bloomed.

That was the curse, the horror of it all. I can see it now. The shining cities, the bridges of purest white, the towers of glass rose again — but everything we built, everything I built had in it a flaw. A shadow. Twisted lines carefully placed by my left hand. Note by note we sang, but each verse hid a darker chord.

And then my greatest achievement: The Machine. My left hand's glory. As I grew in power and fame, my people began to look to me for wisdom. In their grief the Lost could find no satisfaction in the things we built here nor in the friends we gained. I tried to show them the wonder of our new home, but they would not listen. Their hearts grew hollow and sere, and they begged me. My own people begged me. 'Oh, Teon – First Singer! Use your skill to take us back Home.'

'But I cannot. The Dark waits there, covering an entire galaxy with his malice.'

'Then build us a weapon. A weapon of Light that can strike him down!'

I knew it was folly, but my hand itched to build it. A colossus, a pure warrior of light. I could not see…

I fell asleep. How long have I been asleep? My hand.

No. No. It is gone. My left hand is gone.

The blue flower blooms.

It isn't over.

I'm sorry. I'm so sorry.

Jalyx, I'm sorry.

The wood-elf stopped reading. Trowel sniffed in the sudden quiet, and the priest laid a comforting hand on her shoulder.

Rime realized tears were flowing over her folded hands. She hated to cry, but for once she was not ashamed. *Teon. The First Singer.*

Trowel nodded, seeing the understanding in the mage's eyes. "Yes. Teon, the leader of the entire Precursor civilization from beginning to end, if our studies are correct. Creator of the most advanced culture and technology this world has ever known, and these are his final words. His final words that seem to be recorded at the moment of the Precursors' destruction."

"Such a great shame that his final moments were ones of madness and pain." Father Andrew shook his head.

"This is — this is the most valuable object on the planet." Rime looked between the two. "You realize that, don't you?"

"You may be overstating things slightly," the scholar demurred.

"The entire foundation of our history -- of our technology -- is based on Arkanic devices. Every little piece we find, we break apart and make a worse version of it. And the historic implications alone -- the Precursors are not native to Aufero! They came from somewhere else on ships -- silver ships," Rime continued. "In every respect the value of this device cannot be measured. Every company — every nation in the world — will want this. Every word must be studied. Every sentence given to dozens of scholars to devote decades to. Slight remarks made on this recording could hold the answers to questions that have stymied scientists for hundreds of years. This is it. This is the key to the entire civilization. And you came here to sell it. And everyone else came here to buy it, before the rest of the world catches wind of its existence."

The wood-elf managed to look slightly embarrassed. "Yes. It's not the most pure of intentions, I'll admit. One of the clauses I insisted upon is that the translation will be shared with the world ten years from the sale. I'm not holding up the progress of Aufero; the buyer is getting a head start. What is your point?"

"Does any of that sound like a pretty good motive for murder?" Rime picked up her sketch of the triangle and crumpled it into a tight ball.

10

Tottering like a clattering stack of breakfast plates still clumped with waffle residue, forks and butter akimbo, Jonas did his best to help Karis down the long stairwell without making her aware that he was assisting her.

He was thankful that that he'd had the forethought to bring her down the east stairwell, which didn't terminate on a fresh corpse. Karis' heel came down on his toe, and he was also glad that he'd taken a moment to slip his boots back on. As he caught the green-gilled noble again, preventing her from braining herself on the blue-silk wrapped marble baluster, he gazed across to where he expected to see the spreading pool of blood and Funnicello's remains.

He saw clean white marble and no dead dwarf. Soapy water radiated on the floor from a metal bucket. The water inside showed a slight rose tinge. A sponge moved back and forth clutched in delicate hands. The cleaner looked up from her kneeled position, a white cloth tied around blonde-strawberry hair.

"Oh, good. You found her," Neriah said with a relieved smile, then sniffed hard mastering her tears. "I was afraid that you — you know — that you wouldn't."

The squire sat Karis down on the bottom step and diffidently linked her hands around the bottom rail. He adjusted his vest, smoothed his hair, and ran a thumb down the red-cotton strap of his sword case to make sure the hilt looked properly impressive over his left shoulder. Now he had to say something. *Something impressive. Something impressive. Something impressive.*

"I, uh..."Jonas took a step towards the soap-sud princess.

"Drinking her worries away in a closet, like a debutante grounded by her parents," Geranium hooted as he bounced down the last few stairs.

The bard laid his hands on the squire's shoulders, rested his pointed chin on Jonas' head and continued. "No sign of the banker yet, and we pawed through all the underwear drawers in all of the rooms. I even tried on a pair or two just to be absolutely certain."

"I, uh..." the squire's mind desperately tried to change gears from formulating a suitably impressive statement for the princess to formulating a proper response to Geranium's proximity.

"My father took Funnicello into his office. We wrapped him very carefully in the best linens. He used to bleach them twice and hang them to dry in the gardens behind the manor," Neriah reported, eyes still.

"As he would have wished it, I'm sure," Coracle said, patting her seashell as if to comfort it.

"Thank you." Neriah stood up slowly and dropped her sponge into the pink-filled bucket.

Across the lobby, the three actors sat leaning against the wall next to the steel-reinforced doors with its tiny gold lock still winking in the lamp light. Vincent had his head back against the cool stone; Toby was flopped over in his lap snoring. The taller man's fingers idly ran through the sleeping hero's blonde hair. Sand was a few feet aside, arms crossed. The white-haired man looked up inquisitively, but did not approach Jonas and the others.

"No luck, searchers?" he elocuted with crisp consonants across the lobby.

"No, we didn't find anyone besides Lady Karis." The squire stepped a few feet across the lobby in a clever attempt to disentangle himself from the bard.

Geranium sighed with regret and allowed the squire to go free. "He must be up in the Lord's Tower, eating the drapes and touching himself inappropriately, the mad old stick."

"What makes you say mad?" The sea-elf shifted her conch to the opposite elbow's crook.

"Eh, ripping someone's guts out is a pretty sharp sign of diminishing mental returns." The bard leaned back and scooped up his floating guitar. Holding it behind his back, he began to pick out an intricate scale that quavered with comical insanity like a bleeding clown stacking broken wine glasses.

"Are Lady Rime and the others finished with their search?" Jonas asked.

"They've been in the Library this entire time," Neriah replied softly, then her face bent in a small smile. "I imagine Trowel found a few topics she wanted to lecture on. I really don't think that Master Waters is anywhere downstairs either. We've been moving around so much, surely we would have stumbled upon him."

Rime in a library. Yeah, that could take some time. The squire scratched his nose. "Well, I guess I'll check on them, and then we can go on with the search in the Tower."

"Your search is over," a voice groaned from the top of the stairs.

There wasn't a rumble of thunder, but there should have been. At the top of the stairs stood Master Waters. The thin man was leaning forward as if in pain, the top buttons of his long coat mangled and torn open. He was leaning hard on some sort of pole with tattered fabric and metal rings hung against his gaunt hands: an oak curtain rod, thick enough to be dangerous. *He must have ripped it down from somewhere in the house.* Jonas was surprised to find his sword in his hand. The squire wasn't very bright, all in all, but one thing he had learned at the Academy stuck with him. His body knew danger before his mind did. Something in the trader's voice touched an animal nerve, and he never questioned when his hands moved on their own. His hands knew the beast of old, the wolf slinking up to the campfire.

"Master Waters? Are you alright? We've been looking for you," Neriah called.

"Looking. Looking? I've been looking," Waters muttered.

"Neriah, get behind me," Jonas said, putting his foot on

the first step.

The thin trader at the top of the stairs pushed himself up, using his curtain rod as a crutch. All could see his face clearly in the cheery light of the lobby. His face had been gouged, deeply and horribly, from his right temple down across his face to the left side of his chin. Blood seeped from the wound, and he blinked his eyes through a rheum of gore. Jonas took two more steps. He needed to close the distance and keep the bleeding man covered. If he bolted it would be a chase into narrow, unfamiliar terrain.

"Looking for a safe place. Looking, looking." Waters shifted his grip on the curtain rod, leaving a crimson mark. *He clawed his own face. He clawed his own face.*

The bleeding man took a moment to straighten his coat: a moment of common-place vanity. The blood on his hand smeared on the fine ivory buttons. His attention drifted as if he was trying to find his place in a ledger, or in the comforting rows of his paper-stacked office. Then his attention fell onto Neriah's slim form like a debtor weighing his final loan.

"You are safe. Safe. You are safe." The trader hefted his curtain rod, rings jangling.

Then with an unintelligible word, Master Waters hefted his curtain rod and started down the stairs, his gaze never leaving Neriah's face. The violent twist of his hands left little doubt as to his purpose. Geranium cursed and swung Lady Moon-Death into place. The bard's pink-gloved fingers flew into position, notes rippling as he brought his music to bear. A heartbeat behind, Coracle took her huge sea shell in both hands and loudly began to chant the beginnings of a shamanic ritual. "Forces of the Fire, servants to Seto. Forces of the Earth, servants to Jocasta.

143

Forces of the Air, servants to Marrus…"

The bard and the shaman called on their arcane power, but the squire was already moving. Magic and mystery have their might, but steel doesn't fail. *I don't have to sing for it to work, either.* Jonas held his sword flat across his body in a defensive posture. Master Waters was clearly unhinged. He had to find a way to disarm him, hopefully without injuring him. *Well, more than he's already injured himself.*

The squire watched the bleeding trader closely for any sign of him slowing his charge; there was none. Sighing, Jonas tucked his shoulder down and stormed up the stairs. He needed to catch the thin man low enough to topple him over.

Jonas had been in a fair amount of physical altercations: barroom brawls, schoolyard scuffles, quick and quiet bloodletting on the foggy field of war. An emaciated moneylender wielding a curtain rod was not something that particularly concerned him. But the world is a fantastic teacher, ever inventive in the nasty surprises and unfortunate lessons it can devise. Today's lesson was pure, mad ferocity and the startling damage a decorative piece of oak can cause in the hands of one who has left the fear of pain and death behind like misplaced luggage on the ferry.

Master Waters swung the oak rod with a strangled cry, faster than his thin arms should have made possible. It connected with the squire's left shoulder and head with a bone-dense thunk. Jonas stumbled to his right, narrowly missing the marble step with his chin. *Is there a way Lady Neriah didn't see that?* His thoughts rolled around and clattered like dice in a cup.

I should… Fuzzy thoughts were cut short by another blow on his back, and his ribs sang with pain. Then another blow on his left arm, another on his gut making him wheeze with expelled air. Jonas made his fingers stay strong around the hilt of his sword and did his best to push himself up through the onslaught. The curtain rod gave a sharp crack as the end of it snapped off leaving a ragged spear point. No time for thinking, his hands saved him again and pushed off hard -- not up to a standing position but down the stairs, sliding and bumping down the steps and away from the reach of the maddened trader.

"You are getting your ass kicked," Geranium chant-called, his voice already warming to the melody of his power.

"I throw the sand of the moons and the shells of the sun!" screeched the sea-elf amid the rain-shower plink sound of small objects falling.

Geranium's guitar howled into a ringing high note as he sang on. "And apparently Nai-Elf magic is simply awful. Awful elf magic, magic, magic!"

"Bring forth the Eleventh Incantation of Wave and Foam!"

The squire spit out blood and managed to roll out of the way as Waters' curtain rod was already stabbing down at him. He raised his sword and made a clumsy swipe at the rod. Like a snake, the trader avoided the blade and brought the broken end down into the squire's side. It punched through — a shallow wound. Jonas grabbed the rod and held it in place despite the pain. *If he gets it out of me, no telling what he'll do.*

Waters gave one tug on his weapon, then released it. Jonas gaped at the unexpected response, then coughed in pain as the trader began to viciously kick his sides and batter him with his fists. *This is like fighting a rabid dog or a tree in the wind. He just keeps coming!*

The squire still had his sword; it would be easy enough to bring it home into the Waters' flesh. As much pain as Jonas was in, it was all too clear that the trader was brain-sick. It wouldn't be right to cut the man down.

Twang. The rising music of the ebony guitar finally reached its peak, and a dark chord ripped through the lobby. Master Waters stopped his assault as if caught in treacle; his hands moved slower and slower. Jonas got a good look at his one remaining ey — a pinprick of madness dancing on a candle in the dark.

The trader stood up like an unwilling marionette and slowly turned towards the center of the lobby, where Geranium stood, neon pink hands flying up and down the strings of Lady Moon-Death — endlessly spooling a melody of unerring complexity and intricate design. The bard's sharp face was taut with concentration, his grin growing wider and more jagged. As Jonas clambered up, the music gripped him but then let him pass. Master Waters walked down the steps as if pulled by a hook in his heart. The squire's eyes registered Coracle still doing some sort of mad caper off to one side and Lady Neriah standing behind her, but it was difficult to pull his attention away from the music and the pink-haired maestro.

The mad moneylender, blood still seeping from the self-inflicted wound across his face, continued to make his way towards the bard. Geranium the Eruption opened his mouth to sing.

Come and walk
in the garden with me
Come and talk

in the garden with me
Come and walk
Come and talk
in the way
that we used to do
And forget to remember
that we aren't tender
and come
and walk
and come
and talk
in the garden with me

Jonas had heard the song before but never like this. It was deep like the ocean is deep. And dark, like the ocean is dark. Master Waters walked forward as if bound by the mathematics of the universe, as if the song was printed on both his birthing caul and his funeral sheet. And then it changed.

The squire's eye could not follow it, but Geranium did something with his left hand and the music changed. The song was the same, but it was different. *Deeper. Darker. So dark.*

Waters stood tall, then leaned backward as he strained his spine.

Come and walk
Come and talk

The trader began to spit and cough; his one remaining eye bulged.

in the way we used to do

The trader screamed in pain. Jonas shook off his

fascination and ran down the stairs, whether towards the howling man or Geranium he wasn't sure.

and come
and walk
and come
and talk

Jonas was yelling, but it seemed to disappear in the music. He was moving too slow. His eye caught the movement of the Library door as Rime and her two companions appeared, their faces a mixture of confusion and surprise.

in the garden with me

There was a sound — a quiet sound. The sound of a damp paper bag filled with air then popped. Waters' head fell forward, and the music ended.

The trader collapsed onto the marble floor of the lobby. Father Andrew and Trowel rushed forward, jostling the sea elf who was completing an elaborate dance that seemed to involve a lot of turning around in a circle. The priest was the first to reach the trader, but it only took moments for him to confirm what everyone already knew. Master Waters was dead.

Geranium the Eruption stood in the center of the Lobby, hands pushed down into the deep pockets of his long cobalt coat. Lady Moon-Death hovered nearby, seeming to absorb the light. The bard's brown face split in a manic grin, and he sketched a half-bow.

"Encore?" he inquired politely.

WHO WAS VERTON WATERS?

The trader, Verton Waters, was a man of no particular interest.

He made money. He sold things. He bought things. Coins and coffers may mourn him, but no other living soul would.

Perhaps, in the secret alleys and hidden curlicues of him there were some minor glimmers of humanity, of life, of love. Some quiet secrets that the bard's song had wrapped around, like smoke coiling around a tall cedar.

But he worked very hard to conceal them and would expect such diligent extraction of character to be honored. Solitary, drab, and impervious like an ink slash in a ledger.

Let that be his balance.

A zero sum.

11

"Everyone sit where I can see them," Rime demanded.

They were in the Parlor. The wine-sick actors had needed some help and Lady Karis even more so. Lord Bellwether had appeared after several fist-pounds on his study door. The door was thick, and he had not heard a thing. Now the remaining ten guests of the manor sat before the mage with Jonas minding the door as the eleventh.

And I'm twelve. Eggs come in dozens, don't they?

Rime crushed the vagabond thought with her left hand. She had made a quick search of Waters' corpse. The mad trader did not have Funnicello's keys. The guests took their place on the opulent couches, making a vague semi-circle around her. Sand guided his still incapacitated troupe onto a long bench towards the back, and Karis wobbled over and joined the inebriated trio as a calm afterthought.

Most of the guests, still absorbing the brutal death of Master Waters presented chastened faces. All except one — the instrument of the trader's demise — who sat sprawling in a tall-backed leather chair, one knee over the arm. Geranium smiled at her with the irritating smugness of a king of cats.

"Now. How did you do that?" The mage stalked closer to the bard.

"How? Isn't 'why' a more imperative question?" Trowel clenched her fat hands in consternation.

"'Why' is immaterial. Ephemeral. Nothing to base an investigation on. Too muddy and vague. Plus he's going to tell us that part anyway." Rime pointed at the bard, who raised his hands in mock defense. "He can't wait to tell us 'why'. But I want to know how. In this house three murders have transpired. The actress, the butler, and now the trader. Of these three deaths, one has an immediate and inarguable perpetrator corroborated by a brace of witnesses. I find it logical that a man who commits one murder would find it easy to commit another, and a man who can kill someone without touching them would be the perfect suspect in the case of the victim killed in plain view inside a coffin on a stage."

The mage wheeled to face the bard full on, not without a certain sense of triumph. She wasn't convinced that Geranium killed the actress. There were far too many pieces of the puzzle askew -- the chalkboard in her mind was a morass of scribbled notes and dotted lines. But it seemed to wipe the pleased expression off the bard's knife-blade face, and it lead to a more vital line of inquiry. She had entered the Lobby midway through Geranium's song only moments before Master Water's death. She could feel the magic in the bard's song — could almost see the lines of force -- but it was all elusive. *Ephemeral.* Rime had been around wizards a-plenty growing up; understanding their use of magic was as easy as Algebra. *This music. This music-magic. It doesn't operate like anything I've ever seen before. I don't know how it works.* The feeling of incomprehension nettled her. Her ignorance made Geranium the Eruption far more dangerous than she had first believed.

"I didn't kill Darla!" the bard protested, standing up quickly. "Did you hear any music at the play? A drum or a fife or a piccolo? Then you know it wasn't me!"

The white-haired actor had slowly stood and now looked at Geranium with tight lips and the gaze of judgement best suited for an executioner.

"So, you need music for your abilities to work," Rime pounced on the detail.

Geranium rolled his eyes. "Well, duh."

"You can manipulate people. Take control of their physical faculties, even their internal musculature and respiratory system. How did you kill Master Waters?"

"Darling," the bard crossed his arms with slow insolence. "You are a very smart girl. I think you've battered us all over the head with that fact sufficiently."

"Can you affect people's minds? Can you cause direct physical damage? Can you shoot lightning out of that stupid guitar of yours?" Rime hammered on, surprised to find herself breathing hard.

"You know a lot of things. I say it, so you can hear it. It is

152

very important that we all know this about you, yes? You know a lot of things. Things and springs and wheels and the click-clack of numbers falling in a row. But music?" Geranium tapped a staccato beat with two fingers on the pulse of his wrist. "It cannot be known. You can't contain it. You can't weigh it. You can't put it safe on a shelf or bury it down in a hole. There is a reason that the Songs of the Lost still haunt us, that the simple melody in children's games hum and burn in our temples as we clutch the pension-staff and stumble our way towards the grave. There is a reason that I walk penniless and proud down dark roads with only my guitar as companion, as every true Bard of Gate City must."

"What does …"

"Quiet now," the bard raised two fingers to his lips. "Listen and remember. It binds as it breaks; it slips up the tallest castle walls and shivers its way into the darkest of hearts. It burns as bright as the sun, warm as an oven while I stand on the stage. I sing and every eye is mine and every heart is mine and every secret unfolds and my music drinks tears and shines and shines and shines. One song — the right song — one song for every heart. Even if they've never heard it, even if the song hasn't been written yet, there it is, quarter notes and red blood on the parchment. And when the wind is at my back, I can see it. I can hear it."

The bard's eyes shut tight.

"And if I can sing your song, I can break your heart."

Rime interrupted sourly, "Ridiculous."

Geranium smiled. "I broke his heart, that's 'how'. And I was trying to keep him from hurting anyone else, like your pretty sheep-head guardian. Waters killed Darla and Funnicello. I was *protecting* all of us."

The bard had leaned forward with the vehemence of his last statement. He realized it and straightened his spine, face returning to its casual glamor. Rime took note. *I think he is telling the truth.*

"Oh, well that's…" Neriah let her words trail off.

"I was going to assist, but the spirits come in their own time," Coracle said philosophically, patting the large shell at her side.

"Thank you for the intent." Father Andrew shook his head. "Though surely there was another way."

Geranium looked slightly uncertain. "Yeah, I did kind of overreact I guess. I could have just put him to sleep or something."

"Overreact? Cold-blooded execution is a slight misstep in judgement?" Lord Bellwether covered his face with his hands for a moment, then focused his gaze on the bard. "But if it brought the murderer in our midst to heel, then I suppose we are in your debt."

"Oh, you're very welcome." The bard sketched a bow.

Sand still stood, his face granite.

"Okay, stop." Rime crossed in front of the bard. "If anyone starts applauding this fool I will become physically ill. It is possible that Waters was the murderer, but there are several details that contradict that theory."

Geranium spoke to the floor, frozen in his bow. "Oh,

great."

Rime ignored him and presented her argument. *It would be so much more convenient if I could just show them my chalkboard.*

"The most important detail is this. The dwarf bled copiously from his wounds. The trader has a small amount of blood on him, but it all comes from his self-inflicted face wound. Even if we posit that an older man such as Master Waters could overpower and disembowel a much stronger, battle-tested opponent -- in an extremely small window of time — all while escaping and completely avoiding detection. Even if we accept all of that, are we supposed to believe that he managed to avoid getting any of the dwarf's blood on him, or that he took the time in the past half hour to clean himself and change clothes?"

"We do have showers in every room," Neriah suggested.

"That. That is beside the point. My next point," the mage continued, "is that my family has worked with Master Waters for many years, as I've gathered has yours. He has never shown the slightest sign of mental illness in all that time. Are we supposed to believe that he suddenly and conveniently went insane? We have no evidence that he killed the butler or the actress, and now we have no way to interrogate him and gather more evidence because you played your banjo and made his heart explode."

"LADY MOON-DEATH IS NOT A BANJO," Geranium howled in mortal offense.

"Whatever," Rime said with satisfaction. "My point still stands that you are a stronger suspect than Waters."

"You're a stronger suspect. You're like the strongest of suspects," the bard insisted. "And could you please let me have my Lady back?"

As a precaution, Rime had insisted that the black guitar be left in the lobby behind them. It had floated its way to the door and now hovered outside, giving off the occasional arpeggio of disgust.

"Please, please. My friends." Father Andrew stood up and laid a hand on the bard's shoulder to calm him. He attempted to do the same to the mage, but her cannon-fire gaze kept his hand floating awkwardly in the air between them. "We must remain calm, keep our better selves close at hand. The dark works we have seen--and done tonight -- all have their cost. There is reason to suspect Master Waters; there is reason to suspect Master Geranium. But there is reason to suspect us all."

"To the point," Trowel applauded, rocking slightly in her seat. "Until the mystery is unraveled we must give each guest their own measure of suspicion, reasonable doubt, and a modicum of courtesy."

"Yes, we will all be civil to the killer until he is unmasked and apologetic to the victims when they lay bleeding on the floor," Sand said as he shook his head with disgust.

"Or apologize to us all when we find the true killer, who could be none of us." The bald priest smiled at the actor. "I know you are in pain, sir. But please remember, the killer could be none of us, still hidden and scheming somewhere in the manor."

Rime opened her mouth to interject, then shut it as her mind bustled with chalk lines. So far none of the evidence was conclusive for any of the other guests. *A final suspect, a secret guest? Someone that was here before we were, waiting to strike?*

The mage addressed Lord Bellwether. "Would that even be possible? The rest of you have been here for days. Could someone have infiltrated the manor and remained hidden for more than a day?"

The lord's face went still as he considered, his thick mustache barely moving. He looked to his daughter whose face mirrored his own.

"Before this night's events, I would have said it was impossible. But we have already witnessed such strange sights of woe and wonder, such casual slaughter -- how can I be sure? Between the arrival of each guest, the hustle and bustle of our entertainment, Scholar Trowel's fascinating discussions and presentations..." Bellwether trailed off for a moment, and Neriah reached over to take her father's hand.

Trowel's presentation! The box, can't forget. How does it fit into all of this? Rime's mind was covered with chalk dust, and the board itself nearly wrapped completely around the library.

"I can't be sure. And until we are sure, we must consider the possibility. But of this I am sure. There has been entirely too much activity here on the main floor and in the guest rooms," the tired lord continued. "There is no way for a secret guest to have remained hidden, unless they had an accomplice."

"We checked all of the guest rooms most thoroughly," Coracle assured the others. "No big chests or pots, nowhere for someone to easily hide."

Rime shot a quick look over at Jonas. He nodded his agreement, though with a slight uncertain tilt to his head. The mage mirrored the tilt with her head to show she understood. *Pretty sure, but not completely.*

"I see. As I assumed," Lord Bellwether sighed, an old pain settling on his face. "Then for someone to remain hidden, they would need to have made their way to a place in the manor that no one frequents regularly. Or ever."

"Oh, Father." Neriah's voice was stricken. "Mother's Solar."

"Yes. It has remained closed since the day of her death nearly ten years ago. Funnicello would enter once a month to keep it tidy, but no one else goes in. It would be the one place in the manor our supposed secret guest could be hiding. Hiding in a room full of shadows and memories," Lord Bellwether sighed.

"In the tower," Rime said. *The only place left.*

"Well, this is fucking ominous." Geranium pointed towards the door. "Can I get my guitar now, please?

12

Jonas tried his best to concurrently appear: handsome, strong, skilled with his sword, courteous, solicitous, and funny. The proximity of the princess behind him hung like a magnifying glass over him, and her occasional gaze was like the sun.

The squire stood tugging his high collar, in front of the ornate doors that lead from the second floor landing to the Lord's Tower. Behind him, Rime and Neriah walked side by side with Father Andrew close behind. Jonas turned with what he hoped was a properly courtly flourish, his hand outstretched. Rime adroitly batted it out of her way and gripped the large handles of the door in her thin hands. The princess didn't even notice, her face tight with determination.

She's been through a lot this evening. He reminded himself. *Lots of dead bodies tonight.*

A more introspective soul might have found that thought a little ghoulish or distressing, or a sign of a certain numbness to blood and carnage. In Jonas it simply skated across his square-shaped psyche and flopped off the edge.

Neriah had insisted on leading them to her mother's Solar. "It causes my father great pain to think of my mother. I was very young when she passed, but to him it could have been yesterday. I will take you." She had stood up, resolute in her cucumber nightgown.

"But, my dear one, there is a chance of danger, and it is my place…" her father had protested.

Neriah shook her head, errant blonde-strawberry curls shaking free from the clean linen head scarf she wore. "All of this talk of a 'hidden guest' aside, I doubt there is much chance of danger, Father. We are checking just to be absolutely certain. And I am sure I will be safe in the company of Rime. She is a wizard after all. And her guardian, Josh."

How can I like being called the wrong name so much? The squire wondered.

Her father's concerns were further mollified when Father Andrew offered to accompany the three younger guests. Trowel had busied herself with preparing a fresh pot of strong tea from the side table, still heaped with the necessities of light refreshment and entertainment by the solicitous — and now dead — butler. Her left hand shook on the sugar jar, and her pointed silence about the issue made her position clear. The old wood-elf had survived sufficient terror and had no interest in pursuing more in the upper chambers of the manor.

The drunken actors continued to snore, oblivious to the woozy lady in red that shared their couch. A few hours before Lady Karis would have crawled out of her skin to be in such close proximity to the lower caste, but the two grand equalizers of Drink and Sleep kept her close and democratically aligned for the moment. Sand stood watch over the incapacitated trio, his expressive face stern and watchful.

Coracle excused herself to a far corner of the Parlor and seemed to be performing a cleansing ritual that involved a lot of chanting, a gravy boat, and some cherries from the side table. The cherries may have had no religious or shamanic significance as she paused her chanting regularly to pop a few in her mouth.

Rime loudly refused to allow the bard to accompany them at the exact moment that Geranium refused to leave the Parlor. The coffee-skinned bard and the furious mage had locked gazes for what had seemed a small century.

"Just don't let him play his stupid instrument," Rime had ordered Lord Bellwether finally, who raised his hands in assent.

The bard's sulking was only eclipsed by the outraged caterwaul of Lady Moon-Death, still hovering in the parlor.

So four of the manor's guests stood in front of the door of the Tower. Jonas desperately tried to catch Neriah's eye while furiously constructing something suitably pithy and comforting to say.

"Let's go," Rime said and pushed open the heavy door, revealing friendly orange light and a well-appointed set of stone stairs lushly carpeted with a muted blue shag.

Neriah followed close on the mage's heels, leaving the squire in the lurch. Jonas' gaze was rescued by the kind eyes of Father Andrew. The priest patted him on the shoulder.

"I'm sorry that your dwarf-butler died?" Jonas said.

Andrew raised a knuckle to his lips. "See, it's probably for the best that only I heard that. Why not cut it down and start with 'I'm sorry'? And maybe then follow up with, 'Actually my name is Jonas.'

The squire grinned. The priest was a wise man.

Catching up with Rime and Neriah, Jonas discovered that the staircase terminated after only a half-turn into a large room that spread the entire diameter of the tower. It was less opulent than the rest of the manor, with simple chairs and un-adorned tables centralized around a brass fireplace. The flue ran up one wall then disappeared through a cunning grate. It was a sitting room, friendly and commonplace. Neriah turned a dial on the wall, and the room grew brighter. Illumination came from the walls, burn-light glass just as the rest of the manor. A metal staircase was on the far side of the room and spiralled up through the ceiling to the next level.

"You spend a lot of time in this room usually?" Rime appraised the room with quick but focused glances.

"Yes, my father and I take most of our meals here when we have no guests. Funni…" the lady ran a hand across her brow for a moment then continued. "Funnicello would bring our meals."

"But not as much since the guests arrived?"

"That's right. Do you really think there is some sort of crazed murderer hiding upstairs?"

"It is possible," the mage sniffed. "But I think you are right. This is about eliminating a possibility."

"How many levels are there?" Father Andrew settled into a nearby chair with a satisfied groan. "Sorry, old knees."

"Just two more above us. My father's bedchamber and mine are the next one up, then at the top my mother's Solar and the, uh, bathroom." Neriah said.

Rime made a careful survey of the sitting room, walking a slow circuit, lifting up the occasional cushion for closer inspection. Jonas hovered near the table where the priest sat, his eyes orbiting the space around Neriah.

"Is is strange that I can almost imagine the murderer?" Neriah asked the priest suddenly. "It makes my skin crawl; it's like listening to a scary story. I can see him, in a black cloak with a white face, coiled around a corner like a snake."

"Not at all strange." The priest carefully flexed his knees. "The human mind is an amazing organ, and like much of nature it abhors a vacuum. We need there to be reason. We need there to be explanations for things. And now, in this dark and horrible night — a secret guest — a hidden murderer is appealing. It explains all of the death and woe with the added benefit of freeing us from facing the possibility that one of the other guests did these awful deeds."

Jonas tried to imagine the killer but failed miserably. The best he could conjure was a vague outline of a cloaked figure, smiling and laughing,and then he realized he was just remembering a puppet show he'd seen as a child.

"I guess so," Neriah forced herself to smile. "It's just a fantasy, a weird notion in my head. I guess."

The bald priest tenderly massaged his knee and laughed. "I always tell my youngest that ideas are the worst monsters. They appear out of nowhere. They change and grow without any aid. They can change the course of your life, end a love affair, build an empire, leave you shaking and afraid in the dark of night -- but worst of all you cannot touch them. You cannot pull them to you when needed, or push them away when they weary you. So, I tell him…"

"Are you two done?" Rime approached the table, her face impatient.

"We were just waiting for you to complete your investigation, detective." Father Andrew released his knee with a deadpan expression.

"Thank you for telling me that, Father Andrew. I'm sure your children take great comfort from your words." Neriah stood and pushed her chair back under the table with automatic care.

"Well, Jacob kept having these terrible nightmares about a carrot with teeth that hid in the dark corner near his bed, and he wanted a hug more than my wise counsel…"

"Okay. Going upstairs now." The mage turned on her heel and swooped towards the metal staircase, her white half-cloak flapping.

Jonas gave the priest a hand out of his chair and offered a rough apology. "She, well, she's like that sometimes. Well most of the times but worse when she's thinking really hard about something."

"No harm, no harm at all. Let us make haste to catch our intrepid detective," Father Andrew pointed towards the spiral staircase where Rime was already several steps up.

Neriah called up after the mage and started up the stairs as well. "You agreed with me that there *probably* isn't a secret guest, but who do you think is the murderer?"

"Too early to say," Rime replied.

"Early? How many more dead people do you need?" the squire muttered.

The four of them arrived at the next level. The staircase continued up higher into the tower, but Rime was already moving away on the landing, so the other three followed. This level was neatly split into two by a wide hallway leading from the staircase to the opposite wall of the tower. A nice end table held a spray of dark flowers. Windows overlooked the manor grounds, and two doors stood on either side

"These are our rooms, my father's and mine. My mother's solar is on the top level. Do we really need to…"

Rime cut her off, hand already on the doorknob. "Yes, we need to. We are here to investigate the possibility of someone hidden in the manor. We need to make absolutely sure before returning to the Lobby. Investigation is about eliminating possibilities."

"I see. Well this is my father's room, and the other one is mine." Neriah pushed open the door for Rime and stepped inside as if to protect it from an interloper.

"Jonas. Check out her room while we check out the Lord's." Rime instructed and followed the princess, letting the door close behind them.

The squire's eyes locked on the door that lead to Neriah's room. It was a curious dark shade of blue, but seemed to curl into sea-green at the edges. *That is her room. If I walk through that door, I will be in her room.*

There are times in life where someone comes to the edge of the world.

Jonas had never been in a girl's bedroom. His brain clattered, pushing the phantom puppet he had imagined earlier aside, and tried to come up with any sort of prediction as to what he would find inside. The best it could come up with was a vast woodland glade made of pink cotton. And bunnies. There were probably bunnies.

Father Andrew came up alongside and solemnly waved a hand in front of the squire's face. Getting no response, the priest patted Jonas on the arm.

"Do you want me to check it out? I have a son and two daughters -- nothing I haven't seen before."

Did the bunnies sleep underneath her bed, or on a long pillow specifically designed for rabbit comfort? These were questions, and they required his full concentration.

"Okay, son. I'll just check it out then," Father Andrew grinned and pushed open the door, chuckling.

The squire's mind quailed and executed a brisk parade-ground about-face before he could catch a glimpse through the door. He fussed with his buttons for a few minutes and tried to ignore the fact that he was being ridiculous.

The door to Lord Bellwether's room opened first, and Neriah appeared with the mage behind. She was laughing at something that Rime must have just said, and Jonas could not help but notice the triumphant tilt to his companion's head. He also noticed the mage had something held tight in one fist and that she stuffed it down the neck of her dress without the princess noticing. He frowned, but Rime caught his eye with bellicose certainty and talked over any objections he might have been devising.

"Nothing in there, except for a massive bed and various lordly items," the mage said. "I assume that there were no devils under the bed in Neriah's room."

"Uh, well." *I couldn't go in because of bunnies.* "You see…"

"Devil free," Father Andrew assured her, exiting the princess' room.

Was it all pink cotton? Jonas did not ask.

The priest, lady, and mage moved away towards the spiral staircase, and began to clatter up the steps. Jonas lingered and glanced at the mysterious sea-storm blue door on the edge of his world. Then he moved to follow.

13

The Solar of Heart-Break, of lions roaring their last as the flood came. Rime stood in the center of it, her hands still -- both inside her head and without. She was a creature of numbers, of reason and radiation. But something about this place — this room — made her feel sad. She wanted to make notes on the chalkboard in her mind, she wanted to pursue this mystery to its conclusion, but the Solar was a masterwork of grief. It kept her in pause, trapped underneath empty air.

"I don't come in here often, and father never does," Neriah said from the door.

The room was mostly empty; tall glass windows stood as empty sentinels of night along the wall. Rime could see through a haze of rain the dim blur of the white and red moons. A simple couch was in the middle of the room, and a wooden chest was placed nearby. The chest was not particularly ornate but well made. It was easy to guess its contents: yarn, thread, scraps of fabric, hoops for embroidery. *Mom stuff.*

"She died when I was small. I don't have many memories of her."

"My mother did as well,"The mage said with carefully redacted emotion and continued to survey the room. What she had come here to see was in plain view directly above the door.

A piano was pushed into one corner, right against the windows. It was made of deep red wood, kept bright with care and plenty of polishing. A silver candelabra sat on the top, with white candles that had never been lit. During the day it would be a sunny place to play, with a spectacular view of the surrounding forest. Now, the thin burn-light only reflected Rime and Neriah against the dark glass.

Neriah came into the room at last and placed a fond hand on the piano. "I do remember she used to play for me. After she died I used to sneak in here to plunk away at the keys. It made me feel close to her."

The older girl laid a finger on one of the keys, and a deep tone filled the room. Neriah grimaced. "It's the only time I've ever seen my father truly furious. He grabbed me by the arm and dragged me down to my room. I still have a scar on my knee from the staircase."

Rime had no idea how to respond to that. She had made a simple decision to never think of her family again, some time on the road between Carroway and Talbot. It had been an easy choice, and one that she had found completely satisfactory over the past few weeks.

"I'm simply glad that fool Geranium didn't know this was here," the mage changed the subject.

Neriah laughed, warm and uncomplicated with a little

snort at the end. "That is the truth! He'd be up here like a shot, playing dirty songs with one hand and splashing wine with the other."

She has a good laugh. Rime was surprised to discover her own face bending into a smile.

"He is such a pretty man, don't you think? If I told my father even half of the propositions he's made since arriving, ha!" Neriah plunked a high note. "Come on, be honest. Even though he is insufferable, there is something appealing about him."

"I…" Rime's words ground to a halt. She didn't know how to respond to that either.

The mage took a quick look at her mental blackboard. With horror she watched as it slowly flipped over to where she had jotted down a quick note about Jonas some hours earlier. The entire expanse of the blackboard had somehow been filled with an immaculately detailed depiction of Geranium with his shirt off.

"Rime. Rime, are you, are you blushing?" Neriah asked with amazement.

Rime did not answer at first, as she was feverishly erasing the drawing.

"Do you have a crush on Geranium the Eruption?" the older girl demanded with glee.

Rime calmly turned the blackboard back to the proper side, filled with notes and information about the investigation. She had a murderer to find and she was closing in. Everything else was ridiculous and could be safely ignored.

"No," the mage replied and turned to leave the room.

"Uh-huh," Neriah chuckled again and followed.

Rime took one last long look at the final clue she needed: the painting above the door. A painting, done while in the bloom of youth, of Lady Bellwether.

"That is the most amazing bathroom I have ever seen." Jonas shook his head as if waking up from a dream as he and the priest came back out into the common area of the tower's top level.

Father Andrew laid his hands reverently on the three swords embroidered on his chest, then wiped away a tear. "Thank the Nameless that he has allowed me a glimpse at perfection, at the facilities that man can aspire to, the apex of toilets."

"I don't even know how that sink worked!" the squire added. "There were like eight levels of glass, then blue liquid, then that bird, then — was it a basket of muffins in between all those gears?"

"I snuck a couple; they're raisin," the priest confirmed with a slight guilty expression. "And they are delicious."

The final level of the Tower was split in half, similar to the sleeping quarters below. One half was given over to the late Lady Bellwether's Solar, which Rime and Neriah had disappeared in immediately. The other half was the Lord's Bath, which Father Andrew and Jonas had just spent the last several minutes ogling. Jonas had also noticed a trapdoor at one end of the hall's ceiling. The princess had assured him that it was secure and lead to the roof of the tower. The squire had given it a solid pull just to be safe, thick iron chains held it fast with a crude square lock. Apparently, Lord Bellwether had spent his money on the amazingly delicate and powerful magical lock for the front door, but for the roof trap door he had skimped a bit.

The door to the Solar opened, and Rime and Neriah appeared. "So, no hidden guest in the Bath?"

"No, none skulking around the Solar?" the priest replied to the mage's question.

"Not in the least. I believe we can safely discount that theory." Rime motioned towards the stairs. "Let's get back to the lobby and let everyone know."

The princess moved forward and took Father Andrew's arm. "Come, I know your knees are still hurting you. Let me help you down the stairs."

The bald man laughed. "Oh, a lesson on pride, eh? Very well, but I insist that you let me ask you some questions about the facilities in your bathroom."

Neriah laughed her perfect, broken laugh and the two began clattering down the metal stairs. Rime snagged Jonas' sleeve and kept him from moving. She leaned forward until she heard the footfalls move down closer to the next level.

"I've solved it," she whispered. "I know who the killer is. Well, to be technical, I know who *a* killer is."

Jonas' jaw dropped. "You do? Who is it?"

Rime took another quick listen as the footfalls passed down below the bedchambers, then turned back to the squire. "Lord Bellwether. Lord Bellwether killed the actress."

"How do you know? And why would he ask us to investigate a murder if he was the murderer?"

"It's perfectly clear, as soon as I saw the picture of his wife, I…"

For the second time that night, Neriah's voice filled the air. A scream of despair and terror.

Jonas and Rime almost slammed into each other as they both scrambled for the metal stairs and pounded down. The bedchamber level was empty, so they kept going. The princess' sobs clawed at the air and scoured the squire's heart.

The two companions swung around the bend onto the last level of the tower, the sitting room. Neriah was on her knees, crumpled and swaying, while Father Andrew did his best to comfort her.

Lying face down in the center of the floor was her father. A jeweled dagger was buried in his back, and his blood seemed almost purple against the dark tunic.

WHO WAS ELRIC BELLWETHER?

Elric was a gardener.

Outside the grand manor of his family, hidden by the forest's overreaching arms, the rain and the night, was his chiefest joy. A garden of simple stone and proud cedar. Each wooden rail was cut by his own hands, and each flagstone stamped into the earth by his own foot. Jonas and Rime would never see it, but it was there all the same.

As a child, he had crowed with excitement to see green bean shoots bursting from the dark earth. He had clapped with earnest delight when the first round bump appeared on the brushy arms of the peanut shrub. His father, gray bearded even in his memory, had been more than a little put out by his son's fascination with rolling in the dirt. But at his wife's insistence had allowed it and even put on a pleased expression when Elric served his own malformed and tiny potatoes on the immaculate marble table in the manor. His father was a titan of business; his family's money had wandered around the lands of Aufero since 'a week or two after the Precursors arrived' as was the common joke. Elric was much older before he understood the unlikelihood of that statement. But even as a child, even as he dug tidy holes for his tulips, he well understood the vast importance and influence that his family's gold had in the Far Away World.

He understood and, like a child, forgot it often. He had the finest tutors and the best training in the proper duties and decorum of a child of the Heart-Broken Lion. Elric was dutiful and quick. Elric was gifted and pleased his mentors. But no power could keep him from his garden when the day's lessons were through. He brought books on herbs and the lore of the leaf-loving Yad-Elves; he sent for cuttings from the far-flung corners of the globe. Lilies from Marwood, birch from Seroholm, precious golden roses from the court of Caleron. His family's wealth could have bought him any treasure, but all that Elric desired was good, black earth and a new bulb, or curious vines, or tiny seeds. Flowers and plants, exotic and common, shrub and fern: all found a careful place in his garden.

Then, when he was seventeen, he sat at his father's bedside.

His father took his hand, a rarity. His beard was white, and his breath was heavy and thick with the scent of Jembox Mushrooms.

"Are you ready, boy?"

"I am, Father. You don't need to worry." Elric made himself smile. "I'll grow a mustache."

His father laughed with pain, his eyes grave. "All we are is

175

a name. Bellwether, old and proud. The name is in your hands now."

"I know, Father. I know."

And Elric did know. He held his father's hands until they went cold, and he folded them carefully across his still chest. He walked into the next room where the men of business waited. He signed the papers and looked each one in the eye. As they left they called him Lord Bellwether without irony or concern in their voices.

Lord Bellwether had a new garden.

Vines of trade, bulbs of industry, the simple growth of small coin to larger. He found that his new garden could be tended in many of the same ways as his old. New saplings needed extra care, weeds came back even with the most diligent removal, and sometimes plants die and nothing the gardener can do will change it. With care and study, with planning and effort, any garden can flourish. Lord Bellwether spent long hours in his office building fences of paper and laying flagstones of ink.

At the beginning, he still made time for his first garden. He slipped out in the evening with a spade and his watering can or at the dawn with his clippers and a new packet of dandelion seeds. But then the hours grew longer, and he spent much of his time in travel tending the new bulbs of his family's wealth and pruning the dead wood from the old growth trees of their investments. He spent one night in ten at his home, and with a sickened gaze he saw that weeds and rot were creeping into the plants. He knew he should instruct a workman to till it into the earth, but some part of him stood fast. "When there is time I will put it all right again, right after this trip to Gate City," he told himself, and then, "Right after the meeting in Quorum

176

with the Seafoam Trading Company." He told himself many things. As do we all when our heart needs lies to keep beating.

A week of seasons, a month of years. The Bellwether fortune grew under his dutiful and measured watch, and he took some comfort in the satisfaction his father would have felt.

And then, when he was thirty-five, he sat at a table with her. She knew about his money, she knew about his name. She laughed without derision at his mustache. She sipped wine and her eyes were the golden rose of Caleron — her hands on the glass stem were the lilies of Marwood. She was birch and peanuts and green beans, all at once.

Without a thought, he told her about his garden -- about his real one. She sat down her wine glass and stood up. His heart stopped until she said with a peapod smile, "Well, aren't you going to show it to me?"

They had to climb over the wooden gate; it had grown thick with ivy and creeper. He found an old trowel gone to rust and a broken pair of shears. The plants had gone rioting through the years, drunken growth demanding place. Heedless roots and petals and leaves and thorns grew where they would. He found his hand in hers, and her eyes and her lips and the three moons and the green festival of life once more -- all in his hands.

They wed. Two words. A new life, a new shoot bursting from the good, black earth.

He made time; she helped him find it. Under rocks, and in closets, and in the pockets of old coats. They found a fortnight hiding in an old cupboard and a long afternoon mixed in with some loose change. There was so much time to be found, everywhere really.

They had a daughter, and they named her Neriah. She played in the garden and applauded the petunias and squished the earth between her fat pink fingers. Lord Bellwether smiled and bent back to his weeding. His lady plucked blackberries and tossed them through the air into her mouth. She pressed the cluster of wine-dark purple against his lips and kissed him to follow.

And then he was forty-five and sat at his wife's bedside.

And then he was forty-five and sat at his wife's grave.

And then he was forty-five and closed the gates of his first garden for the last time.

And then he was fifty and fifty-five and sixty.

And then he was dead.

14

Neriah's face was buried in the priest's chest. Her muffled sobs only now starting to quiet. Father Andrew smoothed her hair, his face stricken. Jonas stood near the stone stairs that led back into the manor — his hand tight on wooden sword hilt.

Rime sat at the table and was very still. She straddled a chair with her hands steepled on the chairback, eyes locked on the dead man in front of her.

The mage's mind surged with activity, looking at each angle of the mystery on the blackboard. A quick survey of the room had shown precious little evidence in the hurried moments after discovering Lord Bellwether's body. A bit of fabric and some spattered blood suggested that he had been attacked coming up the stairs and had managed to crawl the few feet to the center of the room where he expired. The gold etched dagger was finely crafted, with a sapphire in the pommel. It was distinctive, but Rime was absolutely certain that she had seen nothing like it since arriving in the manor.

No cryptic symbols drawn on the floor in blood. No mysterious scent from the killer's perfume. No confession scrawled on foolscap and crammed into his pocket. The dagger protruded from just below his left shoulder blade. *The killer is left-handed. Maybe.*

Rime rubbed her eyes. They felt heavy and too round like thick glass marbles. It had to be two or three hours after midnight, and she was displeased with her current position in the book. Of all the mystery novels that lay piled in her mind, more than a few had some version of her current predicament. She had followed the clues, built a compelling case, and named a suspect only to find that suspect dead a few page-turns later and a pack of new questions running off into the darkness. Inspector Kyng had always filled the air with some off-color epithets at this point in his investigation and then stormed into his Thinking Closet to eat jam and toast until he worked his way free of the new morass of possibility. The mage considered asking for some marmalade and bread.

Neriah was still crying. *She loved her father.*

The mage turned her gaze inward and stared at the blackboard in her mind. Every inch was filled with chalk lines. Details and conversations and bits of observation, every step of her investigation. Rime's memory omitted nothing but even she had to admit that perfect recall was often a burden when trying to detect patterns in the data. Did her conversation with Geranium have anything to do with the lion figure etched on Jonas' buttons? Were Trowel's box and the Precursor recording more or less important than the color of the curtain rod that Waters had brandished as a crude club? Coracle's chants? Toby and Vincent's relationship? The tiny gold lock that held them all captured in the manor? The symbol on the tile and Funnicello's blood? It was like looking at a thousand candles, each the same color and brightness. Where should she focus her attention?

Rime groaned. She couldn't unravel it all: too many threads. She needed a finite perspective. The same need had driven her to barge into the squire's bedroom earlier in the evening.

"He killed the actress," the mage began. "I'm sure of it."

Father Andrew's neck snapped up and Neriah's tears stuttered into startled silence. Jonas' free hand flew up into his curly hair and gave a brisk tug before sliding down to cover his face in embarrassment.

"I've suspected it ever since Sand told me of her nocturnal visits — a lover inside the manor. He has been a widower for several years, a likely candidate. Of course, nearly every other guest of the manor was possible, so I began to look for evidence that suggested the most promising suspect."

Neriah's head had raised during the mage's words, her face still towards the priest's chest. She did not move as Rime continued.

"And then I saw the picture of the late Lady Bellwether in the solar hanging above the door. Blonde hair, sharp chin, high cheekbones. The actress, Darla, was a wood-elf. Sharp chin, high cheekbones. And with the blonde wig covering her ears, she was an almost perfect match." Rime mused as her fingers tugged on her stripe of white hair.

Neriah stood up and brushed the tears from her eyes. She pushed herself away from the priest gently and turned to face the mage.

"Of course the wig was a slightly different shade of blonde, and the actress' nose was noticeably longer, but in the dark…" Rime broke off as Neriah's fist slammed into her face.

The mage squawked with surprise and half-fell back over the table. Neriah swarmed up past the chair and landed another brisk punch on Rime's left ear. The older girl's face was a stone mask of righteous fury. The pain from her face and her burning ear put down roots through the mage's body and began to spread into anger. Anger coiled its hand around her magic, and it thrummed in her blood. *I don't have time for this stupid girl. It would be easy to end this. A little drop of power, of fire and lightning. A storm.*

Father Andrew and Jonas hurried over and pulled the two young ladies apart. The priest dragged Neriah to the far end of the room, and the squire bodily hauled Rime across the table and held her squirming a foot off the ground.

"Calm down! You've got to calm down." Jonas's voice rasped in her ear.

"Put me down! Put me down!" Rime demanded. *Just a tiny, tiny drop.* The Magic Wild burbled and flowed; dragons screamed in the dark part of her mind. *A storm*, they called. *A storm.*

The mage's eyes blazed with light, and energy crackled around her left hand. She fought against the squire's strength and began to take aim.

"Rime! Rime, you've got to — oh hell." And then Jonas bit her ear with desperate energy.

"OW." She wriggled furiously in his grip until she could face him. "What the fuck was that?"

"You are losing it! You weren't listening. It was the only thing I could think of," the squire protested.

"I wasn't losing anything, I knew exactly…" *What was I doing? I was about to. I was about to kill Neriah.*

The thought was like a tomb of ice. Her anger was gone. Jonas saw the change in her eyes. The blaze faded, and the gathering lightning dissipated from her hand. The squire sat her down, and straightened her white half-cloak with a practised motion. *Something that squires learn.* She thought absently. *For making their knights look pretty on the battlefield.*

Rime stepped forward, crossing the space between her and the new Lady Bellwether.

Father Andrew was finishing some words of consolation or advice, but Neriah cut him off and turned to greet the mage. Her face was impassive and composed. The armor of etiquette shone like poisoned glass. Rime opened her mouth to speak.

"You are cruel. And empty," Neriah said. "And what you've said about my father *may* be true. But he deserved far greater respect than such a cold recitation over his grave."

Rime grimly reached down the front of her dress. She pulled out what she had found in Lord Bellwether's bedchamber. Opening her hand, she presented a strand of golden hair.

"There is no one else in the manor with this color hair. Yours is not even close. The actor's, Toby's, is darker yellow and is cut far shorter. If you hold it up to the light you can see regular striations in the grain. This hair is synthetic. It comes from a wig." Rime let it end there.

Lady Bellwether raised her chin. "That suggests a link between my father and Darla, and it suggests that they may have kept company. But it does not prove that my father killed her. Nor does it explain why we stand here now over his corpse."

The young noble's voice wavered on the last word, but she kept her gaze firmly on Rime.

The mage sighed. "Which is exactly the point I was working towards when you punched me. If we accept as given for the moment that Darla was your father's lover, it does little to explain the other deaths. The pieces don't fit. I can't relate Funnicello's evisceration or Waters' madness at all."

"Even Darla's death doesn't quite fit your scenario, I'm afraid." Father Andrew looked thoughtful. "If Lord Bellwether wanted to hide an affair or an indiscretion, why would he poison her and make her death so public?"

"Maybe Funnicello found out about it? And was going to report it to the garrison?" Jonas offered. "And Master Waters was *also* in love with Darla, and he went insane from grief. OR he was in love with Funnicello!"

Rime shot the squire an arid look. "Covering your bases." She stated with only a teaspoon of rancor.

"Hey, it could happen. People find a way to make things work," the squire replied stoutly.

"It doesn't make sense. Bellwether didn't kill Funnicello. He was standing in *your room* when the dwarf died." Rime crossed her arms.

"And it doesn't explain why my father is dead." Neriah's voice was steel.

"Unless…" the mage's eyes widened and she dashed to the lord's body.

"What are you doing?" the grieving noble demanded.

Rime held up the dead man's hand. She pushed back his sleeve to reveal the naked wrist.

"Whoever killed him took his key to the front door," the priest gasped.

"Just like Funnicello." Neriah shook her injured hand. "Is that what this is all about? Escaping from the manor?"

Rime drew a line on her blackboard and connected two circles. "No. The killer did not attempt to escape, even though they had the butler's keyring. Their purpose is not to escape."

"Then why…Nameless." Father Andrew bent his head in a quick prayer as realization hit him.

"What?" Jonas asked flatly.

"The killer does not want to escape. They want to make sure that no one else does." Rime gave her swath of white hair a vicious tug.

15

The squire took the first careful step down the stone stairs. For the first time all evening, he praised his good fortune to be wearing his travel-worn boots. The thin leather was nearly silent on the stone if he moved carefully. He held his good steel in front of him in a two-handed grip for maximum chopping power. It limited the quickness of his strokes, but it made him feel a good deal more secure as they descended back down from the Lord's Tower.

He had insisted on taking the lead. Rime was best from a distance if it came to battle, and he wanted the priest and the princess as far from the clutches of the shadowy killer that lurked the halls. Jonas could hardly imagine any of the other guests filling that rude outline in his head, but he planned to have a solid grip on his sword when they next encountered anything that moved. The staircase was as well lit as when they had ascended a bare hour ago, but the pools of shadow between seemed all the darker. Did the tireless burn-light glass seem to flicker and dim, or was it just his imagination?

Neriah kept herself rigid and held her head high. The grief hung around her brow like an ebony crown, but she was determined to wear it with all the severity and dignity of her family's name. The squire's heart went out to her, but even he knew this was no time for his faltering pleasantries or quarter-hearted glances.

"Pick up the pace. We need to get downstairs. One of the other guests is the killer, and we need to approach them quickly. It is a small chance, but they may still be flustered or harried by the lord's murder." Rime's voice pressed the back of his neck like an insistent ferret.

One of the other guests. Jonas moved no faster. "And if one of them is waiting on the other side of the door with cleavers and whips, I'd prefer they not hear us coming," he whispered.

The squire grinned. He couldn't turn and see his companion's expression, but the swift click of her teeth coming together was all he needed.

One of the other guests...is the killer. Step by careful step, quiet and sure with his good steel at the ready. *Who could it be? One of the actors? Drunk Lady Karis? Fat Book Lady Trowel? The sea-elf? The pink-haired bard with his guillotine grin?* The squire stopped, his shoulder against the door that led back into the manor. He listened, waiting for his heartbeat to slow. A question formed, and he whispered again. "Wait. How do we know it's not more than one of them? Or *all* of them?"

"We don't." Rime bit the words.

"Great," Jonas replied and pulled the door open a crack.

He peeked through. All appeared just as they left it: the well-lit white marble and brass accents of the grand double-staircase twined with cords of blue silk and the rows of guest rooms on the second floor landing. Jonas made a gesture for the others to wait. Father Andrew kept a protective arm around the grieving Lady Bellwether, and he thought for a split-second that her eye held a tiny amount of concern for him. The squire dismissed it with all his might; he could not afford the terrifying elation and distraction.

Jonas walked out onto the landing, careful and slow. No attack came, and he leaned over the balcony to get a better look down in the lobby. The white tile reflected the burn-light glass. No one could be seen. He held his breath and listened. At the edge of his perception were two sounds: the quiet strum of a guitar coming from the Parlor and indistinct muttering coming from the Library. He turned back towards the door to see Rime already stalking forward with impatience. Jonas sighed and pointed over the rail.

"I hear guitar from the Parlor and someone talking in the Library."

The mage thought a moment before responding. "Let's go to the Library first. It's only been an hour. The majority of the guests should still be where we left them in the Parlor."

Rime gestured, and Neriah and Father Andrew emerged and joined them as they went down the stairs.

"Josh, shouldn't you put away your sword now?" Neriah asked abruptly.

"Don't want to alert the killer." Rime nodded agreement.

"Oh, yeah." Jonas began to sheath his sword, then paused. "Wait a minute. The killer killed Lady Neriah's father, and they know we had to walk past where he was killed to come here, so won't they know that we know that they did that thing?"

"Just put it away," Rime sighed.

The crossguard clicked against the brass fittings of his scabbard and Jonas shook his head to dislodge the over-thorny thought it had tried to formulate.

"And it's Jonas. His name is Jonas," the mage added, stepping quickly to the Library door that stood slightly ajar.

The squire blushed in complete mortification. Neriah gave a stiff bow in automatic courtesy. "My apologies, Jonas. It has been a hectic evening."

"No, I'm sorry, my lady."

"Everyone's sorry!" Rime hissed. "Now come on."

Jonas had a brief second to process several emotions. Few of them were conducive to his ego, but he did feel a generous helping of gratitude towards Rime for straightening that little quandary out for him. The four guests stepped into the Library, and the muttering became audible as they moved through the door.

"...the foundations of the City are strong, and we have built them with due care. For even before the building of the City, there was a time, a moment. A time of beginnings. A time when each spirit was brought to the axis of creation and presented with the First Choice. Each spirit was allowed to choose. The Choice is the crux, of course," the wood-elf Trowel spoke to a room of empty tables and chairs as if addressing a packed hall of students.

The portly scholar's eyes were calm, her mind focused on the topic of her lecture. She had ripped her blouse open, leaving her right breast bare. It hung, a sagging globe against her abdomen.

"And what was the First Choice, I'm sure you are asking yourself," Trowel continued. "Well, this will be a dreadfully banal class if I fill all the gaps for you. Who has an idea?"

The priest shot Jonas a confused glance. Neriah cleared her throat, concern clear on her face. "Scholar Trowel, are you — are you alright? Is there…"

"The Choice was a simple binary," Rime interrupted, taking a seat at the front table. "Serve or Destroy? Each spirit was given form and might and a purpose by the tenets of Creation, but each was allowed this final determination."

The mage — with glacial calm — made eye contact with the other three guests and pointed insistently towards the seats. Jonas had no idea what was going on, but it seemed clear that Rime was handling it. He took a seat and was joined shortly thereafter by the others.

"Very good!" The half-naked scholar chortled. "Of course, this is all nonsense. The tablet was of dubious authenticity and even the translation had several grievous assumptions that reduced it to clever speculation at best. I'm surprised to find this class so well-read! However, it is still fascinating as an analogue to most other cultures' creation myths. Most others always reduce it to the more comfortable 'Good' and 'Evil' paradigm."

She's crazy? Just like Master Waters went nuts. Jonas leaned over his table to whisper to Rime, but she waved him back. He frowned and slid his chair back, freeing access to his sword. Trowel picked up a book from a nearby pile and began to leaf through it with focus. She gave a small exclamation of triumph and ripped out a page. Jonas saw Rime blench.

"Aufero in its cradle. A fascinating time of which we know precious little. My esteemed colleagues — Silverhammer and that gnome he works with — they love to inflame the academic press with their theories about the Precursors, and I will admit…" Trowel took a casual bite of the piece of paper she held, "…that since their technology has become such a dominant force in our current technological development it does bear a certain innate interest."

Rime stood up slowly, and the others followed suit. The mage turned and indicated for everyone to leave the room. Trowel cleared her throat, leaned an elbow on a nearby chair, and addressed her classroom of empty chairs with a conspiratorial tone.

"But in the grand tale of our planet, the Precursors are newcomers. A recent event, even though it was over 2500 years ago. The gnomes, the dwarves, the humans as well, all newcomers. Travellers from Beyond."

Rime opened her mouth then stopped, uncertain. Raw curiosity battled with expedience and she wavered for a moment. They were bare steps from the door.

"Just ask," Jonas whispered.

"Scholar Trowel," the mage called with relief. "Could you

elaborate on that? What do you mean that we are 'newcomers'?"

"But, of course," the half-nude scholar replied with triumph, responding as if the question had come from an empty chair a few feet in front of her. "Even though humanity is the dominant race in Aufero, they are not indigenous to this planet. Our world is a, a nexus, I suppose one could call it. The walls that separate this world from others are very thin. Very thin, indeed. Strange scraps of other places find their way here, wash up on the beach as it were. And sometimes, as was the case with the Precursors, a gate opens and entire civilizations come through. Do you know, I have a recording somewhere that describes their journey in part…"

An expression of vague unease crossed the portly wood-elf's face as her hands quested around her person and on the nearby tables. She continued to lecture, but her growing discomfort was clear.

"Where is that box? The recording? Somewhere...I'm sorry, class. There is a lovely bit of verse that describes the native races of this planet. The translation into the common tongue is weak, but— the box — where did I put it? 'Dragons, Elves, and Goblins in the beginning. All spun from the Balance. Elves for beauty and Goblins for strength and Dragons for will.' Where is that BOX? I'm so sorry, class. The verse is very long; allow me to skip to the end. 'Then the darkness and the storm crept in along the edges of the City. The Elves fell to pride, the Goblins to rage, the Dragons to despair. The City opened its gates lest they fall and brought new pieces to the game.' I can't find it. I can't find it."

Trowel was weeping. "I can't find it. Where is it? I can't find it!"

192

Rime seemed at a loss. Jonas felt the same. *How do you speak to a crazy person? How do you help them?*

"Scholar Trowel, can we help you?" Neriah's voice shook with her concern. "Can we help you look for it?"

"I can't find it. Where is it? I can't find it." The scholar stared at the empty chair, tears rolling down her round cheeks.

16

"What in the world was all that?" Father Andrew asked as he pushed the door of the Library shut behind them.

Rime tugged at her white hair in thought and did not respond. *Two of the guests fallen into some sort of psychotic episode. Waters and Trowel. Impossible for it to be a coincidence.*

"She seemed so lost," Neriah sighed. "What box was she talking about?"

"The box with the recording?" the priest hazarded. "She showed it during her presentations, and she showed it to Lady Rime and myself earlier this evening."

The box. Rime pictured it in her mind. The simple, elegant construction. The Precursor symbol on the lid. "She didn't have it with her. Her purse was gone, and it was nowhere in the Library. Someone took it from her."

194

The mage made some quick notes on her blackboard and crossed out several pieces of evidence that no longer applied. She moved quickly across the Lobby towards the door that lead to the Parlor. The others had to trot to catch up.

"You've got something, don't you Rime?" Jonas asked and she paused, with one hand on the door.

"Maybe this isn't about a jilted lover or family pride. It's about money. Everyone in the manor came here to bid on one item: a box of immense value. A box containing the final words of the Precursor civilization. Each guest stands to gain incalculable wealth and personal influence if they obtain it. The bidding was to conclude tomorrow. What if one of the guests knew they were not going to win? They knew that the consequences for coming back empty-handed were more than they could bear. They would do anything." Rime leaned her ear against the door to better hear the music being played inside.

"So they drive Trowel insane to steal the box, but how do the others factor?" Father Andrew pressed a weary hand against the three blue swords embroidered on his chest.

"I don't know," Rime hissed. "Neriah, did your father want to buy the box as well?"

The older girl replied, relief at this new line of inquiry overriding the stiff propriety that she had leaned on. "I believe so. Master Waters was the main broker for the auction, but he also oversees large purchases made by my father. I know they spent quite some time discussing the box."

"Okay. The suspect takes shape, the 'poor guest'," Rime whispered. "The guest who doesn't have the resources to win the auction. Your father and Waters were obstacles to buying the box. Maybe the actress was killed as a warning to Lord Bellwether or something to distract him from the auction. Maybe Funnicello discovered the killer in the Lobby sneaking into Trowel's room, perhaps to steal the box. We already suspect the use of poison on Darla; maybe the killer used some sort of toxin to drive Master Waters and Scholar Trowel into the fit of insanity that we've all witnessed."

"That's a lot of 'maybe', Rime," Jonas frowned.

The mage doled out a swift kick to the squire's shins. "I know."

The squire grimaced and held his tongue.

He's right. I can't even see the board anymore, there's so much chalk. All in all, this was a most dis-satisfying mystery. Most of her ink-and-paper heroes would already be hot on the trail of the killer, or have sent out invitations to the climactic tea. But she was lost in the weeds. All of her theories seemed reasonable when viewed alone, but together they shot off in a million directions. There was no unity, no grace to any of her possible solutions. Everything she learned made the night's events more complicated instead of illuminated. *I have to press on. At the very least, I'm losing potential suspects at a steady rate. If I wait long enough there may only be one possibility left: Rime Korvanus and the Case of the Oh Nevermind Everyone is Dead.*

The mage shook her head and focused on her three allies. "I'm guessing. I will admit it. But let us focus on what we do know. And let us move quickly before someone chances upon us whispering at the door. We were all together when Bellwether was killed, so that eliminates the four of us. Trowel could be faking insanity to throw us off, but I doubt her dramatic skill -- and her malaise — seems very similar to what affected Master Waters. So, let's eliminate her for the moment."

"Reasonable," the priest nodded.

"The actors, Sand, Vincent, and Toby are possible but still unlikely. They weren't anywhere near when Funnicello was killed, and I can't possibly imagine they would have any particular motive. Leave them out too." Rime counted quickly on her fingers and began to push open the door. "That leaves Lady Karis, Coracle the shaman, and Geranium. Those are our three suspects. We will press them, ask them questions, keep our eye peeled, and hopefully they will reveal something?"

Her voice trailed off as they pushed into the brightly lit parlor. The couches and fine tables waited, and music filled the air from Lady Moon-Death. But where she had expected to find the other guests, she found only an empty room. The black guitar played itself as it hovered above the chair that Geranium had occupied when they left the room.

"Crap," the squire said. "They're all gone. They could be anywhere."

Rime wasted no time but began to stride towards the door that led to the Banquet Hall where the night's events had begun. "We are in danger. Well, *more* danger. Immediate danger. This was a place of relative safety. They would only have left it to either cause harm or to escape it."

Jonas' sword was in his hand, and he ran to get in front of her. "Stay close, Lady Bellwether and Father..."

"Andrew will be fine," the bald priest offered a tight smile.

"'No time for titles on the battlefield', as they say in the Legion."

"Neriah for me," the older girl smiled. "Or you can call me Natalie or Mariah or Nancy, since I mangled your name all night."

"We go to the Banquet Hall first. It's close and the logical place that the actors would have fled. Also, I will finally get the chance to inspect the actress's body." Rime mentally kicked herself for waiting this long and physically kicked open the door that lead into the Banquet Hall at the same moment.

The hall was dark. The stage lights still shone, but the long tables in the audience were festooned with shadow.

This is where it started. The play, me and Jonas dripping rainwater on the floor. Rime did not slow and plunged towards the brightly lit stage. Jonas kept his sword ready right at her heels. The priest and Neriah followed close behind.

The mage stepped onto the stage, shading her forehead to give her eyes time to adjust. Jonas leaped in front of her as a tall figure stepped out from behind the dividing wall at the back of the stage.

"Oh, you're back. Any luck?" Sand asked mildly.

"No hidden guest. We found Lord Bellwether dead. Where is everyone else?" Rime threw the question like a javelin at the white-haired actor.

Sand's eyes widened. *Real surprise or feigned?* The actor came downstage towards them.

"The Lord felled, too? We need to get out of this place.

Never should have taken this engagement," Sand sat down on the edge of the stage. "I've lost enough actors tonight, and I don't want to lose any more."

"Where is everyone else?" Rime repeated.

Sand looked up, out across the darkened hall. "I don't know. Lord Bellwether excused himself right after you left. That professor became disturbed — uncomfortable — constantly tugging at her blouse and wandered off not long after. The bard and the shaman went next, thick as a pair of cats hunting a mouse covered with cream. It was just my boys and me, alone with the drunk dilettante and that insufferable guitar. The music started to make me feel strange, so I hauled up Toby and Vincent and dragged them back in here. If we're going to meet our end, I'd much prefer it to be on the stage."

He rapped his knuckles on the wooden floor.

The music! The bard said that his music could show him secrets, let him control people, drive them insane. Rime felt a mechanical pleasure as her thoughts clicked into place. *Geranium. It has to be.* But it still didn't quite fit as much as she wanted it to. *Or maybe I want it to be him, so I can have my answer and also the delight of beating a confession out of him.* Rime forced herself to calm down. Her emotions — her glands — had not been proper allies this evening. Every encounter with the bard had made her feel strange, had made her react more extremely than she would have liked. *And then I almost killed Neriah. Is that what I'm like?* Maybe, after all, the comfort of having the bard's music to blame for all of the night's murder and strangeness was the most appealing part. *Not the first signs of my own madness.*

"I need to inspect Darla's body. I've put it off all night, and I can't solve a puzzle without all of the pieces," the mage said brusquely. "Jonas, watch the door."

"Uh, which one? There are three. One back into the Parlor, then two back into the Lobby," the squire grunted.

"All of them. Watch all of the doors," Rime seethed.

"We'll help you," Father Andrew consoled him. "Neriah and I."

"Come." Sand stood up weary. "I'll take you to her."

The mage and the actor walked behind the divider to the crammed pile of theatrical detritus. Vincent and Toby were both awake, the younger still clearly nauseated and sick. Each held the other's hand but also gripped blunted stage weapons in the other. Their leader filled them in on the current situation with terse sentences while continuing to move to the gilt-covered coffin.

Rime threw the lid of the coffin back and leaned forward without waiting for any ceremony or permission from the other actors. She surveyed the corpse, expecting to immediately glimpse the final piece of evidence that she needed. The final piece — the last line of chalk. She was horribly disappointed.

Darla was lovely even in death. The other actors had straightened her clothes and carefully arranged her curly hair. *Dark brown.* The wig she had worn was on a nearby trunk, and Rime did not need to look close to match it with the strand of hair she'd found in the lord's bedchamber. Flowers filled the coffin, their fresh scent masking any scent of decay. Rime recognized the flowers; they had been used to decorate the banquet tables during the play. Sand stood behind her and sniffled quietly into his sleeve.

There has to be something. The mage lifted the dead actresses' skirts and pushed back her sleeves. She checked carefully around her neck and shoulders: not a mark, not a scratch. A few old scars long healed. A rough tattoo of a frog on her thigh. *There has to be something. Some clue.* Clearly the killer had not read the same mystery books that she had. It was becoming more than a little frustrating.

"You and the others tended to her after she died, cleaned her." Rime wheeled on the white-haired actor. "Was there a strange scent. A bruise you noticed? Something that didn't belong in the coffin?"

"No." Sand reached into the coffin and touched Darla's clasped hands tenderly. "Only the blackberries."

"The blackberries."

"Yes, she had a sprig of blackberries in her hand. She was bad about taking snacks with her into the coffin for that show."

Rime exhaled and carefully reached into the coffin, pushing back the dead wood-elf's lips. On her teeth and gums were the faintest stain of dark purple. She checked the corpse's fingernails. A tiny sliver of purple was lodged under her right ring finger.

"You threw them away." It was not a question. "They could have been the vector for the poison. We could have matched it with some in the kitchen — or if some grow around the manor grounds."

"Perhaps. But that wouldn't do us much good at the moment would it?" The lead actor reverently closed the lid of the garish coffin.

Rime noticed that the wood was much thinner than it appeared from the audience. Some cunning method had been used to make cheap lumber look like the finest mahogany. She wrote the word 'blackberries' on a tiny corner of her mental blackboard. She realized that the actor was right. She had collected every scrap of information, kept track of every lead, and she still had no idea what was truly going on in the House of the Heart-Broken Lion.

"Rime!" Jonas bellowed. "Doors!"

The mage locked eyes with Sand. "Stay here."

"Nowhere else for us to be in this world," the actor said, hefting a battleaxe that appeared to be made of plaster and tin.

Rime sprinted out onto the stage, her eyes trying to adjust to the shadowed banquet hall beyond the stage lights. Jonas had his sword at the ready with Neriah and the bald priest behind him against the far right edge of the stage. The three doors leading to the hall were swinging wide in unison, and three silhouettes were briefly outlined by the burn-light globes outside. One tall shadow, two shorter.

She made herself stop in the center of the stage. She spread her hands wide and felt her magic coil and seethe, ready to act. The mage allowed herself a grim smile. Rime waited a heartbeat.

"Returned to the scene of the crime, eh?" the bard's cocksure tenor filled the hall as he stepped into the light at the foot of the stage. For one moment his cobalt blue coat gleamed as if outlined in neon. Lady Moon-Death was slung over his shoulder. No notes came, but the instrument seemed to hum quietly to itself with anticipation.

The two smaller shadows came forward and flanked him on either side. The sea-elf Coracle had eschewed her grand white conch for a bandolier of daggers and a wicked looking longsword. Lady Karis' face was a smeared ruin of lipstick, mascara, and vomit. Her purple nailpolish was chipped, and thin fingers wrapped tight around the haft of a brutal looking morningstar. Both women's eyes burned with the green-yellow candle flame of madness.

"I told you they would be here," Geranium smiled. "The murderers themselves, the strangers at the feast, the uncertain bandits. Don't worry, Lady Neriah. We'll save you from their clutches."

Rime took one step towards the edge of the stage.

Her mind hummed with calculations. The actors would only be a hindrance, and neither Neriah or Father Andrew had revealed capacity for combat. It was her magic and Jonas' steel against the two maddened women and the music of the leering bard. Rime appraised her companion. His skill with his sword was solid but not exceptional. He could perhaps deal with one or both of the women, but he would have no defense against the insidious abilities that spooled from the melodies of the black guitar. The priest and the noblewoman would be completely undefended — a vast potential for concentration being diverted. An almost mathematical certainty that the squire would get himself skewered trying to impress Neriah. The numbers flew like doves and then lighted on the bottom line.

Geranium was the mastermind. Geranium was behind it all. And *she* wanted to fight him. One on one, no distractions.

Rime turned her head and waited for the squire's eyes to lock on hers. She spoke very carefully and directly. "I can handle the bard. You can't. Get Neriah and the priest out of here. Do not argue. Go. NOW."

With a crackle of white energy her right hand came up, a fierce buffet of wind pushed Jonas, Neriah, and Father Andrew two-thirds of the distance to the door. The squire always needed a push.

"Now," Rime said and turned her attention to Geranium.

Surprisingly, Jonas did not argue. Instead he immediately grabbed the other two and pushed them bodily out the door.

Geranium laughed a mellow pleased trill up the scale. "Ladies, if you would be so kind. Please go and detain that beautiful boy."

Both women growled in delight and bolted towards the door.

The bard unslung his guitar with lackadaisical bravado and pulled it into place, snug against his pelvis.

Rime smiled, her teeth bright. It had been a long night, full of questions, conversation, careful searching and determined thought. She had restrained her use of magic since their arrival, but now it was time.

"Time to dance, bard," The mage made her vicious smile go wider. "Play something classy."

17

Jonas spun on the marble staircase and took his sword hilt in both hands.

Father Andrew stumbled at the top of the stairs. The princess tugged at his arm, pulling him forward. Neriah's blonde-strawberry hair had come free of her headscarf in their mad scramble. The squire's mind had been evenly split between admiring it, wondering what it would be like to brush it, and figuring out how to survive the fight that was moments away and shrieking up the stairs behind them.

Karis and Coracle swarmed up the stairs. The sea-elf came first, almost bouncing up the steps and spinning her longsword with murderous elan. *She's good with that sword; I can see it in her grip.* The bedraggled noblewoman was just behind. The cruel iron ball hanging from her morningstar clattered against the marble steps. Jonas was about two-thirds of the way up the stairs; the priest and the princess on the landing. He had pushed Neriah and Father Andrew up the stairs on instinct. He really should have thought about it more. The Lobby was the largest open area in the entire manor. *But I couldn't be sure I would be able to keep both of those ladies busy. I need a bottleneck.* Jonas leveled his sword at the approaching women. *They have to go through me to get to the princess and Father Andrew. Pretty good plan for five seconds.* He congratulated himself.

"Keep moving upstairs," he called. "Don't get corner…"

The sea-elf's blade cut through the air in an overhand slice. Jonas blocked and swung her sword hard to the right, smashing it into the marble bannister. He had to immediately retreat two steps up when the morningstar crushed into the step where his foot had just been. Coracle snarled and whipped the longsword forward again, nimbly leaping over where Karis crouched, her thin arms straining against the heavy weapon. The squire kept his guard in place and took another step back up the stairs. *I really wish I had a shield right now.*

"Don't get cornered!" he yelled again over his shoulder. "Keep going up."

It wasn't much of a plan, but it would have to do. His best hope was to keep moving, keeping them as far from Neriah and Father Andrew as possible. Wait for an opening to wound or dispatch his two opponents. Or at least keep them at bay until Rime could mop up the bard and come to his rescue.

Unless she uses too much juice. And passes out. Like she does.

Karis screamed in rage and risked a wild swing of the morningstar across his body. The sea-elf had to skip out of the way, irritation clear on her face. The cruel spikes scored along his left forearm. No bones were broken. His hand still worked, but the wound burned cold then hot as blood pumped. Jonas cursed and backed up again. He was only a few steps from the second floor landing.

"We're at the Tower door!" Neriah called, her breath short.

"Do your best to spare them, Jonas! They are mad; they don't know what they are doing," the bald priest wheezed with exertion. He heard the door slam behind them.

The squire felt the iron grip of his training slip over him. *The Code.* On the battlefield it was safer and quicker to be merciless, to kill your enemy the moment the opportunity presented itself, to take every opportunity. But to attack a witless opponent, to benefit from the enemy's weakness instead of respecting their strength, to fight without honor, went against his training and his nature. *I have to figure out how to disarm them.*

Coracle laughed and battered at his defenses, her sword moving like a sea-snake. Karis was swinging the morningstar again, forcing him to retreat. Jonas lost his balance for a moment and had to tuck and roll across the marble landing to avoid the shaman's blade. *I have to figure out how not to die.*

The squire popped up into a guard position, and felt a pressure against his back heel. He was already at the door that lead into the Lord's Tower. He had bought the priest and the princess maybe a few seconds head start. His plan was not going particularly well.

What would Master do? Jonas parried two more lightning-quick slashes. *Change the board. Make an unexpected move.*

"So, uh…" the squire grunted as he shifted to the side, letting the morningstar slam against the thick wooden door behind him. "Why are you…" Right-hand block, then a kick against the shaman's midsection. "…Why are you trying to kill me, exactly?"

Get them talking, boy. His master's words. *True Villains can never resist.*

Coracle's blue lips parted with derision. Karis had tumbled forward after the morningstar had impacted the door and was rising from her ungainly flop. The cords in her neck and arms strained as she hefted the weapon again. "The box. The box. The box, you fool," she spat, purple eyes wild.

"And self-preservation." The sea-elf tugged a dagger free from her bandolier. "You and your mistress and Lord Mustache have killed enough of us tonight."

What box? Jonas had no idea what she was talking about, but at least they had paused their onslaught. He counted it a tiny victory. "We haven't killed anyone. Coracle, you were with me when Funnicello died!"

The sea-elf shifted distractingly,tapping a long blue finger against her breastbone. Her feral eyes were amused. "That's true. We were becoming quite close. But your partner wasn't there then, and she is a wizard, after all."

Good point. Rime was under the bed then, but is that going to seem like a convenient explanation, or----shit. Jonas spun away from the door as the human noblewoman bellowed and swung the morningstar at his ankles. Karis cursed bitterly as her swing fell short.

"Come on! You're a shaman! Can't you consult the spirits and see that I'm telling the truth?" the squire panted.

Coracle laughed, flipping her sword and dagger from hand

to hand like a juggler. "Oh, the spirits? Oh the Balance, send me your waves and your wind and your fire and your, I don't know, fucking little pebbles or whatever to guide me on my way!"

The sea-elf spun her longsword behind her back and flicked the dagger at him in the same motion. It buried a few inches into his right shoulder.

The sea-elf laughed again. "I'm a thief, you fucking moron. It's a good thing you land-dwellers are all short-sighted racists. My little shows with the shell and the prancing and the chanting? Humans eat it right up, open their doors and their treasure troves and their secrets to Mama Coracle. I consult the spirits and they tell me about their husband's shipping deal, or where the best silver is kept, or who in the Council of Nine can be bribed if you bring him a well-bathed ten-year-old boy. I came here to steal the Precursor Box. And I will fucking have it, if I have to cut it out of your entrails."

"The box. The box. The box," Karis panted in soul-broken despair. "I need it. I neeeed it."

Okay. Jonas pulled the dagger from his shoulder and tucked it into his belt. His blood was ruining the fine white shirt and beautiful black vest he had worn all night. *Okay. These ladies are crazy.*

His plan was not going well at all. His attempt to distract his foes with conversation was only pissing them off. The wound in his shoulder wasn't mortal, but it was painful and blood loss would become a factor soon enough. Time to fall back on his last line of tactical options.

Stupidity.

The squire bellowed a guttural challenge and rushed Karis first. She was still recovering from her last shot, attempting to hoist the morningstar yet again. He bowled her over with his left shoulder and kept moving. Coracle was nonplussed, two daggers drawn and held like a cross in one hand while the longsword hung eager in the space between them. The sea-elf was standing in his path to the tower door. Jonas risked a tricky attack sequence he had been working on the past week or so. It was the one that a devil-kin had used to completely bypass his defenses in a few moves. He wasn't sure if he had it all down, having only seen it once and only then before going face first into the sand. The squire prayed.

Coracle parried his assault with speed and grace. Jonas felt desperation burn in his stomach. *She's too good.* Taking a wild chance, the squire feinted out of the attack sequence then moved into the reach of her arms. The sea-elf's eyes widened with surprise, even more so when Jonas grabbed her bandolier and put his foot on her sternum and kicked out with all the force he could muster.

The faux shaman staggered back, her eyes whirling. Jonas didn't wait. He ran through the tower door and slammed it behind him. The pain from his pierced shoulder chose that moment to catch up with him and roared up into his throat, escaping as a most unheroic whimper. The tower door swung inward towards the stairs leading up. He looked desperately for some way to bar the door. His hand moved without thought and plucked the bloody dagger from his belt. Jonas jammed it in the space between the bottom of the door and the marble floor. He gave the dagger a swift kick to wedge the door as tightly as possible.

The squire stood up feeling faint surprise. *Pretty good idea.* The door vibrated as Karis' morningstar collided on the outside. The noblewoman's screams were muted by the thick wood, but he had no doubt that they would batter their way in soon enough. Jonas turned and ran up the stairs.

The sitting room was dishevelled; a chair had fallen over the cold body of Lord Bellwether. No sign of Neriah or Father Andrew, so Jonas kept running. Up the spiral staircase his feet hammered. The hot pulse of his forehead, arm and shoulder wound dimmed for the moment. He arrived at the level of the bedchambers and managed a strangled call.

"We're up on the next floor," Neriah's clear voice came from further up the metal staircase.

Jonas panted and heaved himself forward. His legs were getting heavy and thick from the quick ascent. He arrived at the top level and collapsed to his knees, gasping. The priest was the first to his side, lined face gray with his own weariness. Neriah came a split second later, as she ripped the bottom hem off her nightgown to fashion a crude bandage for his shoulder. A tiny pulse of delight came from her touch, but the cacophony of pain drowned it out ably.

"You all right?" Jonas managed.

"Plenty of workout for the knees," Father Andrew grinned, his face covered with sweat. "Just what an old man needs."

"I blocked the door, but it won't hold them long. I guess I'll just stand at the top of the stairs and try to hold them off," the squire sighed and began to push himself up.

"Let me tie off this bandage." Neriah insisted, keeping a firm grip on his arm. "We should have made a barricade on the lower levels, maybe the sitting room. We just kept running like frightened rabbits."

"It's okay. It's okay." The squire wished she could spend all night holding his arm and tying the absurd cucumber silk around his shoulder. It was obvious that Neriah had no particular skill in battle medicine, but it made him absurdly pleased to see the silk wound around him. *Like a lady's favor at the Tournament.*

"It's not okay." The princess' face was tight with anger. "My father is dead, and I'm the lady of the house. I have a responsibility, a responsibility…"

Neriah's gaze went to towards the ceiling, and she inhaled in surprise. "The roof. The trapdoor to the roof."

She stood up and pointed towards the small metal square that Jonas had inspected on their last trip to the tower. *An hour ago? Even that long?*

"We climb up to the roof. There's no ladder; Funnicello always had to bring one up from the storeroom when he went out to clean bird shit off the statues. It's the best place right now to defend. They would have to jump and climb through the opening, and you would be stabbing them all the time," Neriah said with triumph, letting the wounded squire fall back to the ground.

Bird shit? Did she just say 'bird shit'?

"Come on, there's no time. Help me break open the latch," the princess continued.

The squire made himself stand up. It was a good idea. The ceiling in the hallway was about eight or nine feet from the floor; Jonas could touch it if he jumped. Neriah was

212

already attempting to do the same and grab the trap door's latch. She wasn't having much success, so she pulled him forward making his heart race.

"Boost me up." And without waiting for any response, she clambered up onto his shoulders. *I am in great danger. I could be dead in a few minutes. I really need to stop grinning like a fool.*

Neriah grabbed the latch and pulled down. Although the simple length of iron chain was still in place, a gust of wind and rain came through the opening. Lady Bellwether was getting soaked, but she kept her grip. "I'll hang on to the latch. Let me hang from it, then break it with your sword."

Jonas complied, not without a little sadness. The princess was proving a cool head in a crisis, even as she dangled from the iron latch like a bedraggled squirrel. He carefully placed the end of his sword against the chain, almost at the limit of his reach. *Don't miss and hit Neriah.* The squire swung. The iron chain clattered but it did not break. A spike of anger formed in his gut. His sword was good steel and it was not going to be outmatched by a stupid iron chain of no particular name or repute. He took aim again and swung with pride-wounded might.

The chain snapped, and Neriah fell to the ground. Rain, wind, and night howled through the dark square. Father Andrew came forward to assist the princess with a relieved expression on his face. Jonas opened his mouth to congratulate her, when a crash echoed through the tower. It was distant and muffled. But it was undoubtedly the sound of two vicious women breaking through a thick wooden door with a morningstar.

Jonas sheathed his sword and grabbed the priest by the shoulders. "You first, Father."

Father Andrew nodded and put his foot into the squire's cupped hands to be lifted up through the opening. It took the old man some wriggling, but he finally got his back end up over the wooden frame. All the while, Jonas could hear the distant sounds growing nearer. Furniture was being upended and feet clattered on metal stairs.

The squire grabbed Neriah and nearly heaved her through the trapdoor. "Good idea. Didn't want to forget to say. The trapdoor," he panted, then leaped himself to grab the edge of the opening and the priest's hands.

Neriah helped haul him up as well. As soon as he was through, Jonas drew his sword again to catch the underside of the trapdoor and swing it back into place. A few inches of chain remained, just enough to wind around the brace on the outside of the tower and hold the door shut.

"Maybe it will confuse them a moment," he offered, as he sank down onto his haunches.

He wanted to lay down for a nap. He wanted to have Neriah hold his hand or perhaps even — if he were to really ask a lot of the universe — have her softly brush his hair with her fingers. He above all did not want to be standing on the top of a huge stone tower in the middle of a thunderstorm with two armed lunatics coming for his blood.

And Rime. She's fighting Geranium right now. I hope she's okay.

Jonas took stock of their surroundings as best he could. It was still a couple of hours before dawn, and the pouring rain made it difficult to see. The clouds even blocked the three moons' light. Only a properly dramatic flash of lightning gave him a reasonable view of the tower's roof.

The roof was circular, about a hundred feet across. At the cardinal directions were four gargoyles: a fierce winged demon to the North, a gryphon to the South, and a pair of armored knights to the East and West. The squire risked a quick trot to peer down the sides of the tower. Smooth, well laid stone ran easily fifty feet to the base of the tower and the roof of the manor proper. Impossible to climb during a rainstorm. Jonas pushed soaking wet hair out of his eyes and blinked as much rainwater away as he could. He crossed back to the trapdoor in the center of the roof where the priest and Lady Bellwether waited.

"I guess now we wait," he sighed and allowed himself to fold his legs and sit.

Father Andrew did the same and pushed rainwater off his face and bald pate. "Take what rest we can until they start knocking."

"Was this a good idea?" Neriah asked Jonas, her lovely face framed by sodden gold and red.

"It was," the squire assured her. "And at the very least, I didn't see any bird shit."

She smiled, and for Jonas that felt like a victory of at least medium size.

18

The bard flexed his left hand, fingers spread wide. He curled them around the neck of his guitar, each touch precise and holy.

"Something classy?" Geranium smirked. "You are in luck."

Rime's eyes blazed with green fire. She could feel her magic burn, but she couldn't see his. Only a slight prickle on her skin told her that it was coalescing. *I need to see what he's doing. I won't miss it this time.*

She felt an urge to attack, to swat him like a fly with his grin still fresh on his lips, but her pride and her curiosity would not allow it. The mage had failed to truly unravel the mysteries trapped within the house, but she would solve this riddle. *Give me your best shot, music man.*

The bard closed his eyes, his neon pink hair and glove bent reverently over the strings. Then, with a lover's touch, he ran his fingers across the heart of the black guitar.

Song of the road, road made of song.
Who knew I would travel so long?
Stories and wind, campfire and rain.
When will I ever see my home again?
When will I ever see my home again?

Geranium's voice cut her to the bone. He had a beautiful voice, yes. But every other song he had sung carried a counter-harmony of pride — a vocal swagger. When he sang now, his voice was raw and forlorn. The song of a traveller half a world from home.

Triumph and travel, teapot and steel.
Won't someone tell me what I'm supposed to feel?
Lovers and liars, heroes and pain,
When will I ever see my home again?
When will I ever see my home again?

He opened his eyes and looked at her, letting his hands carry on the melody, simple and dark. "Yes, I know your song, kitten. I know the song that opens your heart, the tune that breaks," the bard spoke intimate and sure. Rime had never heard this song before. Not once, not ever. Her skin prickled again. His strange magic was growing. Her hands clenched in defense; green fire squeezed between her knuckles eager to burn.

The bard sang again.

I walk through the sunshine, but only see night.
Even in the valley I stand mountain height.

The mage felt alone. Alone on a dark road. She felt her father's apathy, her mother's absence, her brother's hatred. She felt her tutor's bamboo rod slap against her shoulder.

Summers and Winters and Springs made of Fall,
The world keeps on turning and I forget them all.

She was alone. Alone on a dark road. Ahead a moonless sky. Behind fire and ash.

Quiet and quick, I walk alone.
Who knew the cold could marry my bones?

The green flame sputtered in her hands. Her eyes began to dim. *What is the point?* Rime wanted to lay down and sleep and weep and wait for a dawn that would never come.

Mud in the gutters, shadow and flame
When will I ever see my home again?
Never, oh never see my home again.
Never, oh never see my home again.

Her magic slipped from her grasp, and she was alone. Her vision was clouded, but she could see the bard's contented face as he let his song fade off into nothing. Then a discordant note — his left hand gripped the neck of the guitar with ferocity and a strange expression crossed his face. Another twang. A violent, angry note. His hands moved faster and faster. The dark melody he had spun around her was cast aside with vicious glee. Rime was still mired in the place he had sent her, hovering over the edge of sleep. She watched with bemusement as the shadows in the corner of the room seemed to thicken, then expand. The mage stood in the center of the brightly lit stage, but the shadow *reached* out towards her. Long tendrils uncoiled, almost boiling with the energy of the bard's furious music.

I should. The first black tentacle wrapped itself around her ankle. It felt like a cold towel, damp and forgotten on the bathroom floor. *I should.*

218

The shadows stretched across the stage and swallowed her in a foul, writhing cocoon.

I should.

I should.

Her left hand clenched. A tiny gout of green flame appeared, small as a star on the belly of night.

I should — burn.

And she did.

Emerald flame poured out of her, biting and tearing at the shadows. The black tendrils erupted like torn husks or shattered corn stalks before a wildfire. *How dare he.*

Rime lifted off the floor, her flame growing brighter and brighter. The bard continued to play, his eyes terrified. His hands moved faster and faster as they called forth more shadow. More for her to burn.

HOW DARE HE.

The Magic Wild sang in her blood and found Geranium's shadow song a perfect symphony. Rime's anger reached down into it and pulled out more and more fire.

She flew high above the stage and poured rivers of verdant flame down on the shadows that had sought to contain her. The bard played feverishly, but he could not call forth enough darkness to extinguish her. She smiled her vicious smile and launched herself directly at him.

Geranium reacted immediately to her coming; his hands danced into a new melody. Lightning rippled along the length of Lady Moon-Death, then arced through the air towards her. Rime laughed and batted it aside. The bard's music sailed into a melody of eight-fold intricacy. Lightning came for her again in a web. The mage clapped her hands together, creating a gust of wind that tore the net of light asunder.

This man had confused her. This man had tricked her. This man had manipulated her and had the temerity to think he owned her with his song. He had the foul heart to crush her with despair and shadow. Rime made her fire burn hotter, and she crashed into the bard's cobalt coat.

The two of them flew across the room as Rime's fury pushed them past chairs and skidding along the marble floor. A grand banquet table broke against Geranium's back as she pushed on. Only when the bard's body slammed against the stone of the far wall and the guitar strings were silent did she stop.

Both of her hands were buried in his coat, the fabric twisted by her grip. The black guitar was between them, its strings gone cherry red from the heat of her flames. Geranium's coffee-skin was blistered and charred.

"If you're going to do it…" the bard sighed as blood poured from his mouth onto Rime, "…don't dawdle."

Is this who I am? Rime thought floated across her rage. *Is this what I am?*

Her right hand tightened, and the flame in her left hand burned hotter than the sun's mercy. Without restraint or remorse, she punched into his right breast. Her magic seared through his silly blue coat and tore through flesh and bone. Rime reached into the bard's chest and screamed.

Geranium's eyes went wide with the pain, then locked on hers. They seemed to change with the clarity of death's approach.

"Girl, girl, girl…" he struggled to speak. "You have to listen. Have to listen. It wasn't me, me, me."

Rime felt her magic begin to cool, as well as her anger. The first waves of exhaustion began to radiate from her center. She pulled her blood-soaked hand free from the bard's chest and did her best to wipe it off on what remained of his coat. "What are you talking about?" she asked, tired and sick to her stomach.

"It wasn't me. It was…" the dying man choked and then continued. "This is not my music. Like with Waters. It came through me, somehow."

Geranium tried to flex his left hand to demonstrate, but his arms would not obey. The bard's delicate fingers scraped against the wall. He leaned against the stone wall as his life flowed out of him. Rime looked down at her own left hand, covered with his blood. Quiet and clean in the middle of the flame and blood, chalk scraped a line across her mind.

She went to her library. She went to her blackboard, to the notes she had made all night in her hunt for the murderer. She held up her left hand, clean in her mind, and placed it lightly against the blackboard. The chalk letters began to move. orienting around her fingers. Words she had thought unimportant, details she had noticed but not understood. The way that the bard's left hand had moved when he killed Master Waters. The claw marks on the trader's face from his left hand. The dagger that killed Lord Bellwether from a left-handed assailant. Scholar

Trowel's torn clothes, ripped by her left hand. And Funnicello---

Rime sucked in air. She was back in the darkened hall with the dying bard. Her mind shuddered. The dwarf's injuries, the vicious tear across his abdomen. She had been unable to identify the weapon. But looking at her bloody hand, she was sure. It was exactly the sort of wound that would be left if the dwarf had reached into the flesh of his own stomach and ripped his own guts out with his left hand.

Geranium nodded, the barest of movements. "You understand. I see."

She had been looking all night for a killer, for a systematic plan or process. She had been looking at the evidence all wrong. The deaths were not parts of a plan nor cogs in a machine. They were *symptoms.*

"I'm sorry," she made herself say to the tall man. "I didn't realize."

"Eh." Geranium said, a tiny echo of his swagger still remaining. "It happens."

"Your magic, I still couldn't understand it. It was great. It was great." *Weak words for the innocent man you just murdered.*

Geranium's eyes were clear and free. "In the End, the only Magic left will be Music."

"What?"

He did not answer because he was dead.

Rime turned away and walked towards the lights of the stage. She would think about the bard's death — his words, his music — when she had time.

The people in the manor had been affected by something. If she thought of the effect as symptoms of a disease, it made the puzzle stand on its head and become clear. The left hand was the key, the prime signifier of the effect.

Just like the recording in the Precursor Box. Just like Teon.

Only people that had heard the recording were affected: Lord Bellwether, Funnicello, Trowel, Coracle, Karis, Geranium, Master Waters. The actors were clear; they were not invited. Neriah had said that she had not attended the presentation, so she should be free from the recording's influence as well.

Rime sat down on the edge of the stage as calmly as she was able. *Jonas didn't hear it either.* It was a small comfort.

But I heard it. I listened to it all. It's why I almost killed Neriah. It's why I just killed Geranium.

A particle of doubt. *But I've killed before. It's not that cut and dried. It seems to amplify your natural mental state, or maybe reduce inhibitions towards certain types of behaviour. Or maybe--*

The empty hall rang with the sound of her hand slapping into her forehead. She had done it again. She had forgotten one of the guests.

The priest. Father Andrew Gallowglass. Servant of the Nameless God. He heard the recording too. I have to warn Jonas!

Rime stood up, then stopped.

What's more dangerous? An old man with no weapons…

The mage crossed back onto the stage with her mind made up, but she finished the rhetorical question out loud.

"Or a wild mage with a demon inside?"

Her words hung in the empty hall. She knew the answer. Jonas was on his own.

Rime closed her eyes and returned to her library to do battle.

WHO WAS GERANIUM THE ERUPTION?

In the hush of the hall, the black guitar hung from the dead man's neck.

The strings were frayed and seared, frail from the heat of their master's death.

But still. They began to play.

A slow song. A song of change, a wander-song, a song of fear and joy.

With the slow care of a crumbling stone, Lady Moon-Death sang his story.

It was a simple song. One that would sound familiar, or seem to belong to the earliest recollection of childhood's fog.

A laughing child became a girl, then a boy, then a woman, then a man. She decided to be many things but most importantly a god. The stage and the music and people and the songs and the lovemaking and the wine and the endless rise of the road. But the music most of all.

It was a good song. It knew much of pain but more of glory. Each note exactly where it needed to be, where it must be. The pure melody of sunset. Sundown wind through the trees, the never-king cry of the gulls, the murmur of the sea.

It was a good song. And that is all any true bard of Gate City would wish.

The guitar's strings at last gave way, snapping and splitting. The great instrument played his song to the last.

None were close enough to hear it, no record of it in the mind of man.

But still.

It played all the same.

19

"They seem to be keeping pretty quiet," Father Andrew said, his voice pitched to be heard over the rain.

"Yeah," Jonas shivered. His borrowed finery was well-made and handsome, even with his blood smeared all over it and the strip of Neriah's dress wound around it. But it was useless against the rain. He missed his smelly brown cloak, resting comfortably downstairs folded over the back of a chair. Jonas wondered if his cloak was pleased to have missed the night's murder and misadventure or was fuming in boredom and complaining to the bedspread.

It had been several minutes since they had pulled the door shut behind them. The first minute had been filled with nervous panting, his hand tight on his sword. But then the rain and the cold overrode the immediate fear.

"Do you think they are just waiting us out?" Neriah shivered from where she sat. The three of them had taken shelter behind the winged gargoyle on the northern edge of the tower. It provided scant protection from the wind and rain but was ever so slightly better than nothing.

The squire gingerly began to ease out of his vest. The wound in his shoulder throbbed, but the bleeding seemed to have stopped for the moment. He held the black vest out to the princess.

"I know it won't help much, but here," he offered.

"Thanks." she smiled and shrugged into the sodden garment.

Jonas laid his sword across his knees and tried not to think about how cold and wet he was. *Since we left the Banquet Hall, this has just been a series of bad plans.*

Father Andrew grunted and let his head fall forward onto his breastbone as if in prayer.

Poor old guy. Jonas sighed with concern. *All this running around can't be good for him or his knees. Blech.*

"Shall we tell stories?" Father Andrew spoke without lifting his head.

"Uh, stories?" The squire pushed wet hair out of his face.

"Yes, stories. Something to pass the time. We have nowhere to go and nothing to do but soak and stew. It'll take our mind off the rain." The priest raised his head and waggled his eyebrows cheerfully.

"I think that's a good idea," Neriah said, her teeth

chattering.

If the princess thought it was a good idea, Jonas thought it was a good idea.

"Okay, sure."

"I'll go first." Father Andrew stood up straight and splayed his hands on his knees. "And you must forgive me, I am a simple preacher at heart. It's been too long since I've had a captive audience — young souls to guide."

Neriah chuckled. "We're quite a small flock, Father."

"Oh, you'll do just fine." The rain filled his slow intake of breath. "And if you do not mind, I would like to tell a tale of home; of Gilead, since it feels very far away right now."

Jonas' heart twitched. *Very, very far.*

"Have you been there, my lady?"

"A few times — in years past — to visit my mother's family. My name is Gilean. It is a beautiful place." Neriah smiled.

"It is. It is, indeed," the priest took a breath. "The green plains and the hills of bare granite. Hidden valleys and villages, and the jewel of it all, Corinth. The city of white spires, of cobblestones and steel. Legend's backyard. Glory's oldest pair of pants. Heroes as common as pennies. Gilead is an old country, a proud nation, always on the brink of destruction by the tides of Evil. There is a saying that Gilead is the anvil where the hammer falls. Darkness falls first and falls hardest on my home. Over the years we have grown strong to stand up against it. The Iron Legion, the Swords of the Faith, our army and our shield most bright. Every war, every campaign, every time that Good draws a line in the sand -- you will find Gilead in the vanguard. The greatest heroes to stand against the shadows of our world have always been sons and daughters of Gilead."

The soaking wet noblewoman leaned close to hear Father Andrew's next words. Jonas was struck dumb. His pulse hammered in his temples.

"Once upon a time, there was a knight of Gilead. He had fought in many battles, slain many monsters, and won more than his share of glory on the fields of valor. But there was one foe before which he had little defense. I speak, of course, of Time." Father Andrew spread his hands, then wiped rainwater from his eyes once more. "He had become old. His hair was gone, his beard was white, the strength of his thews and the brightness in his eye were all but run out. Time is a patient thief, and it had ransacked every part of his larder. All that remained him was a little wisdom, a little wit, and a sword of great worth."

"Oh, what a sword it was! It shone bright silver even in the darkest of nights. It was blessed by the moons, they say, and no evil could bear its touch. The old knight had won it years before and now in his latter days it was the final token of his glory, the sacrament of his honor. Younger knights spoke of it with awe. Tournaments were held for the bare honor of touching the fabulous blade. The royal advisors called for the King to command the old knight to forsake the blade and pass it on to some greater, younger champion. But the King refused. 'It should only be borne by a true knight, pure of heart and noble of purpose. I know of none more fitting than he. Let him bear it until the day he sees fit to pass it on, or until the gentle embrace of Death takes him.' And the advisors were chastened and quickly found something of great importance to take care of on the opposite side of the castle."

Neriah snorted, forgetting the rain. Jonas was more still than the winged statue they sheltered beneath.

"If the Fates were kind, and all tales had happy ends, and lives of justice and sacrifice were properly rewarded, this would be the end of the tale," the priest grimaced. "But sadly, that is not the world we find ourselves in. The old knight took a squire — a young boy from a poor family — a kindly gesture for the aged champion to take on one final pupil. He took great care to instruct the boy in all the duties and lore of his order. Strategy, Swordplay, the care of Armor, the code of Honor that binds all true knights to their duty. But the squire paid little heed to his master's tutelage. He had eyes only for the shining blade."

Master...I... Jonas' heart was full of rain.

"Oh, he coveted it. Lusted after it. Dreamed of it. His hands were ever taking the shape of its grand hilt, his head filled with visions of the great deeds he would perform when it was his. He would be a Hero, the greatest knight that Gilead had ever known." The old man leaned forward. "Until at last he could bear it no more. He waited for his master to drink his fill of wine, then watched the old man totter up the stairs to his room at the tower's crown. When he was sure that his master was sleeping deep, he crept into the old knight's bedchamber. With a dull kitchen knife best suited for peeling potatoes he thrust into the old man's heart, and with the old man's blood on his hands he grasped at last the shining blade..."

"Lies! It's a lie!" the squire screamed and surged towards the balding priest.

Jonas had no plan, only the pain inside of him could not

allow another word to be spoken. If he had taken time to formulate a plan, it absolutely would not have included Father Andrew's left hand grabbing his throat while the priest's right seized his sword and pulled it away. But that's what happened anyway.

Father Andrew gave the squire a quick shove, the force belying his age and weariness. He held Jonas' good steel in his right hand and leveled the point at the gasping squire. The priest's left hand rose up to his own forehead, knuckles tensing as he pushed into the taut flesh. With a quick motion, the priest gouged a quick furrow with his nails that ran from his left temple down to his chin. Blood seeped from the shallow wound but was washed away immediately by the furious rain.

"There. I have it. We are safe, my lady." Father Andrew's face sagged in relief. "I don't know what took me so long to remember."

"Remember? Remember what?" Neriah stood up, her face alarmed.

"We've been hunting all night for a murderer, and there's been a murderer standing right next to us the whole time. That was a pretty good story you told after the play." The priest jabbed the sword in the empty air to punctuate. "The way you fight — you have the mark of the Legion all over you. Born and bred in Gilead — I'll bet you've even sat in the temple when I've performed the service."

Jonas said nothing but stood up grimly. The rain came down harder.

The bald priest advanced, his grip sure on the squire's sword. "And 'Jonas'. A common name to be sure, but not so common. You are the right age, son of Gilead, half a world away. It was you, wasn't it? You killed Sir Pocket. Sir Matthew Pocket, the greatest hero of the Age. You killed him and stole his sword!"

The squire took an involuntary step forward his anger sharp.

"No, my son," Father Andrew turned his wrist and pulled the squire's sword into a textbook Roland Grip, an older style offensive stance. "It has been many long years, but I served my spate in the Legion as well. And this old man still has enough skill to cut you down."

"Father Andrew, I don't understand," Neriah said desperately. "How can you be sure? And your face -- why did you hurt yourself?"

"I am fine, my dear," the priest dabbed absently at his bleeding face with the dripping fabric of his sleeve.

"I don't think you are, Father," the noblewoman insisted.

"I am fine. It's this foul, murderous creature that you should be concerned with. I knew Sir Matthew! I knew him! How could you have killed that wonderful old man?" Father Andrew demanded.

"It." Jonas' mouth popped open. "It wasn't like that."

"What was it like? What was it like when you stabbed the greatest knight this world has ever known in his sleep, then slipped into the night with his sword? Did you sell it? Did you sell it in some back alley when the guilt became too much, when you realized that a filthy traitor like you could never wield it, that your every touch was an offense against the Nameless?" The priest was screaming as the cords of his neck strained against his taut skin.

His left hand rose and softly coiled around the hilt of the squire's sword. The priest's eyes were wild.

"I should cut you down right now. I should…" he groaned as if he was tensing every muscle in his upper body. Jonas stared at him, lost. *He's got a two-handed grip. It's almost like he's trying to attack with his left and hold fast with his right.*

"Father! Father Andrew! There is something the matter with you. You have to calm down," Neriah saw her words were not catching the priest so she lobbed her next ones at the squire. "He's like the others — some madness. There must be something we can do to reach him."

The priest continued to groan and heave, his hands locked in a stalemate. His lips were drawn wide in a rictus, his eyes whirling and furious. *Fight with words?* Then his eyes fell on the priest's chest. Three swords enclosed by a blue circle.

Rage. Fear. Despair. The three weapons of the human heart, bound in a circle of faith.

"Only once," Jonas said in the dark and rain. "We walk through this world only once. Only one life is given by the Nameless."

Father Andrew's hands continued to clench and struggle on the sword's hilt, but his eyes cast around like a man seeking a path out of a dark wood.

The squire took a breath and began the prayer from the beginning.

"Time and wave, sun and wind, night and fire, moons and stone."

234

The priest's lips twitched.

"We walk through the world only once. Only one life is given by the Nameless. It is a gift, a burden…"

"…a challenge, a duty." Father Andrew whispered, almost lost in the sound of falling rain.

"To not waste it. To serve the Highest." The squire paused with hope.

"To the end of our road, with our Honor intact." The priest finished, his voice thick with strain.

The old man closed his eyes. Then, with a sudden spasm he dropped the sword to clatter on the stone roof of the tower. Without opening his eyes, he hugged his arms close. He spoke very quietly. Neriah and Jonas cautiously approached to hear.

"Bind me," the priest whispered. "There is something *in* me. I cannot hold it long, so bind me quick."

Jonas pulled free his belt and tied the priest's hands behind him. Together, he and Neriah helped the priest sit down with his back against the winged statue.

"It's easier if I keep my eyes closed," he said, slowly and carefully. "I'm like a mouse tiptoeing through a room full of cats. Just don't want to be caught."

"Are you in pain?" Neriah asked. "What is causing this?"

"I was so angry at you," Father Andrew continued to whisper. "So sure. So certain. It was right to kill you. It was the only solution."

Jonas turned a worried glance to Neriah. "Angry?"

"I don't know what is inside me or how it got there." The priest's face crumpled in pain. "Ahh. Almost had me. Some devil or demon or spirit of evil. You must get away from me before it takes me again."

"We have you well bound." Neriah laid a comforting hand on his shoulder, which only made the balding man wince.

"Lady Neriah, he said 'angry'," the squire continued.

"I don't think I'll know it's not me," Father Andrew said with calm terror. "Or maybe it is me."

"He got angry, so angry that he was ready to kill me," Jonas labored on.

"What's your point, Jonas?"

"That's the same thing that happened with Rime tonight."

The rain drummed on the stone tower top. Jonas stood up, walked two steps, and picked up his sword.

"I have to go back downstairs," he said. "I have to check on Rime."

Face stricken, Neriah looked up from her place at the priest's side. She followed him to the trapdoor that lead back down into the tower. "But Karis and Coracle, Geranium, Rime herself if she's been taken by this madness!"

The squire nodded. "I know."

"But…" Neriah bit her lip before continuing. "But I'll have to stay here. With him."

Jonas looked across the space to where the old man sat, with his chin on his breastbone again.

"Alone." Neriah's eyes were wide, fighting back terror.

The squire sighed. He was leaving her in a miserable, dangerous situation. If he was killed, she would have no defense against the insane guests that roamed the halls below. He didn't have the imagination to solve this sort of quandary, only the bone-certain knowledge of what he had to do.

"I'm sorry, Neriah," Jonas said. "I really hate to do this. But I'm her guardian. I have to save her. And if she's gone crazy, well, she's way more dangerous than Father Andrew."

"Okay. Okay." The young noblewoman forced her spine to straighten as she fought back the fear, lovely and resolute in the rain. "I understand."

"Here." Jonas pulled free the crude bandage she had made for him. *My lady's favor.* "Tie this around his feet just to be sure."

"Good idea."

"I'm heading down. I'll make a lot of noise, keep all the attention on me. You wait here until dawn, then--" he swallowed, *Am I leaving her to die?* "Wait until it's quiet, and…"

"I get it," Neriah nodded. "Go. Don't worry, we'll be fine. Go."

Jonas backed up slowly towards the trap door. It took some effort to tear his gaze away from the princess. At last, he did. *Got to make some noise right from the start.* He took his sword in both hands and took a quick leap. He would come down on the trapdoor with both feet. The bang should be more than enough to get the two armed women below's attention.

"Okay. Stop," a voice said.

THIS IS MY CHAPTER

And everything did.

The rain stopped falling. The squire stopped falling, his feet a few inches above the trapdoor. The wind stopped. The clouds stopped. Neriah and Father Andrew were as still as the statues that quartered the tower. The three moons shone down, perfect and still.

"Now, what are you doing? What are you doing, son of Gilead?"

Jonas found he could move his face ever so slightly. He cast around for the speaker, but somehow he already knew.

She was leaning against the gryphon-statue at the southern rim of the tower. She was naked, of course, her skin shining with the pebbled water from the rain. A thousand-thousand drops of water hung in the air and waited for her word.

The Gray Witch stretched like a bored cat and sauntered slowly across the tower.

"So, tell me," she cocked her head. "Why in this welladay world are you running downstairs to save that girl?"

"How are you even here?" Jonas found his voice. "Are we going to do riddles this time?"

Her brown eyes sparkled. "No riddles, no challenges, no tests. Just the question. Why save the Girl Downstairs and not the Girl Upstairs? This one's a good bit prettier."

The Gray Witch pointed at Neriah's frozen form, then twined her fingers in the squire's hair. "I am here because I wish it. I hold in my jaws the strands of Possible. If Time is a book, then I touch every page. This is my chapter." She spread her gray arms wide.

"Okay." Jonas was completely lost. "I just told Neriah: I'm her guardian."

"Well, good enough for me. Run along then."

The squire sighed. He was still frozen in midair.

"Did you know, noble guardian, what would happen if you stayed here instead?" The witch smirked. "You would save the life of a Lady, pure and virtuous. One without the blood of unnumbered men wet on her hands. One who truly deserves and needs your protection. One who has lost father and home to steel and madness. Is that not a more fitting task for a Hero?"

"Are you saying that Neriah will definitely die if I leave?" The squire's mind reeled.

"Am I?" The Gray Witch sounded bored. "Why not save her instead? The Girl Downstairs has sold your life enough times. Why give it away again? "

"Urghhh. I don't know!" He was frustrated, tired, and still bleeding a bit. The witch's words confused him. "Look, I made my choice. And I see what you're getting at, and it's nice that you're looking out for me or whatever, but…"

"Quiet. Quiet now. Or your heart will splinter in my grip." The Gray Witch leaned in close, almost breathing in his open mouth. "Do not dare to ask. Do not dream to judge. You do not know what I am. Do not paint me to suit yourself."

"Yes ma'am." Her brown eyes opened like wells of stone, her gray skin sharp as slate-razor.

"You stole a kiss from me, boy," she whispered. "It was most rash, most unexpected. You are marked, never forget it. Now answer me — why?"

Jonas gave the only answer he could. "Because she's my friend."

"Oh. You fool." The Gray Witch turned away. "You silly, silly fool."

She turned and walked back towards the southern statue, speaking over her shoulder.

"If you live to see the dawn, remember this. The wild mage serves no master but her own will. She leads you to your end and will not shed one tear when you fall. She is leading you home, son of Gilead. Every step brings you closer."

"She wants to go to Gilead?" Jonas' veins turned to ice.

"To the throne of the king. Go. Go. Go *now.*"

The Gray Witch clapped her hands high in the air.

The rain fell. The wind moved. Clouds whirled across the moons.

And Jonas fell through the trapdoor.

20

Rime stepped into the library of her mind.

This place was her sanctuary, her bastion. She had built it, page by page, with knowledge and stories and the words of scholars long dead. A bulwark against the cyclopean terrors that writhed in the outer dark. The mage came here often. For study, for relaxation, for a simple escape from the light and clamor of the world. A brilliant child's dream. Never before had she come to this place in her head with caution or concern or fear.

Until now.

She stood in the center of the library and turned a slow circle. Everything was as she left it. The room-spanning blackboard covered with chalk notes on the investigation. The pile of mystery novels next to the windows of her eyes. The long rows of white shelves with lines of books neatly arranged. Friendly green numbers floating about, engaging in some sort of advanced calculus soccer game.

The eight waved her over, but she did not move.

Here, alone in her mind. Rime could admit that she was terrified. The thought that something *else* could be in here, in her safest place. It was supreme violation: that everything could appear normal, that she could make decisions, think her thoughts, but some other force crept in the shadows and twisted her will to its own purpose.

This is how Teon felt. She remembered the fearful exhaustion in the Precursor's recorded voice. *To be insane and not know it. To be insane for all the long years of your life and only realize it at the end.* But something more wrapped her heart in itching burlap. *I am dangerous. Dangerous at my best. If something truly has control over me…*

She did not finish the thought.

Rime took a step forward then stopped, uncertain. *How do I find something that's inside my mind? How do I fight it?* She looked around the library again, her eye catching at last on the green numbers and their game. They had stopped playing, and were waving and gesticulating feverishly to get her attention. The four leaped up and pointed emphatically.

It was behind her.

It had been behind her the whole time, every moment since she listened to the recording. Rime swallowed and clenched her fists. She would not give this thing the satisfaction. With deliberate care she turned to face the final guest of the House of the Heart-Broken Lion.

It was tall — twice her height, black cloak -- stooped shoulders. Its head was that of a fierce bird. A spray of feathers shot high into the air like a crown. Its arms were long — dangling almost to the floor — and ended with thin black talons. White feathers fell and adorned the floor like snowflakes. Its long bill was sharp, head cocked to the left. Its eyes were nothing.

The mage clenched her teeth, then made them relax. "What are you?"

The bird-head dipped, almost as if amused. Its blank eyes held her gaze, then looked down to its black-cloak chest. A square of brass with rounded corners appeared. With a flicker of light, the square was full of rain, then snow, then it hummed a slightly lighter shadow than the thing's tall bulk that surrounded it. Words appeared.

i am the servant

"The servant? The servant of what?" Rime blinked. It was some sort of screen and the words were in the common tongue.

of the dark

The mage narrowed her eyes. *That is pretty vague.* The feeling of disappointment grounded her. Whatever this thing was, it could talk. That helped her feel as if she had her feet on some sort of solid territory.

"Okay. What is your name, then?"

name
name
name

The screen filled with letters, numbers, and various symbols. Slowly, characters began to disappear, leaving only a few shining dimly on the creature's chest.

option

"Option?" Rime looked up at the bird-head. It inclined its bill with apparent pride.

The mage caught a flash of light come from the blackboard behind her. She risked a quick glance. Three letters burned with inspiration. 'O' 'T' 'I' *The letters. The letters that Funnicello scrawled on the floor. OpTIon.* This thing — this demon — it was the one, the true murderer. Somehow the dwarf had known, had tried to warn the other guests. Rime tried to stay calm. She turned back to face the Option.

yes dwarf knew

Rime saw the words in the thing's chest. *It's inside your head, stupid. It knows what you know.*

~~~~~~~~

She took the strange line of symbols to be the Option's laughter from the amused shake of its feathered head. *But I don't know what it knows.* She needed to keep asking it questions, anything that might eke out an advantage.

"How did you do this? How did you make the dwarf kill himself, or Trowel go mad, or the bard kill Waters?"

i do not make
i do not kill
i am servant

"You did something." The mage remembered her anger at Neriah. "You use what is already in people's heads. Their anger, their fear, their suspicions. You make negative

246

emotions more intense."

simple explanation

"Am I offending you?" Rime scoffed. "Well, I'm sorry to malign your craftsmanship."

i reach
i touch
i am the option

"But why?" The mage hated the question. She had spent some breath earlier explaining that motive was immaterial, but she simply could not resist.

i am a servant
of the dark

"The Dark." *Why not call it The Vague? If I could narrow down where this thing came from, I might have a chance. Is it a devil, a demon, some spirit or lost god?* "But what does it want, this thing that you serve? What are you trying to gain?"

you
~~~~~~~~

Rime took a step back despite her need for iron control.

it has been long
since i spoke
strange to speak
i came with him
with the light one
the one who sang

The mage grappled with the strange words. *The one who sang — Geranium. No! He means the Precursor from the recording. It means Teon. But that was thousands of years ago.*

i have grown weak
smaller and smaller
down the long years
hard to serve
difficult to reach
to touch

The foul, tall bird-head of the Option leaned over her, bill inches from her face.

but now i am fresh
i am new again
the tale told again
i walk in new minds
i am strong and sure
not an echo of an echo

One arm, birch-frail and skeletal, rose. A thin, black talon came to rest, ever so gently, on her breast.

i touch you
i reach you

Rime gaped, her mind emptied by fear. It was true. She had no doubt. Her heart and her power were in this thing's feathered grasp. The tip of the talon seemed to burn.

you are special
all of this
tonight
to find the strongest
like the light one
the one who sang
you are a storm
and your heart is a thunderbolt

248

we will serve

The Option's talons dug into her tunic and pulled her up face to face. The bird-head opened wide, and its eyes were empty. She could not see the screen in its chest, but she understood the next words all the same.

we will serve the dark
together

Then with the lightest toss, the tall black thing in her mind threw her away. She flew away from her her library into the outer dark where she had never dared to walk: the cry of dragons and the coils of madness.

Rime fell into the midnight of her mind.

21

Jonas hit the ground with a large thump, nearly staggering over his own feet. The trapdoor banged against the roof with a metallic thunderclap. There was no one waiting in the hall, but the squire felt he had made a sufficiently intimidating entrance. *Not quite as good as the Witch.*

He swung his good steel into a defensive position. Rain-wet hands held sure on the old wood of the hilt. The squire was profoundly disturbed by the witch's words and her very appearance. *Gilead. I am marked. Neriah's death. What was she getting at? Why is she even here at all?*

Jonas did what he often did when encountering mental turbulence. He ignored it. Slid it quickly off the square edges of his mind and moved on.

The squire sprinted down the long hall towards the spiral staircase leading down. He had assumed that the murderous sea-elf and the maddened noblewoman would be waiting right beneath the trapdoor; his clamorous entrance had been designed to give him a slight advantage. As most of his plans, this one was proving to be of little value. His opponents were not in the hall, which meant they could be anywhere.

He peered down the metal staircase for any signs of ambush. Just empty air. The next two levels were dark. Only a dim illumination glinted off the metal of the staircase. The squire decided to keep moving. *They know I'm up here, after all, and there's only one way down. No point in being shy. I have to get to Rime.*

He stormed down the metal staircase two steps at a time. The squire briefly considered checking the bedroom level as he passed, but since no one swung a morningstar at his head, he decided it was safe to assume that his foes were further down. Jonas did notice that someone had methodically smashed every lamp on this level, and only one burn-light globe puked out light from its shattered glass. Enough light remained to see his feet and the stairs, but not much more.

Jonas pounded down the stairs into the sitting room. The globes were all smashed here too. Only a small lamp still spilled golden light across the wide room. The squire skidded to a halt; the wide expanse of shadowed chairs and half-seen couches made him wary.

Another lamp flared on right next to the first. Jonas blinked and a third came on, just below it. Then the lamps stepped forward, and he saw the wicked edge of a longsword pass in front of them.

More lights ignited, and Jonas realized that the lamps were Coracle. The outline of her form was burning a lambent gold, the curve of her legs and arms shone. The gold light followed the whorls of her skin, a sunburst, a meteor, a comet. The sea-elf's blue skin was flat black in the shadows. It was as if the night sky had come to seek his death.

"Took long enough," the thief laughed.

"Yeah," Jonas replied with flabbergasted pith, then looked around in the shifting light of her celestial skin. "Where's your friend?"

"Eh, she wore herself out a bit. It's just you and me," Coracle cooed.

The squire took quick stock. The area between him and the sea-elf was mostly open; only a few fallen chairs posed possible obstacles. A question wormed its way out of his mouth. "Why did you cry when you came to my room? Rime said that sea-elves can't cry."

"Oh," Coracle spat. "Tears make people stupid. They're busy looking for a handkerchief for you instead of minding their purse."

Fair enough. Jonas step forward carefully, his blade held low, inviting a quick attack. The thief was a better sword-hand than he, there was no doubt. *I need her to over-extend, to give me an opening. And then I have to make the most of it.*

"I'm just a thief after all. I might even let you live if you tell me where the box is," she smiled.

"That's why I'm going to win." Jonas took another step forward.

"Really? Why is that?" Coracle spun her longsword. Golden light glimmered on her blade then went dark.

The words of his Master came to him then, and he spoke them with a tired smile.

"Because you fight for gold. I fight for steel." Jonas spurred himself forward into a quick trot, closing. "I'm fighting to save my friend."

The squire kept his blade low, trying to look inexperienced. *Not hard to look that way.*

The thief took the bait. She laughed at his platitude and slashed out with her vicious sword. A glint of light on steel told him that she had tossed a dagger at the exact same moment. The squire's hands moved faster than his thoughts and saved him again. He managed to catch the incoming dagger with a quick upwards swing, which batted it into a dark corner. He turned his body just in time, bending his good steel over his head in time to block the sea-elf's attack.

Jonas blinked. *That is the coolest thing I have ever done.*

The sea-elf gave him no time to enjoy it, instead landing a vicious kick on his kidney-area. He swallowed the pain and took one hand off his sword to grab her shining leg. The squire grunted as he shoved hard with his shoulder, flinging the thief away, and sailing over a nearby sofa. He heard the sound of metal striking stone, but not the telltale skitter-slide of it tumbling away from her grasp.

Her light shone over the sofa, and he gave himself no time to doubt or consider his next course of action. He dove headlong over the sofa with arms wide. Some part of him did pray that the thief wasn't laying pointy side up.

The gleaming Coracle rolled out of the way, so he landed flat on the stone floor. Air whooshed out of him. He did manage to get three fingers on her sword blade and wrapped them up tight, ignoring the edge's bite. He was stronger than she was. This was his opening, and he had to make the most of it.

He pulled her towards him, blood and pain erupting in his hand. Coracle hissed, her free hand clawing for his throat. The tired squire tried to come up with a strategy. *To grab her hand and keep her from choking me, I have to let go of my sword -- or I could...* He brought his sword hilt down on her temple as hard as he could. The sea-elf gasped in pain and her muscles slackened. Jonas winced sympathetically and brought his sword hilt down again. The thief relaxed against the floor unconscious.

Jonas let go and wearily pushed himself up to his knees. He watched the lights go out in the room as the sea-elf's bioluminescence faded with her consciousness. The squire was out of belts to tie up crazy people, so he left her where she lay. His forehead throbbed.

A moment later, the squire edged down the stone stairs to the manor proper, while his free hand idly dropped red blood on the clean floor. Many of the lights on the second floor landing and the Lobby had been smashed, but the high chandeliers still provided enough illumination to see. Jonas quickly deduced by the distinctive circular impact patterns that the morningstar had been used to destroy them. His theory was supported by the morningstar still hanging from a globe near the steps and Karis laying on her back immediately adjacent.

The dour woman was surrounded by glass bottles: wine,

254

liquor, even a few dusty beer bottles. Many of them were half empty and liquor spilled all around her in puddles of alcohol of a dozen shades. She was flat on her back and choking. Vomit had filled her mouth, and she was too intoxicated to do anything about it.

Jonas sighed and tromped over. Without pause, he flipped the woman over and pounded on her back. She coughed weakly, then with more force expelled dirty liquid. Her purple-colored nails seemed out of place in the wet miasma of her self-destruction.The squire dragged her a dozen feet away and laid her face down. Karis took a sobbing breath, then passed into unconsciousness.

With no more time to spare, Jonas ran down the marble stairs and pressed his ear against the doors of the Banquet Hall, listening for the sounds of some sort of climactic musical battle. Jonas heard nothing. His heart skipped, and he pushed the door open.

The hall was a smoldering ruin: tables broken and chairs shattered, a black mark of ash and heat radiating from the stone wall between the two main doors. The squire could barely recognize the tall form of Geranium standing as if nailed to the wall. His beautiful blue coat was scorched and torn, and a vicious wound burned on his right breast. The black guitar, Lady Moon-Death, hung silent from his neck. Every string was blackened and broken.

Then he saw Rime.

She was standing in the center of the stage, the only brightly lit spot in the room. The stagelight made her white half-cloak blaze, as did the stripe of white in her hair. Jonas exhaled with relief and walked quickly towards her. The mage's eyes were closed as if she were thinking.

"Hey, Rime. Rime! Are you okay? I mean, I see you took care of the bard, but…" the squire stopped talking.

The mage opened her eyes.

"Hello, Jonas," she said.

He didn't know how he knew. He didn't want to know, but somehow he knew.

This was not Rime.

22

The mage opened her eyes.

All she saw was black. She was laying flat on her back in the unknown wilderness of her mind. The ground felt spongy and stuck to her hands and arms. It gave a slight resistance as she sat up and tore herself free from the ground.

Rime turned in a slow circle, forcing herself to remain calm. All she saw was black — no glimmer of the library on any horizon. Only the certain impression of enormous shapes moved in the dark: monsters, dragons, creatures beyond description. *Me. All of it me.*

When Geranium had played her secret song, this was the place his melody whispered. When he had called the shadows and tried to crush her, this was the place she compared it to. But now — standing alone and lost — it was worse. Far worse. She felt herself begin to sink, but she made herself take a few steps. The ground clutched her like a lover, reluctant to let her go.

She had no idea what to do. This was what she had hidden from her entire life. This was the madness of the Magic Wild, the dragons in her head.

~~~~~~~~~

The Option. It was with her, somewhere close. Laughing.

Rime surged forward, desperately fumbling for anger, or spite, or determination. Anything that would warm her, help her beat back the dark. Her hands closed on empty air.

you are special
there is so much
dark
in here

She felt hot tears pulse down her cheeks. She was powerless. No magic, no library, no Rime the Wild Mage. Just a scared little girl wandering in the dark.

i can touch so much
i can reach so much
through you

The mage tried to think. A spark of her that was still Rime.

"Will you let me see? At least? See what you do?" she queried the darkness, hoping that the little flame of wit would go unnoticed.

Black talons closed over her shoulders. The Option was

behind her. Of course it was.

if you wish

The Option pushed and she could see a glimmer on the horizon. It pushed again, and she could just make out the rim of her library and the windows of her eyes. The black-cloak bird silhouette of the creature was invisible in the dark, but it stepped in front of her, then backhanded her with a long tree-arm. Rime fell back, and the black earth of her mind wrapped around her with a contented sigh. *I have to get free, push and fight to get back to the library. There maybe I can do something, fight back, anything.*

~~~~~~~~~

The Option laughed again, and Rime sank a little further. She strained against the gravity of her madness, but she could not move an inch. She was sinking — sinking forever.

The light of the library glowed, cool and comforting past the thing's form. Rime locked her gaze on the light streaming from the windows even as the black earth slipped over her mouth and nose. She would look until the end.

Something moved outside the window. Something in the real world. She made her eyes focus to see what approached. Something was a young man in a filthy white shirt. He had a sword in his hands and a stupid mouth open to ask a question. *Jonas. Come to save me again.*

Rime sobbed into the black. The squire would be the Option's next victim. He would be torn apart by her magic in a heartbeat.

Stay calm. Jonas realized that his brain was giving pretty good advice considering the situation, but he was absolutely incapable of following it. Whatever madness had filled the heads of the priest, the thief, the noblewoman, the scholar, and the bard was now looking at him through Rime's eyes.

"What took you so long?" Not-Rime asked. "Where are Father Gallowglass and Neriah?"

The squire knew better than any how dangerous the mage was. Her magic was an unstoppable force; a fight here was impossible. Even if he stood a chance, he knew how angry she would be at him if he got even a scratch on her body while some demon was riding it. The thought of her anger made him smile. And that gave him an idea. *Like Father Gallowglass…*

Jonas lowered his sword and snorted.

"Are you kidding me? You let yourself get taken over by the crazy-demon? Really? Well that is just great." The squire rolled his eyes. "I fought all the way down here, like that blonde guy in the play, and you've already given up. That is beautiful. Beautiful."

"Jonas, I don't know…" Not-Rime spoke but then stopped as an uncertain expression formed on her face.

It's working. "It's just so low class, I guess. I mean, everyone else in the place goes nuts, sure. But you? Guess you aren't as smart as you thought you were." *That should get her good and pissed. I really hope this is working.* Jonas made his eyes go wide in mock-surprise. "Except, *I* wasn't affected. Oh my,

260

I don't even know how to say this, but does that mean I'm better than you?"

Not-Rime took a step forward and her eyes began to glow.

"... *better* than you…" Jonas' voice came as if carried by the wind.

Rime clenched her teeth mainly to hide the fact she was grinning. *That stupid ass. THIS is his plan?*

Her right hand closed, sunk down deep in the black earth. And she found something. Her hand closed on something solid, something real. It felt like a handle or maybe a pole.

She lifted her hand out of the muck and saw what she had found. It was a sword. It was Jonas' sword. Her only weapon against the Option. *A stupid sword?*

And her friend. Rime smiled.

The Option had moved on, making his way to her library, her seat of power. She could see the bird-head outline of the thing ahead. The mage set the sword point down and used it to push herself out of the black. The earth's grip was strong, but the sword gave her a place to lean. Rime tore herself free and started to run. The black around her seemed to vibrate as if the dragons all began to hum at once.

In my head, are you? Think you control me, that you beat me? Rime's feet picked up speed, barely touching the black earth.

Not this time. Not now, not ever. The sword was cumbersome and heavy; she had never used one. The mage put on more speed. She was flying over the black earth chasing the Option. The dragons' hum became a battle-cry. She dodged a monstrous form that emerged from the black nothing. She went faster. A nimbus of white light surrounded her.

The Option was already in the library, and the green numbers were scattering and wailing like over-dramatic bees. Rime saw the Option stretch forth its talon and her own hand moved outside the window. It crackled with power.

Rime shot forward, a comet, and plunged the squire's sword deep into the Option's black-cloak back. The dragons of madness all sang — a perfect harmony — a chord that echoed and lingered.

how
how

"It's an old magic. You wouldn't know anything about it," she growled. Rime gave the sword a vicious twist.

no
i am new
i am servant
i am ready
ready

The Option began to shrink as if dissolving through the floor. Rime kept the sword steady and watched with deep satisfaction as the bird creature sank before her.

i am
i am not done

i am not gone
an echo
of
an echo
can
still
serve

The black cloak and bird-head dissolved and slipped through the cracks of the floor. The green numbers flew towards her in a celebration-cyclone of mathematical glee. The three got so excited in the emotion and tumult of the moment that he made untoward advances toward the six, and received a brutal slap for his temerity.

Rime kept her focus on the floor to make certain that no particle remained of the creature. She took a breath and leaned on Jonas' sword. *Will I ever be sure? Will I ever really be sure?*

"...and you smell funny! And, uh, your penmanship is so, so bad?" Jonas attempted with unmodified panic. Not-Rime continued to advance lightning gathered around her outstretched left hand. *No more plans. Ever.* Staring down bright, crispy death, he realized that was going to be an easy promise to keep.

The mage blinked and took a breath. The lightning faded from her hand. She looked up.

Jonas sighed with relief and sank to one knee. "Thank you. Thank you. You're back, right?"

"Yep." Rime said.

The mage took a step forward and folded roughly to a sitting position. "I'm really tired," she said.

"Did you win?" the squire asked.

"Well…" the mage smiled. "Let's say that *we* won."

23

The surviving guests gathered in the Parlor. Rime had insisted.

"It's traditional. The investigator reveals the cunning details of the mystery and takes questions from anyone who's confused about how brilliant they are." The mage crammed a thick scone into her mouth. Jonas did not argue.

The defeat of the Option seemed to break whatever madness had held the other guests in its grip. They were battered and bruised, but in command of their senses.

The actors had emerged first. While they had not been "infected" as the mage had taken to calling it, they had been put in a catatonic slumber by Geranium's songs. Vincent and Toby did cartwheels and handsprings at the news that they would not soon be murdered. Sand smiled and shook both Jonas' and Rime's hands.

Next they had discovered Trowel abashedly trying to repair her torn blouse with a length of yarn excavated from her voluminous purse. The wood-elf had finally given up and walked behind a bookcase to turn her blouse completely around. This covered her front but left a long swath of her fleshy back exposed. The squire was surprised to notice that she had a large tattoo of a leering naked gnome sitting in what appeared to be a large crock of carrot stew.

"But where is the Precursor Box?" Trowel asked as she spread lukewarm jam on a piece of bread. "It is dangerous, yes., but still an invaluable article for scientific study."

"It was stuffed into Geranium's pockets, along with the keys to the front door," Rime replied. "I'm afraid that all three were destroyed in our conflict."

"How? Metal keys and a box of Precursor design…" the scholar began.

"There was a lot of fire." Rime did not elaborate further.

"Poor Geranium," Neriah sighed.

The new lady of the manor had arrived in the lobby bare minutes after Rime and Jonas had slumped to the stage in exhaustion. She had ignored the squire's instructions to wait for dawn and stopped off in her room to grab a large curtain rod as a weapon. "It worked for Master Waters, after all," she had said.

"A great loss," the priest added, a spray of grapes in his hands. "I will remember him in my prayers — to the bard's eternal annoyance I am sure."

Father Andrew had been no worse for wear when Neriah

and Jonas had trooped back up the tower to retrieve him. Completely mortified by his actions and soaking wet, he had pulled the squire aside on their way back downstairs. "What I said, about Sir Pocket..."

"It's nothing. No need to talk about it." Jonas cut him off, and the priest's measured gaze as he walked away spoke volumes. He did not broach the subject again.

Now they all sat in the parlor, and in the time-honored tradition of those who have survived madness, murder, and mayhem, they all sat stuffing their faces with the leftovers from the night's banquet.

Coracle held a bag of ice to her temple. A vicious purple bruise covered most of her face. Karis snored on a nearby couch, oblivious to her rescue or redemption from insanity. She was free of the Option's influence but not of the astonishing quantity of alcohol she had consumed.

"I'm still not sure I understand," the sea-elf began from behind the ice-bag. "What was this thing that got to us? A devil?"

"I'm not sure," Rime admitted with vast reluctance. "It claimed it came with the Precursors, and they were an impossibly old race. Hell is real — and so are devils and demons — but this was something else. Something else entirely."

"And we were taken — sorry — 'infected'..." Father Andrew reacted to the mage's raised eyebrows. "Just by listening to the recording?"

"Yes. *That's* why Jonas, Neriah, and the actors were unaffected." Rime tossed a grape at the squire's head to underline her point.

"But how can that be?" Neriah asked, still doing her best to wring out her soaking blonde hair. "How can something so powerful get into your head with just a few minutes listening to an old story?"

"Old stories have that effect even without the Option," the priest shuddered. " 'Words, words, words', as they say. It seems to me that this creature is more like an evil idea. And there is nothing more potent or insidious than that, my lady."

"That. That was what I wanted to say," Rime complained.

"And are we safe now? There's no chance that it will return to plague us?" Trowel interjected with obvious concern.

Rime chewed on a bite of scone for a moment in the sudden silence.

"It's not gone," she said carefully, then held her hand up when every gaze in the room spun to her in fright. "I'm not saying that we will all one day dance like puppets on a string, as we did tonight. We all were exposed to a fresh source of the infection -- like jam fresh out of a jar."

Rime held up a pot of strawberry jam to illustrate. "Over time the original infection spread and spread, growing thinner by the years. The Option has always been with us, since it fell to earth with Teon — or waited for him to fall. 'An echo of an echo' ringing down the centuries, hiding in the corners of every mind. If the original disease could pass with just a story — if the Option is just an idea — that's not something you can eradicate. Every thing that Teon made, every story that he told, carried the slightest shadow. And since we are heir to that technology, to that world, the Option is in all of us. "

The guests looked from one to the other. It was not a comforting thought.

"What did it want?" Coracle asked.

"I'm still not sure." The mage rubbed her tired eyes. "To destroy, clearly. But it seemed important that we destroy ourselves. That our own hands — our own works — be our undoing. It claimed it was a servant."

"A servant of what?" Sand asked quietly.

"The Dark." Rime shrugged. "Whatever vague, nebulous thing that is."

"As much as it pains me to lose such prize of historical merit, I take some comfort in knowing that the fire destroyed the sound crystal and the translation. I would caution you all to not repeat any part of Teon's words that your memories retain -- and perhaps to avoid telling any part of tonight's tale. We are all carriers now, if I may extend the disease metaphor," Trowel mused.

"How did you defeat it?" Father Andrew nibbled on a biscuit. "Jonas helped me push it back for a time, helped me remember my faith."

Jonas leaned forward with a pleased expression. "Yeah, Rime. How *did* you defeat it?"

"Please stop patting yourself on the back," Rime frowned. "You helped, certainly — a bit. A very tiny, tiny bit."

"He reminded you of your faith?" the priest asked.

"Something like that." The mage scowled as Jonas' grin grew ever wider. "I think it's time for us to go."

A general groan of disappointment filled the Parlor. The survivors rose and clasped the mage's and squire's hands. Of the thirteen guests of the manor, only seven remained. Coracle put down the ice-bag and shook Jonas' hand but not without whispering a venomous threat in his ear. Karis snored on the couch. The actors each gave Rime a parting gift, as they viewed her as their direct savior. Toby gave her a green comb, and Vincent a skull pin from the Wizard Black's costume. Sand placed a copy of *41 Plays - 39 Good, 2 Bad by Cranberry Scott* in her hands. It was dog-eared, and the margins were crammed with blocking notes, scene descriptions, and some lewd doodles. The mage was honestly delighted as it was a book she had never read. Trowel placed a motherly kiss on the squire's head and advised him to get a haircut. Father Andrew gave both travellers his blessing, but the troubled expression would not leave his face every time he looked at Jonas. The squire excused himself and ran back upstairs to his room to collect his gear. The borrowed finery of Lord Bellwether hung in tatters on his shoulders, and he was eager to get back into his travel-stained tunic and smelly brown cloak.

Neriah pulled Rime aside. The mage grimaced, as she knew what the lady would ask, but found herself regretting the cold facts in her head.

"Funnicello killed himself. Geranium killed Waters. You killed Geranium," the older girl said with forced calm. "Who killed my father?"

Rime sighed. "Coracle did. The dagger matched the others she had on her belt, and she hasn't been able to look you in the eye since she came downstairs."

"Okay. Okay." Neriah smoothed her hair back. "I'm angry. So very angry. What do I do?"

The mage's eyes widened. *I have no idea.* "Well, you could kill her."

"I — I can't do that. She was under the control of that thing. She didn't know what she was doing."

She did know what she was doing. That's how the Option works. It takes what's already in your head and makes it worse. Madness, fear, lust, pain. It can't make you do anything that you didn't secretly want to do anyway. From what Jonas said, she believed that Lord Bellwether and we were the true killers. She put him down out of self-preservation. Rime looked into the new Lady Bellwether's anxious face, and decided to hold her tongue.

"That is true. I'm about to break the lock and open the front doors. She will disappear as quickly as Jonas and I will, I imagine. You will need to summon the 3rd Regiment from Carroway to clean up and handle the investigation. We can't get wrapped up in anything that official." Rime stopped and reached out and took Neriah's hand. "I'm sorry about your father."

"Me too." One tear slid down the older girl's lovely face, then a look of exhausted determination came over her. "But tell me the truth. Did my father kill the actress?"

Rime frowned in annoyance. "That, I actually don't know. I couldn't find any more evidence on her body, only some residue on her hands and teeth where she had been eating blackberries."

"Blackberries," Neriah nodded. "My — my mother loved blackberries."

One final line on the blackboard connected two names.The mage considered leaving the noble with some sort of thin comfort but decided against it. She took both of Neriah's hands and held them palm up. Rime leaned in close and spoke.

"I will never be sure one way or the other, and if it comforts you to believe your father died an innocent man, I don't fault you. But he was infected by the recording just as much as anyone else, and the Option had plenty of pain and regret to work with. I can't prove it, but I think he gave these blackberries to his lover with his right hand after poisoning them with his left."

Neriah nodded, and willed away her tears. Rime was impressed.

"Thank you for being honest with me," Lady Bellwether said and took her hands away.

"Of course, my lady," the mage bowed with true respect.

"I won't lie to the Regiment when they come to investigate, but I will keep your name out of it as much as I can."

Rime grinned. "Okay. I understand. I'm going to go break your front door open now.".

THE LAST CHAPTER

Jonas flopped down the right-hand stairs, as he straightened the brown cloak around his shoulders. He saw Rime glaring at the tiny gold lock that held the front doors shut. Her hand-me-down cloak and dress were remarkably clean and un-scorched, so the squire stuffed her old clothes down in his satchel but left her travel boots out. He dropped them ceremoniously next to her, but she was too focused on the magical lock to pay any notice.

The squire turned and saw Neriah standing alone at the base of the stairs opposite the ones he had descended. She had not changed out of her simple green nightgown, and her blonde-strawberry hair was still lank and damp. But she was a princess still.

Jonas crossed the Lobby, and Neriah smiled faintly as he approached.

"Hey, Lady Neriah. I, uh, just wanted to say that I'm sorry about the tower."

She smiled, just a hair too polite, and his heart cracked like old glass.

"I understand. I do, truly. You care for her very deeply. She is lucky to have a friend so devoted. I wish the both of you joy."

The squire opened his mouth. Then closed it. Then opened it. Then closed it. *But, I don't - it's not like that with, Rime I mean, but you, but me, but but but….*

The proper response would have been to nod with dignity and restraint and bow a silent farewell. Instead, Jonas opened his mouth again and said some things. The worst plan of the entire evening.

He watched her face as words tumbled out of his mouth. He had no idea what he was saying. Whatever he was saying wasn't working. The Lady's face was still and cool. But beautiful, so beautiful. More beautiful because he had seen her shivering in the rain, and running in the halls barefoot, and dealing with her grief with the strongest will he had ever seen. She was still a princess in his head, but she was also a Lady, and a person, and a wonder. He foolishly tried to say all of those things.

The squire ground to a stop. He had no idea what he had just said. Neriah smiled faintly, a hair less polite, and turned and walked away. The door to her father's study closed behind her.

"I ruined that," Jonas said to the stairwell.

Warm laughter came from the door leading to the Parlor, and Father Andrew followed it. The priest clapped him on the shoulder and took the sting from his laughter with his gentle words. "The Nameless guide you, son of Gilead.

The human heart is a box of riddles, and it can take a great deal of time, wisdom, and luck to unravel them. Your own as well as the hearts of others."

"Yeah, okay," Jonas smiled back.

"If you return to Gilead some day, you will be welcome in my home," the priest said carefully. "The tale I told is common in that country, but I believe you have shown the worth of your character this night. I would like to help you tell your own tale when you are ready."

Return to Gilead some day. The squire said nothing. The priest's kind words lashed at him. He took the priest's hand and kept his eyes to the floor. *But it's true. I did it. I killed my Master. He was the best man I'll ever know, and I killed him.*

"Only Once," Father Andrew said.

"Only Once," Jonas echoed.

The squire walked back to the main doors where Rime still peered at the shining, golden lock. Jonas squatted next to her.

"Done embarrassing yourself?" Rime thumped the lock with her index finger.

"Shut your face," Jonas sighed.

"Eh, she is pretty," the mage smirked and let it drop.

Rime's eyes blazed with a cool, blue light. Her hands took on the same shade as they began to glow. Then with a pleased tilt of her head, she thumped the lock once more. The golden lock shivered, then clattered to the floor.

Every bolt, flange, rod, and screw disassembled in an instant, as if pulled apart by a master engineer on his workbench.

Jonas and Rime each took a handle and pulled the heavy steel doors open. It was an hour after dawn, the sun smiled at them with an expression of faint surprise. It had not expected to see them again. The night's rain had left the walk muddy and the tall cedars dripping. The two travellers stepped out of the House of the Heart-Broken Lion.

"Where to now?" Jonas slung his good steel over his shoulder.

"First?" Rime pursed her lips. "First we rob a bank."

EPILOGUE

The thin fire crackled in the brazier, choking on the damp marsh wood. The leather-clad rogue had passed his time in various ways: eating the food that remained, napping, stacking up bowls and cups into replicas of various famous castles and keeps throughout the land. If there had been a book he might have read it. He was that bored.

The first few hours of his vigil had been eventful enough. He had been buried up to his nostrils in the white sand. A torturous time of wriggling, inhaling and exhaling, slowly working his chin free and then his neck — then he had finally been able to lean forward with his squashed-coral horns and use them as crude spades. Sideways patted them affectionately. Perhaps his horns weren't pointed and pretty like the devils in monk's manuscripts, but they had served the purpose well. *I would've had to eat my way out if it wasn't for you guys.*

The devil-kin sighed and jabbed at the struggling flames.

This job had not ended as successfully or as lucratively as he had hoped. He had watched the two kids fly away on his wyvern. The squire and the wild mage had beaten him. Him and his companions.

At least he didn't end up like Cotton. The assassin had never particularly liked the seer, but tripping over bits and pieces of her was the least pleasant way he had passed the last couple of days. Sideways had seriously considered swinging himself up into the saddle of the one remaining wyvern. Seriously, seriously considered it.

Stay paid. That was one of the few rusty rules he still carried, tucked in his back pocket next to his banged up morals and moth-eaten dreams. The assassin had been paid, so he would stay that way. His employer had given him very specific instructions if certain unexpected events came to pass. The most important at the moment was: *Wait three days.*

He pulled the brazier out of the blue pavillion where he could at least watch the sea. The damp wood and pitiful fire were not served well by the steady ocean breeze, but his boredom needed something. The sound and motion of the waves would do. He had even skinned free of his armor earlier in the afternoon, splashing and whooping in the chilly water, naked and orange like, well, a naked orange.

Sideways stared at the waves and thought about naked oranges. And naked women. And naked women eating naked oranges. Then he thought about oranges wearing clothes. Suspenders, long johns and beanies, mostly.

The sun slowly dipped behind him. Long shadows stretched across the beach. The waves beat against the sand, regular as a heartbeat.

Then the waves went flat. The devil-kin bit his tongue in alarm. He had been waiting for something like this, but somehow he was still surprised. The water was as smooth as a mirror. The shadows, harbingers of sundown, reached out across the sea.

Then, the white sword.

It rose from the water catching the final golden gleam of the sun on its featureless surface. It was perfect and required, more necessary than the wave, than the sand, than the devil-kin and the sun.

But it needed a bearer. From a few paces away, the body of Linus twitched. It had laid cool and dead as a stone the past days; his heart's blood had run out and was absorbed by the thirsty dunes. Sideways had first worried about keeping predators and pests away from the body, but nothing had even come close. The gray knight's corpse was hallowed ground, protected.

And now it was moving. Before the devil-kin's eyes, one arm came up, gray gauntlet shaking with the effort. The white sword moved. As constellations turn in their orbit around the secret lacework of the galaxy, so did the white sword move: calm and slow, without doubt or apology.

Linus' body jerked and shuddered. From where he sat, Sideways could see the old man's lips move and his eyes fly open. The white sword settled into place, hovering above the knight's shattered breastplate. The vicious slash across the knight's throat began to close. Ribs and bone reknit. Thin flesh appeared to cover the gaping horror that had been his chest.

Sideways crept closer — but not too close. Close enough

to hear the knight's first words and see the tears gathering in the corners of his eyes.

"Please, no," Linus said. "Let me go. Please. Not this time. This time, let me go."

The white sword waited.

Linus blinked and took a long breath. Both of his hands raised and iron gauntlets closed over the white sword's blade. The knight pulled himself up until his forehead rested against the blank metal of the sword.

The gray knight took another long breath, as if mastering himself. "It still has me," he whispered.

Linus' eyes opened, and he slowly turned his head toward the devil-kin. His eyes were sharp. "Good work, assassin. You have earned your coin."

Sideways scratched his chin and shrugged. "You ready to get out of here?"

"Soon," the gray knight sighed. "I am weak. I will need to gather my strength. Eat and sleep."

"And then…" the devil-kin hesitated. "…and then we head to Gate City for a symphony, some expensive drinks, maybe dancing?"

Linus smiled, but it was pure reflex. It did not touch his eyes.

"And then we begin the Hunt anew," The iron gauntlets tightened on the white sword. "We bring that child down, whatever the cost."

Sideways nodded. He wasn't really surprised. He looked out across the sand and water. The waves had begun to crash again, as regular as a heartbeat.

THE END
FOR NOW

JONAS AND RIME

WILL RETURN

IN

ASTEROID MADE OF DRAGONS

AUTHOR'S NOTE

If you are interested in hearing Geranium's death song in our world, then avail yourself of the mysterious *Fate is Only Once* by Henry Taussig. Mr. Taussig does a fair version of the song on the track 'Rondo to Death'. If you listen close, you can even hear the strings snap at the end.

80851036R00161

Made in the USA
Middletown, DE
18 July 2018